Double Steal

A Danny and Carol Alexander Mystery

Dave Kamper

D0552952

DOUBLE STEAL

Cover Art by Drew Design, lauradrewdesign.com

Author Photo by Michelle Chambers Photography, michellechamberphotography.com

Editorial Assistance by KMH Editing, kmhediting.com

For Jojo,
who made me feel like I could do this,
and who makes it worth doing.
I love you.

Chapter 1

The Guy Who Was Walking Right Behind Him When It Happened got off the train at Union Station and exited on Jackson, heading into downtown. The mid-September morning air was fairly crisp even as it promised to get warmer by midday. The Guy buttoned his sport coat and semi-dramatically shivered as he left the overheated warmth of the station.

Foot traffic was heavy as always, a human stream of the generally well-dressed heading over the bridge and into the offices of the Loop. The noise of car horns, most blown in the spirit of polite insistence rather than New York-style outrage, formed a familiar background noise for anyone not listening to an iPod or shouting into a phone. The Guy Who Was Walking Right Behind Him When It Happened was doing neither of those. He was a little too anxious for all that.

He glanced to his left as he thought he saw a familiar face pass the other way in the crowd, but it wasn't who he thought it was. Happened at least once a day when he walked in from the station. He stood with the crowd at a corner waiting for the light.

He tripped as he stepped off the curb. Didn't fall, didn't drop anything. Just staggered for a step or two like an idiot. People snaked around him, like water around the rocks, no one missing a beat as they flowed along with their fellow wage-earners. For just a moment a shadow of failure fell across his heart, but only for a moment. He jerked himself aright, patted himself down with his left hand to make sure everything was there, tightened the grip on his satchel in his right, and kept on walking.

This wasn't a day he was going to let his demons chase him. Too many times he'd been cheated out of opportunity. Not this time. *Not this time,* he repeated to himself as he straightened up a shade more and accelerated around someone trying to scarf down a granola bar as they walked.

As he crossed yet another crowded intersection, though, the thoughts came back, and he slowed. The Guy wondered if there wasn't something wrong with the order of the Universe. When given a fair chance he always succeeded. It's just that fair chances were so frequently denied him.

Well, not today, he reminded himself. An unpleasant odor wafted from a sewer grate and The Guy hurried past, turning his thoughts away from the past and towards the future. He saw the glint of a gold watch on the wrist of someone ahead of him and it was bait – *yes, I'll get a watch like that.* This time, in a year, his company was going to be rich, and the glory would be his.

In his mind, he deserved this one. He knew that if this went through he'd win all the glory. Even if it fell apart, he had been marked as having Vision. Determination. Moxie. The kind of stuff that helps you to go places. Gets you nice watches. Sunny vacations with tropical drinks. *Yes.*
Having cheered himself up significantly, he strode a little more briskly, feeling the blood flow to his chilly extremities as he took bigger, more excited strides down the street. Today he had left no room for error to creep in. All he had to do was make it seven blocks in the course of the next three hours, and he would be on time for the meeting of his life. The meeting that would Make him.

The experience of walking down a crowded city street full of morning commuters is improved by the possession of a certain amount of élan. The Guy Who Was Walking Right Behind Him When It Happened began to get into the spirit and relish the ebb and flow of these morning crowds. A quick dart to the left to get around an older tourist. A burst of speed to get through the intersection before the light changed. The subtle camaraderie of the crowd, a peloton worthy of the Tour de France, individuals changing places, drafting in the middle of the pack, then taking over their turn in the lead as the oncoming contraflow proved too overwhelming to the frontrunners.

Six blocks left. Now he found his opportunity to cover some real ground. A tall, broad-shouldered man in a black overcoat swept past him on an eddy of current, and The Guy slipped in behind him. This man knew no obstacles. His lengthy, imposing stride made the crowds melt before him as he moved. He commanded the scene, barking loudly into his phone as he waded forward without once losing track of the crowds around him. Five blocks to go.

The Guy Who Was Walking Right Behind Him When It Happened eagerly followed, covering more and more ground. With his path cleared by the man in the black overcoat, he had more time for his mind to work, and he began working through the presentation in his head again. They reached the next intersection. Four blocks left.
All of a sudden, the man in the black overcoat jerked his body and seemed to pitch over to the left. The Guy Who Was Walking Right Behind Him When It Happened tried a stutter step to get around him, but as he did he glanced down. He saw a mass of red on the side of the man's head, and open, vacant eyes. He froze. He heard a scream, then another, and then an ocean's roar of sound and panic as he realized his perfect day was going to be perfectly ruined.

*   *   *

Detective Frank Gaffney hated his job today.

Of all the annoying and frustrating characteristics about crime scenes, there were four he hated above all others. Nearly every scene had at least one. Many had two. Three was rare but not unknown. But four? All of them? At one time? He wasn't ready to swear to it, but he didn't think he'd ever had a crime scene superfecta before, despite a long and successful career in Homicide.

Frank's eyes swept up and down the street. He bit the little clicker on the end of his pen and tried to take in the spatial dimensions. He was certain that the first characteristic of the superfecta was true: no murder weapon. In an enormous percentage of homicides, the murderer is kind enough to leave the weapon behind for the police to find. So many possibilities. Fingerprints. DNA. Registration numbers. Pieces of fabric or debris. Something about which witnesses can later say, "I saw a crossbow like that in the defendant's house." And so on. You get the weapon, he told the cadets at the Academy when he lectured there, and more often than not you got your killer.

He knew what *kind* of weapon it was, to be sure. A gun. The hole in the side of the man's head proclaimed that immediately, long before the medical examiner showed up and confirmed it. Either a pistol at close range or a rifle from a distance. The lab folks would tell him which. Problem was, it almost certainly wouldn't matter one bit. The odds were that weapon was in a sewer grate, a dumpster, or the Chicago River by now. If you didn't find the weapon within the first hour, your odds of finding it went down the tubes.

Of course, Detective Gaffney couldn't be sure they wouldn't find the gun, because of the second dreaded characteristic: an outdoor public crime scene. Looking around him at the urban jungle where he stood this morning, he silently blessed those fools who committed their murders in houses, garages, or hotel rooms.

Confined spaces with limited access, they made it easy for him to compile a list of who had been in and who hadn't. Indoor crime scenes were the best. Perhaps surprisingly, most murderers were dumb enough to kill people in a location that could be linked to the killer, and of that number an awful lot left personal information behind.

An outdoor location ruined so much of that. There were no fixed boundaries. People, even murderers, instinctively resist taking things out of a room or out of a house. They subconsciously feel the boundaries of space, and it often requires forethought and determination to remember to take things with them. In a public outdoor location, there was no fixity of place in a killer's mind. No reason to leave useful evidence behind, or to fall back on well-worn domestic habits that could give something away. The killer in the outdoor space feels the possibilities. At least this close to the lake, he thought, there's a nice breeze.

Characteristic Number Two, of course, largely explained the presence of Number Three – the lack of an immediate suspect. Indeed, Gaffney – in nights spent contemplating past cases while buffing scratches off an old Ford Thunderbird in his garage - had given consideration to reducing the number of Characteristics he hated about crime scenes to three, by merging numbers Two and Three together, but he found he too many exceptions to justify it.

The public at large would be astonished at how many murderers were stupid enough to linger around the scene of the crime, often for very long periods of time, so that they were there when other witnesses, or even the police, showed up. The number of killers apprehended with the gun still warm in their hands or the blood still fresh on their shirt boggles the mind. Sometimes, Characteristic Number Three meant a body discovered all by itself, in a wooded park or the trunk of a car or floating in water.

To his own surprise, he realized he would have preferred a lonely floater to what he had now. This body was lying on one of the busiest streets of downtown Chicago on a sunny morning with thousands of people within a few hundred feet of him.

And no less than fifty who claimed to have seen what happened.

And that was the worst, Characteristic Number Four, what he hated most of all: the huge crowd of witnesses, all with their own story, their own perspective, their own way of making his life difficult.

It would be wrong to say that Detective Gaffney hated witnesses. Far from it. His magic number was two. One witness could too easily be discredited – it was certainly better than none, especially if it was an Honest Citizen, but too much could go wrong to make one too reliable. If you got to three, then the odds were high that one of them would remember things just a little differently than the others. Sometimes three was great, especially if two of them were a couple, because they told their stories to each other and ironed out the differences so it sounded better on the witness stand. But two was perfect. Two witnesses were the standard the Ancient Romans had required to prove murder. It made perfect sense to Gaffney, who had an appreciation for the old ways of doing things.

But fifty?

For one thing, most of them were lying, even if they didn't know it.

"I saw it all with my own eyes, officer, I really did," one of the fifty was saying to a uniformed patrolman. Gaffney stopped stewing to listen for a moment, unconsciously straightening his tie.

"Well, what did you see?" the officer asked, notebook at the ready.

"I heard the screams, and I turned…" Gaffney shook his head and moved on. If he didn't look until after the screams, then he didn't see a damn thing. Okay, he probably wasn't choosing to lie, but the odds of him having anything useful to say were close to zero.

For another thing, half of them were just there for the thrill of it all.

A thirty-something blonde, in a black skirt two inches shorter than it had any reason to be (and heels two inches higher), was telling her story to another uniform. Gaffney didn't even have to listen to know what was going on. She was suppressing manufactured tears, heaving huge gulps of air, and speaking in far too loud and clear a voice for someone who was genuinely upset. With every other word her eyes darted, looking to see if she had caught the attention of the television cameras that were halfway up the block trying to get a glimpse of the action. She had even done a stage cheat; she was turned about thirty degrees away from the officer and towards the cameras so if they saw her and her distraught (but still attractive) features, they would have a good profile shot to go with the on-camera interview she was obviously hoping to draw.

But the biggest problem with so many witnesses was that there was simply no way for him to tell the wheat from the chaff. He had six uniforms and three detectives taking initial reports from the throng; anyone whose story sounded like they had a nugget of information would be taken to the station for a fuller statement. How could he be sure that they were picking up the most useful tidbits?

While those nine officers worked their way through the crowd, there was also no way for them to prevent the other potential witnesses from talking to each other. Not in a public, outdoor crime scene like this. Which meant that by the time they were interviewed, people were picking up on each other's stories.

Some of these witnesses hadn't even been there when the crime occurred. The first officers on the scene had only been able to establish a perimeter about thirty feet across – the morning crowds were too thick for anything more. By the time enough cars arrived to seal off the crime scene a half-block in each direction, there was no way to know how many people within that perimeter had been there the whole time, how many had joined it, and how many had kept on walking to work, unaware they had seen anything important.

Even if one person *had* seen the whole thing, understood what they were seeing, and remembered it with crystal-clear memory, it might be days before the investigating team could separate this one story from all the others that sounded just as – or more – plausible. With so many potential witnesses (whose stories were, he ruefully reflected, so much fodder for a future defense attorney), he would have a hard time pursuing hot leads.

Another four officers, with more on the way, were beginning to work their way through the buildings surrounding the crime scene with windows that might have looked out. This was almost certainly an exercise in futility but they had to try. The odds were small but someone with a vantage point provided by two or three stories of height, if they saw something… Gaffney knew that if anyone had really seen something he would have heard by now. This case was automatically political. This wasn't a drug murder in a bad part of town. This was a well-dressed African-American businessman of some kind, in the middle of the Loop, during rush hour. This was as high-profile as murders got.

The medical examiner arrived and with a brisk precision did her duty. She reported her initial findings to Detective Gaffney, who learned nothing and felt no better about his day. After checking with the uniforms and detectives Gaffney's partner, Mike Levin, walked over to compare notes.

"Well, what do we know, Mike?" Gaffney asked, beginning their usual ritual. He flipped the page on his pad and clicked his pen unconsciously several times. Levin had out his tablet and his finger scrolled down the notes.

"Driver's license says Willis Marden. Forty-four, African-American male, six-four and two-forty. Home address is Naperville. We've got a call to local PD to go to his house and find next of kin. No business cards on him. Tonya is running the name through the system."

"Medical examiner says cause of death was gunshot, probably rifle," Gaffney added. "Death must have been instantaneous. Do we know anything about where he was headed?"

"Not yet," said Levin. "He was walking east, probably from Union Station." Both detectives flinched. If he had been there, then they were probably on the hook for hours upon hours of grainy surveillance camera footage, looking for signs of him and any companions he may have had. Mind-numbing, tedious work that almost never paid off. Joy.

Gaffney looked over Mike's shoulder and commented as his partner began swiping through the photos on his tablet. "Well-dressed fellow. Those are pretty nice shoes. Some kind of professional, I'd say. That doesn't tell us much, but I wouldn't be surprised if this was his normal commute. Why did he get shot today?"

Levin nodded and dropped the only useful new piece of information Frank had heard so far. "He had something big going on."

"You get something from one of the witnesses?" Gaffney didn't even attempt to hide his surprise.

"A little." Levin clicked off the photos and back to his notes page. "The guy who was walking right behind him when it happened said he was talking very loudly on his phone. He didn't hear much, but he swears Marden said something like 'today I get all of this settled'. He's heading to the station to give a full statement. Wasn't too happy about it, but I think he was on the level."

"Pretty vague stuff, though," Frank said, chewing on the end of his pen and scuffing his shoe absentmindedly as he processed what he was hearing.

"We've got Marden's phone. The number he was calling was a 312 area code, so somewhere in the city. Jessica's running that down, too."

"Guess that's the place to start." Gaffney looked around him. The body was being removed, the witnesses were being sorted and transported, and his best lead was a phone call that probably had nothing to do with what happened.

"You do always say you want to work the big cases, right, partner?" said Mike, gently mocking him. "You were pissed for a month when Strommen and Fehn got that Navy Pier shootout."

"Which was recorded on four cameras," retorted Frank, once again tugging at the knot on his tie to make it stay centered. "Just annoys me that they get handed a no-brainer but because the victim's the Mayor's cousin it's suddenly a huge deal."

"They almost got a medal for that shit," Mike agreed, as he had the previous ten times they had had this conversation.

Frank was too lost in thought to notice the sarcasm. He muttered more to himself than his partner. "I mean, we had four more clearances than them last year, and five more the year before that. And they're the ones on the ten o'clock news."

"Grass is always greener on the other side of the precinct, isn't it?" He punched his partner in the arm.

Frank snapped out of his reverie and gave Mike a sheepish grin. "Right you are," he said, but his heart wasn't completely in it.

Mike evidently decided to let it go, returning once again to business. "This has got to be a professional hit, right? I can't make it figure any other way. To shoot a guy in the middle of the head, walking down a crowded street..."

Gaffney interrupted. "Of course, we're assuming that..."

Levin rubbed his forehead, "Yeah, we are. If we're wrong about that, then we're really screwed."

"In about a million..." Gaffney stopped. His phone was vibrating. He fished for it, feeling his sport coat tighten across his back; he was between sizes again and had chosen today to go smaller. After five buzzes he worked his phone out. Headquarters. "This is Frank."

It was their lieutenant, Jenny Halloran. "You still there?"

"Yeah. We'll be done soon, I think. We've squeezed out all we can."

"You're going to want to stick around for a while longer." There was a slight edge to Halloran's voice that told Gaffney his bad day was going to get worse.

He caught Levin's eye and put the phone on speaker so he could hear. "What's up? Tonya find something on the phone call?"

"We should be so lucky. I just got off the phone with a federal prosecutor. Mr. Willis Marden was scheduled to testify in front of the grand jury investigating Alderman Stringfellow. Today."

"Oh, hell." He shook his head in frustration.

"Tell me about it," Halloran said. "I'm sending you Mueller and Wright, and as many uniforms as we can spare. You need to redouble your canvass. Someone hit a witness in the biggest corruption probe Chicago has seen in a decade. And we've got to figure out who and why, and soon."

"This is going to suck on so many levels," Gaffney murmured as he hung up. He looked over to see Levin raising his eyes heavenward and shrugging in resigned irritation.

"There's no winning on this one. This is so political it's toxic."

Frank nodded. "And here's us with a superfecta of a crime scene. This can't get any worse."

Levin shook his head. "Sometimes this job is just no fun, you know?"

Gaffney paced slowly around in a circle as he bit the clicker on his pen. The crowd seemed to have grown even larger, and the uniformed officers looked smaller. The morning sun was becoming warm on his balding head, and the tight black sport coat was encouraging perspiration. Too much information. Too many people. Too many motives. Too many ways to piss important people off. He'd seen careers end this way. Good police, caught up in a case too big for anyone to handle unscathed. Sometimes failing to clear the case is what cost them. Sometimes it was the act of solving it.

He knew with the instinct of a seasoned veteran that Alderman Stringfellow was a crook of some kind, but it didn't stop the man from appearing in public places, getting his photo taken, smiling with leading business leaders, the Mayor, and even sometimes the Superintendent of Police. Gaffney had a passing acquaintance with the Superintendent. He didn't know him well, but before they guy made it to the top they'd briefly worked the same precinct. He'd tossed back beers with him a few times. The Chief was a good man. He wanted the job done right. But would he really want it done on this one?

Gaffney stopped his pacing and forced a few deep breaths. Need to stay calm. Treat it like any other case. Work the evidence, work the leads, take it one step at a time. Document everything. Run down every lead. Keep the bosses informed. Nothing to the media. Be smart, work smart. It's all he knew how to do, anyway.

He turned to his partner, who was talking with a crime scene photographer. "Guess we're going to be on TV after all," he said to himself, once again straightening his tie. A frisson of movement from the crowd indicated the next wave of uniforms driving up. He jerked his head in that direction to get Mike's attention. "Let's go."

Chapter 2

The line of the shadow was just about perfect. It was about twenty feet away from home plate, making it forty feet from the mound, pretty near where the ball would break. The hitter would face not only a curve ball, but a curve ball that moved from light into shadow at just the wrong moment. It wasn't much of an advantage, but Danny Alexander understood the importance of using every conceivable aid to get an out.

He stood on the mound, shuffling his feet a little in the dirt while his fingers found the right grip on the ball. As he shuffled, he held his head low. The casual observer could be forgiven for thinking his mind was elsewhere. He looked, indeed, like nothing more than an aging middle reliever stealing a moment's rest in between pitches. He was more than a little proud to be able to give that impression; it helped that it was also true. But while he seemingly lolled about on the mound his eyes were focused on the other team's dugout.

The batter wasn't so subtle. He was looking there, too. Earnestly. He needed lessons in stealth. At least he had the presence of mind to make it appear as though he was looking at the manager, instead of who he was really looking at – a backup utility infielder sitting all alone on the bench, a picture of boredom.

Danny had spotted the signal caller after about three minutes on the mound. His casualness was too forced. He didn't get up or move around but his hands, feet, and head were constant movement. Fidgeting. He wasn't going to play today but he sat doggedly on the bench, never moving. He clearly wanted to stand, stretch his legs or talk to his teammates, but instead he was stuck where he was, in the role of transmitting signals from the manager to the batter. The gesticulations of the base coaches and the managers were all a decoy. The little guy on the bench was the key. A moment ago the utility infielder had taken a sip of water and spit it out. Danny Alexander smiled inwardly. That spit was the signal to the batter. Swing away.

That meant a curve ball. It had been many years since Danny had a fastball that could get by a batter primed to swing. Even in his prime, too long ago, even that one glorious season when he won eighteen games and came in fifth in the Cy Young voting – when he was well-known enough that his wedding had gotten a brief mention on SportsCenter - his fastball was never his strong suit. No, Danny was what is known as a finesse pitcher, which is a nicer way of saying he threw junk and hoped the other guy was fooled enough that he didn't hit it too hard.

In the grandstand, Carol Alexander watched her husband's curve ball dive across the plate and noted with satisfaction the wild swing on the part of the batter. Two strikes now. Carol wasn't able to read the signs but she knew Danny had it pegged, and that was his advantage. She knew he would love to strike the batter out but hoped his pigheadedness wasn't having the best of him today.

Sadly, it was. Danny saw the young hitter (young enough to be a son, he reflected ruefully) tense his shoulders and squeeze the bat tighter. His weight shifted ever so slightly forward in the batter's box, and he rose up just a notch on his toes. Danny knew this batter wasn't even aware his stance had changed, but it had. The guy was higher and more in front of the plate than normal. His hands were spread out more – he was still touching the knob at the bottom of the bat, but he spread wider. As he got into his final stance, he was just a touch more upright. His bat just a shade less wound up. Not much: an inch at most.

But baseball is a game of inches. The hitter had done what hitters had done for time immemorial when they had just swung and missed and had two strikes on them – tighten everything up just a notch, sacrifice potential power to increase the chance of connecting with the ball. Be defensive first. Don't strike out.

Danny Alexander had built and lengthened his career around such moments. He didn't need to strike the guy out. He didn't need to play the game the hitter was playing. All he needed was an out. It didn't matter how. The situation was perfect for his two-seam fastball, a sinker. In the strike zone but low, on the inside of the plate. The youngster at the plate would probably hit it, but he would be too far forward so he would be swinging down, chopping, a sure grounder to short for the third out. Danny knew this. His eyes saw the intensity, the eagerness, in the batter. A ground out to short was so certain he would have bet on it, if baseball's ancestral phobias hadn't forbidden the act.

But he'd also seen something else and it gnawed at him. The home plate umpire, Bruce Friedkin, had been in the majors even longer than Danny. Danny had pitched many times with him calling the game. Bruce was not a young man any more. It was the eighth inning and he'd been crouched back there for too long. He was starting to drift upward. And, just like the hitter, with two strikes he leaned a touch closer, forcing him to move his head slightly more to the left to get around the catcher.

Friedkin now had a blind spot. A minute one to be sure, but Danny was certain if he threw another curve ball, this time on the outside, curving even farther out, there would be a moment – right as the ball passed from light to shadow – where Friedkin's view would be partially obstructed by the catcher. Not even fully obstructed, but just enough to cause Friedkin to shift to watch the ball in. If Friedkin moved, this late in the game, Danny knew the ump's mental picture of the strike zone would be dislocated. For that brief moment, Friedkin wouldn't be sure where the strike zone ended. In that situation, he could be expected to fall back on the umpire's instinctive desire to keep the game moving. If it was close, he'd call it a strike.

The hitter, on the other hand, now had an excellent idea of where the strike zone was. As soon as he saw the curve ball begin to hook, he would check his swing, knowing the ball would be outside. But Bruce Friedkin wouldn't be so sure, and there was Danny's opportunity.

Up in the stands Carol sighed quietly as she watched Danny on the mound. "Idiot," she muttered to no one in particular. Bruce Friedkin wasn't the only person out there who was getting older and more tired. Sunlight glinted off the strands of grey that were shot through her brunette hair as she leaned forward to collect her things.

Danny turned the ball in his hands, felt the mental click of the perfect grip. He leaned in, took a breath and went into his windup, his back, arms and legs moving in harmony. He reached the apex and then began to unwind. Right leg pressing, left foot planting and springing, his hips, back, and shoulders pushing through the base provided by the legs. Finally, the arm, rocketing forward, with the elbow and the wrist breaking just at the last moment, to create the unnatural spin of the curve ball, which left his hand rotating forward.

But not rotating enough. A curve ball is supposed to break on its way to the plate. This ball didn't. It sailed right on through, a mid-speed pitch right across the heart of the plate. Well, that's not quite accurate. It never made it to the heart of the plate. It was intercepted by a wooden baseball bat that sent it deep into left-center for a stand-up double.

The inning ended in time, but not after that same batter, who in Danny's mind should have been angrily contesting the called third strike from the bench (and who in Carol's mind should have grounded out to short), scored on a sharp single to right. Sometimes one run makes all the difference.

In the locker room after the game Danny heard the news he'd been expecting. The news he'd heard from three different teams the last three years. The news that had made him make sure Carol came to town for this series so he wouldn't be flying home alone. He knew it wasn't personal. Just not enough space on the roster, not with that lefty kid from Nashville with the split-fingered fastball itching for his chance to play.

For all of baseball's pomp and circumstance, these things are handled quietly and quickly. The next morning, his locker emptied, his uniforms turned in, and their bags packed, the Alexanders flew back to Chicago. At about the same time they touched down, Carol's brother, Detective Frank Gaffney of the Chicago Police Department, was beginning to interview his first suspect.

Chapter 3

"Let's go," said Phil Swigert, attorney-at-law and professional jackass. "My client has nothing pertinent to add to your investigation, which you know perfectly well, so ask your questions. The Alderman has constituents to serve, and dinner with Congressman Linwood this evening." The disrespect dripped from every word, but the polite smile remained undimmed.

It had taken days of painful bureaucratic navigation for Levin and Gaffney to be in a room with Robinson Stringfellow. It wasn't even something they had wanted. Neither of them had any illusions about the effectiveness of interrogation in these circumstances. They knew, and all their fellow officers knew, that Stringfellow would only talk with a lawyer present, and would then say nothing of consequence.

But it had all hit the fan less than an hour after the murder, when the *Chicago Sun-Times* website, and then WBBM, had reported the murder victim was going to be a witness in the Stringfellow corruption probe. The brass had been content, for that first golden hour, to let the detectives lead the investigation in their own way. Once the story became public, they couldn't keep their noses out.

A horde of journalists had descended on the City Trust and Guaranty Bank, where Marden was a senior accounts manager, because the *Sun-Times'* source revealed that at least five other employees from the bank had also been subpoenaed to testify in the ever-expanding investigation. The half-truths and incomplete stories told to the paper by people at the bank – random employees who knew nothing about Marden, Stringfellow, or grand juries, and were just trying to sound important - had only complicated things in the public eye, and increased pressure from on high to get a quick result.

By that evening, "senior police officials", more interested in covering their own backsides than in helping the investigation, were telling any journalist willing to waste the ink that, clearly, Alderman Stringfellow should have a chance to clear his name, soon, and that meeting with him would be an early priority of the investigation. And so the detectives began an elaborate kabuki dance with lawyer Phil Swigert. Of course my client is eager to cooperate in any investigation. Please send us a list of questions and we'll look them over: anything we can offer we will. No, thank you, my client prefers not to come to police headquarters to be interviewed; such a location bespeaks a degree of complicity in this tragic crime. No, that time is not convenient. Neither is that one. Saturday? I'll check. Fine, that one will work, but know in advance that our time is short. An hour? We never have that much time. We'd prefer fifteen minutes. Well, okay, thirty, but no more.

The next challenge had played itself out for Gaffney and Lieutenant Halloran in the form of countless hours of truly pointless turf battles with the local FBI office, since Marden was a witness in a *federal* criminal investigation. The logic of that did not escape the Chicago Police Department, but as a matter of honor they fought to retain the case file in their possession – and by the skin of their teeth they had so far succeeded. In this instance, Gaffney, Levin and Halloran were completely in sympathy with senior police officials (anonymous and not), none of whom could bear the perceived indignity of seeing the FBI take over a murder case in their town. It is hard to have too much sympathy for their position, but such things are ever thus in the world of competing bureaucracies.

Desperate for anything to use in the interview with Stringfellow, the detectives had moved quickly. A rail pass inside Willis Marden's suit jacket confirmed that he had, in fact, been coming from Union Station when he was shot, and so a team of uniforms had met up with the Station security team and gone through the dreaded video footage, without result. No shadowy encounters with unidentifiable figures. No mysterious women in a romantic embrace with Marden. No briefcases switched while sitting down on a bench. No envelopes of cash passed discretely. No obvious signs of deadly assassins following at a discrete distance. Nothing. As they had predicted.

Finding out all this nothing had taken a huge amount of time, as had analyzing the witness statements. Their number of "witnesses" had grown, not shrunk, as people called in who had been there when it happened but had not stayed around at the crime scene. In all, more than one hundred and ten statements were now on file, none of them providing anything that appeared to be of much value. Gaffney was nothing if not methodical on the job but in a case like this *methodical* was effectively a synonym for *stuck*.

He'd been through Marden's home but found nothing that immediately seemed relevant to the case. The tech department was working in Marden's home computer. Nothing yet.

Naturally, once the news was made public, the police had to spend their time looking into the City Trust and Guaranty Bank. All the bank's senior employees had been called to testify before the grand jury. The hope was the proverbial hot lights of a courtroom – and the subsequent threat of a perjury charge – would bring some facts out that hadn't been discovered. Not yet.

And so, three days in, with nearly two thousand hours of police work already devoted to the case, they sat in the conference room of Swigert's luxurious law office, face-to-face with main person of interest, with nothing to talk about.

Alderman Robinson Stringfellow was tall and broad-shouldered. He had features that could only be described as chiseled, although Gaffney realized looking at him up close that he was younger than he'd imagined. Couldn't be over forty-five, but the overall appearance was much older. He may have even, Gaffney realized, colored his hair to *make* it grey. His gray suit fit his frame just so, and it was expensive enough that it didn't look that expensive. No jewelry, not even a tie clip. There was no flash to him. His walk, his posture, all spoke confidence without bragging or arrogance. Several years ago, Robby Stringfellow, as he used to be known, was an earnest and by all accounts effective and intelligent supervisor in the Public Works Department. He'd taken on the Machine to win his first election, worked himself and his family and friends to the bone. It was hard, Gaffney felt, to truly dislike a guy who put that kind of effort into something. Except for the part where he was as corrupted as a half-empty carton of potato salad left out in the sun. There was little sign of Robby in the Robinson who sat behind the desk in his lawyer's richly-appointed office.

Frank had gone a size too large with his suit today, instead of too small. He easily reached into his pocket to pull his pen. "Alderman Stringfellow, your primary checking account is with City Trust." He shifted his eyes from the paper in his hand to look his quarry straight in the eye. "Is that correct?"

The alderman's voice was smooth and mellow, with no trace of strain, but there was the unmistakable shadow of a sneer playing on the corners of his lips. "It is."

"And you have a savings account there, too, am I right?"

"I also financed my house from City Trust, though I think they sold the mortgage on to Chase or another multinational. But I'm sure you know all that." The attitude was patronizing but controlled. You don't have anything on me. Thanks for playing, rookies. He smiled only with his mouth.

"Detective Gaffney," interrupted Phil Swigert, shoving himself into the conversation so forcefully it was almost physical, "Alderman Stringfellow has never made any secret that he is a patron of City Trust and Guaranty Bank. He is proud that he gives his business to a neighborhood bank that invests in the community instead of some large multinational that sends its profits overseas. Please don't waste our time. Get to the heart of the matter."

Frank gave the attorney a hard look, but both of them knew there was nothing behind it. He jerked his head almost imperceptibly in his partner's direction.

Levin went to the next question on their pathetically small list. "Did you know Willis Marden?"

The alderman made a point of acting like he was trying to remember, in the same sort of way parents pretend they have forgotten it's their child's birthday. "Well... I'll tell you. I can't be too sure. I don't remember the name, I know that." He flashed the detectives a display of whitened teeth. His eyes didn't smile.

Gaffney tried to act like he wasn't a little impressed with the performance, and pushed across a collection of Marden photographs. "Do you recognize him? From the bank or anywhere?" asked Levin.

Stringfellow screwed his face together, then stared at the photos for a long fifteen seconds. "Hmmm... I've got to say, I just can't be sure. I mean, I go in the bank a lot. Not that big a place, you know? It stands to reason that I've probably seen him, maybe even talked to him. But I just can't remember doing so." He bit his lip as if in deep thought, but Frank could see even from across the table that Stringfellow was stifling a laugh.

Levin leaned in a little. "You might have but you don't remember? Are you sure you can't recall meeting him, not even once?"

The constructed drama continued as Stringfellow went through another round of trying desperately hard to remember what everyone already knew he was going to say. Finally, he shook his head in an excellent impression of disappointment. "I'm sorry. I really am. I wish I could say one way or the other. But, like I said, I met a lot of people in that bank. If I've seen him, or talked with him, I just don't remember. Sorry." He shrugged, suddenly looking like a twelve-year-old boy who'd forgotten his homework. His eyes, in marked contrast to the rest of his expression, stared mercilessly at the detectives. They also, Frank realized, had a certain element of merriness behind them. Stringfellow was having a good time.

Levin pulled a thick wad of papers from another folder. He passed some of them to Swigert. "This is a copy of your closing papers from the mortgage you took out on your home eight years ago. Look at the tenth page – the one that's tabbed." It was a signature page. Even in scrawled cursive, the name of Willis Marden was visible.

This was, naturally, a complete surprise to the alderman. "Well, huh! How about that? There's his name, right there!"

"So you admit you've met him, at least once. Is that right?"

A tone of wonder and astonishment now, eyes wide with innocence. "I can see why you must think that. I really do. And maybe you're right. But that was eight years ago. That closing is just a blur in my memory. There were four or five people who came in and out of the room, signing things and giving me things to sign and handing me forms and so on." He leaned back and spread his arms in a shrug.

"You're saying you don't remember meeting Marden?" Levin and Gaffney, who (as you'll recall) had expected absolutely nothing out of this interview, were nevertheless boiling inside. If he admitted he knew Marden, then that made him look just a touch more fishy. If he denied meeting him, and Levin or Gaffney were later able to find a witness able to put the two together, then his credibility was damaged, having possibly lied to the police. This middle course, on the other hand, gave them nothing. His failures of memory would sound plausible to a jury. As he listened, Frank cast back to his own house closing years before. He couldn't remember any faces, either.

Stringfellow kept up his act. "I won't kid you; I didn't follow half of it, but I trusted the bank and so I signed what they wanted me to sign. If one of those folks was this Willis Marden, I sure can't remember either way. I don't know how many other ways to say it." The last line was delivered slowly, almost in a monotone. He once again flashed a toothy grin, but his eyes now flashed malice. He was too proud to play the innocent forever, but too practiced to let it get out of hand.

For all the fun on television, this is in fact how most interrogations go. Gaffney and Levin knew that, in the absence of hours upon hours of time to drill into someone's tale, finding cracks and exploiting them while building trust and a false sense of security, most people were able to cling to a story for a short interview. And Alderman Robinson Stringfellow, after all, had years of experience telling tales to newspapers, constituents, and probably any number of attractive women.

Suffice it to say, after their allotted half-hour had expired, the detectives had failed to crack the witness.

"Well, gentlemen," Phil Swigert said as he gestured towards the door, "I'm glad we were able to be able to be of assistance." Swigert was all smiles. Stringfellow looked almost sorry for them. "If you should need to talk to my client again, please do not hesitate to give my office a call. Failing that I'm sure you'll respect his privacy."

Gaffney choked off his first thought for a reply, and smiled politely in return. "And I'm sure, if you think of anything that might be of assistance to our investigation, you'll stonewall as long as you can before telling us."

Phil Swigert took four quick steps around the edge of the desk in a flash. He stood close to Gaffney, looking him right in the eye, unblinking. But his tone remained measured, almost paternal. "Detective, I'm disappointed in that remark. We met with you of our own accord, against my better judgment, despite no charges being filed and no warrants presented. The accusation that we are trying to stonewall you is beneath you and the Chicago Police Department." He stayed where he was, close, his face (still smiling) just inches from Gaffney's.

Gaffney leaned forward, hard. After a moment, Swigert blinked and moved back just a hair. Gaffney stopped smiling. "We both know why Willis Marden was killed. Maybe today we don't have the proof, but don't go thinking for a minute that you've won one over us." He grabbed his papers and strode towards the door. He looked back over his shoulder. "We've barely started looking. Taking a few bucks is one thing. Murder is another. *Someone always talks*. When we find them, you'll see us again." He slammed the door as he exited.

Levin smiled as they walked down the hallway. "Good thing you got out the door when you did, Frank. If he'd had a chance to reply he'd have ruined the nice moment you had there."

Frank grimaced. "Nah. He was happy enough having a veiled threat like that on the record. He can use it to claim we're biased when this thing goes to trial."

"So it's a win-win, eh? You get to feel all tough for ten seconds, and he gets ammo for appeal. Good to see things even out like that. Brings balance to the Force."

Frank ignored the jibe. "Sure wish we had something real on Stringfellow. I gotta say, it just doesn't feel…"

Levin nodded as they reached the lobby of the law office. "I know. For him to escalate from graft to murder…"

"It's quite a leap," finished Frank. "Not everyone's got murder in them, and I just…"

He opened the door. "Oh, crap."

Three television cameras, four photographers, and a horde of reporters stood in the parking lot of Swigert's firm, ringing the doorway. As Gaffney and Levin emerged, they closed ranks and began shouting questions.

"Did Alderman Stringfellow offer any statement?"

"Have you made an arrest?"

"Do you have a suspect in the case?"

"Did Stringfellow know Willis Marden?"

And so on. Gaffney and Levin shook their heads, not even risking a No Comment as they eased their way through. Frank reached up to straighten his tie. Halfway into the mob, the questions suddenly stopped. They turned and saw Stringfellow and Swigert emerging from the building.

Frank suddenly felt incredibly stupid. This whole affair had been designed for Stringfellow to give this press conference. Show him as cooperative, denying involvement in the murder, eager to help the police. And the next time someone stuck a microphone in his face he could say - in all sincerity - that he'd answered all the police's questions and they'd had no reason to hold, arrest, or charge him with anything.

Damn. Levin shot him a look and shook his head in equal parts frustration and admiration.

The politician looked demure and composed as his attorney told the reporters that while his client would make a statement and answer a few questions, he had to get back to the people's work. Then Stringfellow stepped up to a podium which had magically appeared from inside.

"The loss of any life before its time is a tragedy." Every millimeter of his expression spoke only sadness. "I support and welcome the police investigation into the cruel and shameless murder of Willis Marden. Today, I was pleased to meet with these two fine detectives..." - Gaffney and Levin tried to hide behind the CBS cameraman – "and offer my help in their investigation. They assured me that..."

The shots were loud, quick, unexpected. Frank spun halfway around. A reporter from the *Tribune* fell backward, knocking into him. Both headed for the pavement as others hit the dirt around them. Frank cried out involuntarily as his elbow took the brunt of his fall.

No more shots. He rolled to his side to get clear of the reporter and looked around. Mike Levin was on one knee next to him, face grim, automatic in hand, scanning the parking lot.

Gaffney cursed the pain as he tried and failed to get his gun out of its holster. "Did you see anything?"

Levin shook his head but didn't interrupt his slow sweep. "No. Four shots. Sounded like a pistol. At least fifty feet away. Call it in."

Gaffney pulled out his phone, aware that at least two other reporters were doing the same. He looked around. Alderman Stringfellow and his lawyer were on the ground, heads up and moving. They seemed unhurt. He didn't hear any cries or screams. Every person he saw seemed to be moving.

You'd think these things would be easier to figure out, but it took a full twenty minutes after the ambulance arrived to confirm that first impression. No one, it seems, had been shot by anything. Leaning against the trunk of a squad car, an ice pack on his elbow, Frank watched the chaos unfold around him. It had been a long week, and as soon as they finished here he could head home. He was in the middle of reupholstering the seats on a fourth-generation Ford Thunderbird. He'd never worked on a 1965 T-Bird and was hoping to finish them so he could start tinkering with the disc brakes; it was the first year they had them. There was nothing more to be done here, but if he got the seats done then he'd have accomplished *something* this week. *I want more excitement,* he told himself, *just not today.*

A score of rookies from the police academy were picking their way slowly around the perimeter, looking for footprints, shell casings, or anything else. The TV reporters were all on camera, trying to interview each other to add an air of objectivity to their reports. Those not interviewing or being interviewed were giving statements to uniforms, although none of them knew anything useful either.

Alderman Stringfellow and Phil Swigert were talking to Levin in hushed but firm tones, demanding constant police protection, given that they were obviously targets for assassination. They looked genuinely shocked and surprised.

Lieutenant Halloran pulled up in an unmarked car and walked over to Gaffney, dressed in street clothes. "You all right? I came as soon as I could."

He checked to make sure his shirt was tucked back in and nodded. "Just banged myself up pretty good. Mike's been shot at before. He handled it better."

The lieutenant smiled wryly. "Any sign of the shooter?"

"Not a damn thing. No shell casings... hell, no spent rounds yet, either. We're canvassing the neighborhood but nothing yet. Sound familiar?"

"At least this time no one was shot in the head and killed. You've got that going for you."

"You know this doesn't make any sense, right?"

Halloran slowly turned her head, surveying the crowd. "Yep. Marden was presumably killed to prevent him from testifying against Stringfellow. Hard to understand how trying to kill Stringfellow fits the pattern."

"Unless someone is afraid Stringfellow's going to talk. Implicate them in something bigger."

"But if they were really worried about that, they would have..."

Frank finished for her. "Made sure they did the job, not scared him with wild pistol shots in front of a bunch of reporters and two detectives. And don't bother asking. We tried right away. He still isn't talking. If he thinks someone else is out to get him, he's not scared enough to talk to us."

"Yet."

"Yet," he agreed, but without enthusiasm.

"The captain is breathing down my neck for a report. The folks upstairs must be having kittens; calling every hour for updates. Anything substantive I can tell them?"

Gaffney gave her a sympathetic shake of the head. "Tell him one of your lead detectives knows how to react to gunshots, and that the other has an incredibly sensitive funny bone."

Halloran rolled her eyes. "And nothing on the shooting."

"Nothing on either shooting. I know," he said, earnestly. "How hard are the folks upstairs making this for you?" He didn't need an answer. "Thanks for having our backs."

Gaffney saw Halloran's brain began working overtime to find a way to dress up "we're nowhere with this investigation" in more appropriate language. She furrowed her brow. "We don't have a lot of wiggle room on this, Frank. Either we make some progress or we're going to end up working the overnight shift in Lost Property." Frank knew she was both kidding and being serious, but he couldn't tell in what proportion.

Levin came over and looked at the expressions on Halloran and Gaffney. "We seem to be going in the wrong direction here, partner."

"Yep."

"Here's a thought: what if Stringfellow set this up himself?"

Gaffney considered the idea, biting the clicker on his pen. "Could work... fakes an attempt on his life to garner sympathy in the public eye, put us on a false scent... we're really closing in on Rockford Files territory here."

"Give me another theory that makes sense."

Gaffney began counting off on his fingers. "One: jealous husband. Stringfellow's got to be a bit of a player, right? Guy sees on TV that Stringfellow's going to be here..."

Levin nodded. "Because Stringfellow called the media."

"He rushes over, fires some wild pistol shots and runs off. Two: Swigert's the target. This guy's a lawyer for half the bad guys in Chicago. He's got to have a flock of enemies."

"Who choose just this moment to try to kill him?"

Gaffney shook it off. "Three: the shots are totally random. Just happened to be happening near us. That's why we didn't find any spent rounds. They weren't fired our way."

"That's really a stretch in this neighborhood."

"Four: A stunt by one of the reporters. Fired off blanks to scare up a story, add some color to things."

"I could buy that, but the shots sounded too distant."

"Five... hmmm... Nope. No five. Four is what I got."

Levin considered for a minute. "Two and three are crap, but one and four are just crazy enough to have something behind them. If either is true, though, then the shooting has nothing whatsoever to do with Willis Marden. That seems a little hard to believe."

Gaffney nodded thoughtfully. "It does, I agree. So, it still seems like we're nowhere, but I gotta tell you," he shook his head ruefully, "I don't think I can really see the forest for the trees here. We're juggling footballs – the brass, the media, the public – and duking it out with the FBI and slimeballs like Swigert. So many moving pieces..." He sighed and tapped his pen against his teeth.

Levin looked at his partner. "Are you thinking of calling them again?" He didn't need to say to whom *them* referred.

Gaffney shrugged. "They'll probably get into it even if I don't, once they see my name in the news."

"Are you talking about your own personal Sherlock, Detective?" asked Lt. Halloran, peering at him through disapproving eyes.

Gaffney shrugged a little sheepishly. "Sherlocks, I suppose. He'll have some ideas, for sure. Probably Carol, too. And God knows I'm going to hear about them whether I like it or not."

"I don't like bringing civilians into a case this big," she responded firmly. Frank couldn't quite tell if it was an order or an opinion.

"Look," he said, straightening up and squaring his shoulders. "I'm not talking about the two of them seeing the case file or Danny walking through crime scenes. He'll come up with his ideas on his own – Carol will do most of the research and he'll just make some insights. I don't see the harm in hearing what they have to say."

"What exactly do your sister and brother-in-law bring to the table, Detective? I don't want to see this case blow up in our faces. No one up the ladder noticed her face in the corner of that photo in the Trib, but they might."

Frank reddened. "Ah... I didn't think you'd seen."

"She wanted to march with Black Lives Matter, that's her business, but if we let her or him near this case and they screw something up, get noticed?"

Gaffney understood. *Everyone* was watching.

But this was his case.

"Jenny, I want to get their take – his and hers. You know how I run my cases. Every lead. Every angle. Every idea tested, turned around, looked at. I've had more than fifty pairs of eyes on this, and we are as far away from a real clue as we were ten minutes after Marden was shot."

"Detective," she said, kicking the formality up a notch, "I don't want..."

He interrupted, "Lieutenant, I need to be able to run my case the way I want to run my case." He reached up, found his tie was straight, and looked his boss in the eye. The look of chagrin that had been on his face since the shots rang out was gone. "God knows he can be a blowhard sometimes, but Danny has real skills. He's still playing because he knows how to read situations, find small clues. He sees everything, and for everything he tries to find meaning. A lot of it is bullshit, but I *need* some meaning on this case."

Halloran's face was getting red from holding back a retort, but he was on a roll.

"And Carol, well... Carol's frickin' smart. And in a nice, grounded kind of way. Sure, a lot of what Danny's doing is just guesswork, but he knows how to guess better than anyone I've ever met, and then Carol can take that bull and run it down like no one else. So the Department doesn't like her politics. I don't love them either sometimes, but it doesn't make her any less smart. I'd really like to bring them in, Lieutenant. Let them say what they have to say. It'll be one conversation, maybe two at most, but I value their perspective." It was a long speech for Gaffney, made all the worse because he was heaping praise on his brother-in-law.

She shook her head, just this side of angry. "I don't like it. You're not some country bumpkin cop, and neither is Mike. The two of you are the best homicide team in the city, and I don't buy it when you say you 'need his perspective.' You have the resources of the whole department to tap. We don't need the crazy they'll bring to this."

He bit the clicker for a moment, then shook his head. "You're right about one thing. Mike and I are the best damn detectives you have. We got that way by using our professional judgment. Mine tells me I want to hear what Danny and Carol have to say. If you're not okay with that, then you need to remove me from this case and get someone else. The media's watching," he added, "so I'm sure Gil Strommen and Barry Fehn will be happy to work it."

There was a long moment as Halloran looked at him and Mike. Frank waited. *Did I push that too far?*

Halloran sighed. "Fine. See what he has to say. No confidential material, right?" He nodded. "When will you talk to them?"

"Danny was playing in New York, I think. Carol went with him. She said he was probably going to get cut last night or tonight. I'll see them when they get back home, if they're not already there."

They all turned and got back to work.

Chapter 4

Frank pulled up to the Alexander house around eleven Monday morning. As he had expected, his last two days had continued to be frustrating, exhausting, and wholly unproductive.

A police officer, he'd been told long before, was only as good as their informants. Every snitch, dime-dropper, stool pigeon and whistleblower in the city had been cornered by someone in the last few days and pushed to tell what they knew. All for naught. Gaffney had long lamented the fact that the criminal underworld did not always operate according to free market principles. There was a demand for leads on this case, at a very high price, but the criminal marketplace failed to provide the supply. Adam Smith would have been disappointed.

The upshot of all the blocked paths was that the unlimited supply of manpower he'd had at his disposal was being eroded. Crime didn't stop in the big city, after all. And straight from the Department of Irony the shots fired outside Swigert's office had pushed the Mayor to demand twenty-four-hour protection of Alderman Stringfellow for the time being.

Five days was a long time in the murder business, when Lieutenant Halloran told him he had to give up Mueller and Wright for a few days while they worked a stabbing on the West Side, he wasn't surprised. When his request for overtime for six uniforms to canvass commuters on incoming trains at Union Station was cut to three, he knew they had their reasons. He and Mike figured they had, at most, another two weeks before they'd have to pick up new cases, too. And he was no closer to a suspect.

Carol opened the door wearing a stylish but restrained black dress, gave her brother a hug, and chatted with him as they walked back to the kitchen. Danny Alexander sat at the kitchen table in a well-pressed black suit and tie. A blizzard of printed a news articles was scattered all around the kitchen table and floor, and a laptop hummed. He was turning off his phone as Frank entered.

"An offer from another team?" Frank asked conversationally, as he poured himself a cup of coffee.

"Nope," answered Danny, "Gerry said he thought there was a rumor that I might go to San Francisco, but they just called up a couple of closers, so that's done. The other folks have mostly made their moves already. I've got some time off."

"Well, then, interested in taking a look at this Marden business?"

Danny gestured around to the piles of papers like a lord surveying his fiefdom. "We already are." He stood up. "I just got off the phone with Mike."

"Levin? My partner? Why?"

"I had a question for him. He'll text me the answer as we drive. Finish your coffee. We've got to be there by noon."

"Where?"

Danny ignored the question. Carol patted Frank on the arm, gently turning him back towards the door. Danny placed a few dishes in the sink and followed right behind. "Catch me up a bit on the case," he said, a little too gregariously. "The papers don't have a lot of new detail. It was a rifle, right?"

They walked into the garage and packed themselves into Carol's car. Frank looked at the bumper stickers but thought better of it. "Yeah. A Remington of some kind, we think. The bullet was disfigured, though; even if we found the weapon, I doubt we could match it." Gaffney couldn't remember the last time he'd ridden in the back seat of a car. The seat belt was too low. Annoying.

Carol pulled out of the driveway. "Anyone hear the shot?" she asked over her shoulder.

Detective Gaffney rolled his eyes. "Don't tell me you don't already know the answer to that." Husband and wife in the front seat sniggered.

Frank fished out his mobile phone with a sour look on his face. He clicked to his saved case notes, transferred laboriously from his notepad as a way to revisit what he'd written. "Eleven people claim to have heard the shot. Two are sure it was from close range. One is absolutely certain he saw it come from a taxi a block up the road, notwithstanding the fact that there would have been at least fifteen people between Marden and the cab. Two know for a fact that the shot came from the south, two others from the west. Three others are positive they heard multiple shots, and one is dead certain, as certain as we are that the sun will rise tomorrow, that Marden pulled a pistol out and shot himself in the head."

Carol chuckled. "Any of them at all credible? I watched the ten o'clock news from that night on the web. That cute blonde woman looked a little too rehearsed for my liking."

Frank nodded. If there had been an audible shot, he would have gotten a hundred reports instead of just eleven. "My guess is the gun had a silencer of some kind. They're not too hard to make. If you google it you find all kinds of sites that explain exactly how."

"And the phone call?" Danny asked.

"Jessica in our office traced the phone call to a law firm downtown. It was Marden's attorney."

"Anything of value?"

"Only that Marden planned to claim complete innocence of wrongdoing at the grand jury later that day."

Danny twisted in his seat to look back at his brother-in-law. "What is the status of this grand jury probe?"

"You know who Robinson Stringfellow is, right?"

"Chicago alderman. Suspected of corruption."

"Because that's really new," chimed in Carol.

"Target of a shooting a few days ago," added Danny.

Gaffney shrugged. "Can't be sure about the shooting, but by reputation he's more corrupt than most Chicago politicians. The feds have been looking at him for months, and the grand jury is sorting evidence. They've already heard from more than seventy witnesses, and my guy at the US Attorney's office thinks that's less than a third of the total. It's one of the biggest investigations they've had for years. Half a dozen other aldermen, three or four state legislators, a whole host of people in the city's purchasing office, maybe other folks... they'll all get caught up in it."

"What are we looking at, crime wise?" Carol asked.

"The usual," said Frank. "Bribes for influence on city contracts, sweetheart deals on land speculation, hiding his income by using family members, the usual. Potentially kickbacks from some city employees in Stringfellow's ward. Lots of money, basically."

Danny nodded. "Do they have enough to convict?"

"That's the tough part to figure out," said Frank, clicking his pen/stylus as he thought through his answer. "Part of the reason this grand jury has been sitting so long is that Stringfellow's pretty damn smart about this. The paper trail is confusing and spotty, the witnesses are all a step removed from him, and he's been smart enough to be disciplined in what he says to who, so despite 500 hours of wiretapped conversations they don't quite have it."

"Where does Willis Marden fit in?" Danny asked. His eyes were bright and shining, eager for news, like a child opening up a big present under the Christmas tree. Frank had seen Marden's body lying in the street, and his face flushed at Danny's enthusiasm.

He shook his head. "Nope. No more. Not until you tell me where we're going."

Carol checked her blind spot, then smoothly changed lanes. "We're going up to the northwest suburbs."

A sour grimace. "I figured that. Where?"

Danny actually winked. "Give me just a minute more. The papers said that Marden's bank is suspected of wrongdoing. What do you know for sure?"

Sometimes the relentless tide of his brother-in-law was just too much to resist. Gaffney rolled his eyes and struggled silently, for a moment, then shrugged his shoulders in resignation and explained. City Trust was Stringfellow's bank for his mortgage, checking account and so on. While the feds suspected it was being used for some kind of money laundering, they had yet to find anything real.

"And now," Gaffney said, in the air of someone speaking to a small child, "now you need to tell me where we're going."

Danny's phone beeped. He swiped the screen, read for a moment, and a brief, satisfied smile flashed across his face. "We're going to a funeral," he said as he tapped out a reply.

"What!?"

"Don't be so shocked," Carol said. "Funerals happen every day."

Gaffney threw his hands up in exasperation. "Yes, but usually you only go when you know the person who's died."

Danny reached into the pocket of his suit coat and pulled out a sheaf of papers clipped together. He sorted through the pile for a moment, extracted one, and handed it back to his brother-in-law. "Get to know him."

Gaffney looked down at an article from the *Chicago Sun-Times*, from the morning after Marden was killed.

C.L. man carjacked and killed outside closed amusement park
By Sam Richter

A Crystal Lake resident, Mark Bucholz, was found dead near the parking lot of the former Santa's Village Theme Park in East Dundee this Thursday evening. He had been shot, the apparent

*victim of a carjacking. His car, found nearby, had been
ransacked.*

*The victim was a 2005 graduate of Cary-Grove High School. He
joined the US Army in 2006, and served in Iraq in the aftermath
of Operation Iraqi Freedom. He married Janet Waters in 2010,
and leaves behind a twenty-month-old son, Jacob Paul. Mr.
Bucholz worked as a benefits coordinator with the law firm of
Owens, Hampton & Picard in Chicago.*

*His brother-in-law, Paul Ellsworth, speaking for the family, told
the Sun-Times that Mr. Bucholz was a dedicated husband and
father. "Mark cared about his family more than anything in the
world," he said. "It's devastating to all of us. We're all in shock.
He was great brother and a great friend."*

*Co-workers at Owens, Hampton told police that he had left work
soon after arriving, around 9:00 Thursday morning. He
originally had the day off, but had come to the office in the
morning to catch up on some paperwork. His family was
expecting him home later that morning so they could spend the
day working on home improvements, Mr. Ellsworth told the
Sun-Times.*

*The East Dundee police say they discovered Bucholz's body
around 3:30pm after a routine police patrol discovered his car, a
2011 BMW, being stripped by at least two unknown males in
the parking lot of the former Santa's Village. The young men –
described only by the police as "persons of interest" - fled at the
approach of the police. The body was lying in the woods next to
the parking lot of the decommissioned theme park, which has
been closed for more than ten years. The car was parked in the
northwest corner of the lot, obscured from the road by trees and*

44

shrubs. This property has been the site of many petty crimes over the past five years.

At the time of writing, the police had not announced the names of any suspects. Given that the estimated time of death was between 10:00am and noon, the two males who were stripping the car are not considered likely to have been associated with the crime, but the police are eager to interview them. Three car jackings have been reported in Kane County in the last five weeks, and the county Sheriff's office is investigating links between the crimes.

"Thanks, Danny, really, but I've already got one homicide I'm working. Seems to me the Kane County Sheriff and the East Dundee police have this under control. Why on earth are we going to this funeral?"

Carol answered over her shoulder as she waited out a red light. "His wallet had been taken and the car rifled but they got his ID from fingerprints and the VIN on the car." She turned onto a side street. "We're almost there. We made good time."

Danny continued. "Still no suspects, and no gun, either. His car had I-Pass, and the paper said he was recorded passing through the Barrington toll stop at 9:44, so not much time passed between his driving and his being killed. I think it's a right at the light, sweetie."

"Yes, darling. I know," Carol replied. They pulled into the parking lot of a funeral home. A few mourners were making their way inside.

"Better let me put your badge and gun in the glove box, Frank," Danny said. "Not going to help us much if people know you're a cop."

"Help with what?" Frank demanded with exasperation. "Why are we here? What does this have to do with my case?"

Danny opened his door and swung his long legs out, then twisted his head to look at his brother-in-law with a confused expression. "You really don't know?"

"No, I don't know."

"This is the guy who killed Willis Marden. Straighten your tie. We're going to a funeral, for God's sake."

Chapter 5

Frank was in the process of removing his seat belt but he stopped and stared at Danny. He was at a loss for worse until he finally burst out, "What in the hell are you talking about?" He was speaking much more loudly than he intended as he got out of the car.

"Marden's killer. This is his funeral." Danny Alexander wore a smug expression that in other circumstances would have merited a sock in the jaw.

"How in the hell can you say that..." Frank was shushed by his sister. A forty-something woman in sandy blonde hair was walking towards them across the parking lot with an astonished expression.

"Danny Alexander?" she asked. Notebook in her hand.

"Pretty rare for people to recognize me without my uniform and cap on," he answered, not really showing the annoyance Gaffney could tell he felt. "You're either a real baseball nut or a reporter."

"Sam Richter. *Sun-Times.*" She put on a nervous smile and extended her hand. It was a nice hand. Frank couldn't help but notice.

"My wife, Carol, and her brother Frank." Hands were shaken all around. Danny and Carol exchanged a glance.

"What's a sports reporter doing at a funeral?" Carol asked, in a voice half an octave higher than usual.

"I moved from sports to crime reporting two years ago. Less travel. I'm surprised I recognized you. Are you related to the Bucholz family?"

"Friends of Janet's," Carol said, with a hint of sadness in her voice. "We had fallen out of touch but my family used to know hers, and, well, you know." She paused and bit her lip, then shook it off and looked up. "Is the paper doing a story on the funeral?" "Probably not, but I try to get out to
the funerals of victims I report on. Helps me stay connected to the story."

"Sure, sure" said Danny, solemnly. "That's pretty smart." He and Carol began slowly inching their way on opposite sides past the reporter. "Look, I don't mean to be thinking about these things on a day like this, but I don't want to pull any focus from the real story, if you know what I'm saying, so, ... well, if you do write about it..."

Richter nodded. "I'll leave you out of it. It'll only mean too much attention on the family, and they don't need that. He was just a working stiff who was in the wrong place at the wrong time," she added, looking off towards the pavement.

"Exactly. Thanks for being understanding." He extended his hand. "We'd better get inside. We're a little later than we wanted to be."

"Sure. Take care." She smiled and headed out into the parking lot.

Frank followed her with his gaze until she was out of earshot, then whipped around. "Friends of Janet's? How worried should I be that the two of you lie so convincingly?"

"Don't sweat it, Frank," said Danny, a bit dismissively. "We're on the good side, after all."

"That's debatable. How are you going to explain to Janet that you are friends of hers?"

"We won't have to. People ask who you are if you crash a wedding, but no one asks at a funeral. We'll just keep to ourselves and look solemn and no one will ask us a darned thing." He opened the outside door and gestured the others to go in ahead of him.

"If we're keeping to ourselves, then why are we here?"

"Look around. See who's here. That sort of thing."
Frank fumed at the colossal waste of time while Carol dawdled over the guest book. She seemed to take an inordinately long amount of time to fish a pen out of her purse when there was one right there. He was red in the face by the time they walked into a large viewing room, with a large gathering milling about, speaking in hushed tones. A closed casket sat in the front of the room. On top of it was a photograph of a clean-cut, short, and athletic-looking man holding his infant son and smiling. The three of them paused for a moment, looking at the image in silence.

Danny broke the pause first. He leaned in to Carol. "We need a relative. Not immediate family. Who looks like a first cousin?"

She nodded in the direction of a gathering of short, thin people standing together in one corner of the room. "I'd say they're a good bet." Frank couldn't help but notice that Carol was right. Not front-and-center enough to be immediate family. Frank guessed cousins.

Danny arched an eyebrow. "Care to join us in our work, Frank?"

"I still think you two are being incredibly stupid, but I'd be lying if I said I wasn't curious. What are you planning to say to them?"

"One question, that's all," replied Danny. Frank once again felt that a sock in the jaw would not have been out of line.

Danny led the three of them in a roundabout fashion towards the corner, exchanging quiet glances and nods with the people they passed. They stopped near the presumptive cousins.

Danny hunched his shoulders a bit, so that he looked less tall and athletic. He waited a full minute, then looked over to a twenty-something man in an ill-fitting black suit. He nodded, waited for the nod in return, then put his hand out.

"Hi, I'm Dan. I used to work with Mark."

"Tony Bucholz. He's my cousin."

"I'm so sorry for your loss." Danny clasped his hands together in front of his waist and bowed his head, as if mastering a deep sadness.

"Thanks. It's been pretty hard on everyone. Uncle Mark and Aunt Cheryl are just devastated."

"Do his parents still live around here? I thought for some reason they'd moved to Arizona a few years ago."

"No, they still live in the old house in Fox River Grove. Uncle Mark's still got five or six years at the school before he can get his pension."

"Sure." Gaffney watched as Danny stood silently for a moment, looking around. "Such a sick kind of coincidence, isn't it?"

Tony gave a shrug. "You mean about how he used to work at Santa's Village when he was in high school?" He was facing the wrong way to see the look of surprise on Frank's face.

"Yeah."

"Just dumb luck I guess."

"I suppose. How's Janet doing?"

Tony raised his eyes in the direction of a blonde in a shapeless black dress, holding a child in her arms. "I don't think it's really gotten real for her yet. You know?"

"Yeah. I suppose I should go over and pay my respects." They shook hands again. "Nice to meet you."

He took a couple of steps back to Frank and Carol. "Okay, let's wait a few more minutes and then work our way out. You got what you needed, right?" Carol gave a subtle thumbs-up.

"What was that?"

"Carol had something to do here, too."

"I suppose you're not going to tell me about it."

"Good guess."

"How did you know he used to work at Santa's Village?" Frank asked.

"It's what made most sense to me."

"You're going to have to do better than that." Frank gritted his teeth.

"Yeah, yeah. When we leave. Mike is meeting us at a café nearby in twenty minutes. We'll go through it all…" He stopped suddenly. Frank and Carol swiveled as they saw five men approach. Their bearing, their serious expressions, and general appearance marked them as ex-military.

The first one extended his hand. "Hello, I'm Andrew Ernst." He indicated the men with him. "We served with Mark in Iraq. Did you just get here?"

"Yes," said Danny smoothly, "My wife is an old friend of Janet's family." He introduced her. "This is Carol, and her brother Frank."

Ernst respectfully shook hands with both of them, then reached into the pocket of his suit coat and pulled out an envelope.

"We're collecting for a donation on Mark's behalf to a charity for military families. Lots of people never even got their spouse home from over there, and they could use the help. There's an address on the envelope if you can send anything in."

"Thank you, thanks so much," Danny mumbled, taking the envelope and turning slightly away. "We'll send a check." He shook hands again and started away.

"If you send a check…" Frank began.

"I know," said Danny. "We can't leave any permanent mark of our presence here."

"We'll give some money to the Purple Heart Veterans," offered Carol as a solution. "They do good work."

"Kind of cold, though," remarked Frank under his breath, as they headed out. "Aren't we going to pay our respects to the widow?"

"No," said Danny. "Fewer people who notice us here the better. Come on. My conscience is starting to feel jumpy about the stories we have to keep making up."

Chapter 6

Danny and Carol must have felt a little more guilty than they let on, because they drove in silence to the restaurant as Frank tried to figure out their game. Levin was waiting for them, pacing back and forth in front of the café.

He held the door open for them. "Danny, God knows I like you, but this has got to be the wildest idea you've had yet. You think this guy killed Marden, don't you?"

"Louder, Mike. I don't think the back of the restaurant heard you."

"Sorry." He lowered his tone as they took seats. "Frank, any of this make sense to you?"

"You knew about this before I did." He shot his partner an accusing look, but Levin smiled back. "They just took me to the funeral. What did he have you doing?"

Danny answered. "I asked Mike how much gas there was in Bucholz's car when it was found. The paper didn't report that."

Frank looked at Levin, who raised his eyebrows and nodded, with the air of an indulgent parent.

"What the hell does that have to do with ... Look, enough playing around. We've got a murder to solve and half the brass in town watching every step we take. Get to it. Why do you think this guy killed Marden?"

Carol jumped in, her voice filled with the excitement of discovery. "Here's the nickel version: it's the only thing that explains his own murder. First rule of assassinations, you know. Kill the assassin."

Gaffney waved his hand. "Uh, uh. None of this *post hoc ergo propter hoc* crap." Carol stifled a giggle. "What, I can't throw a little Latin around now and again? You know exactly what I mean. Come on, take me through what you've got."

They paused their conversation as the server came up to their table and took drink orders.

Danny could hardly wait until she left. His voice trembled with excitement as he began to lay it all out, talking quickly. "Bucholz worked at the law firm of Owens, Hampton and Picard. I've never been there, but I've heard of them. They're a really big firm. Worldwide reach. Couple of hundred lawyers, high profile clients, lots going on. Know where the offices are?"

"I'm assuming downtown."

"Office building not quite a block from where Marden was killed. On floors four through nine. My guess is five hundred feet, maybe four-fifty."

"That's a long way for a rifle shot," Levin observed.

"Not for a guy trained by the Army," chimed in Carol. "We're thinking he was probably a sharpshooter or something."

"Strike one," Levin retorted. He had talked to the Kane County Sheriff's Office this morning. Bucholz was in the military, yes, but he was in a logistics and supply unit. Not a front-line grunt. Not a sharpshooter. Gaffney gave his partner a congratulatory nod. Didn't do good to let the amateurs think they could do this all on their own.

"Still, he could have kept in practice."

"Pretty thin, though," said Frank.

"Of course it's thin," said Carol, interrupting, but with a smile. "We just got back in town twenty-two hours ago. Internet is all we've had so far. Give us a break already, would ya?"

Gaffney picked up from his partner. "So, here's your story: Bucholz goes in to work, gets himself to a window, and kills Willis Marden from long range with a rifle. Where did he get the gun?"

"I take it..." Danny began, glancing at Levin, who shook his head.

"Right. Nothing registered in his name."

"He could have gotten one in Wisconsin without a permit and without registering."

Frank failed to conceal an eyeroll. "Again, thin, but I'll allow it. Let me guess. He shoots Bucholz, jumps in his car and drives to Santa's Village, a place he was familiar with from his younger days."

"It's not really on his way home," said Danny. He seemed a little peeved that Frank was telling the story for him. "Had to have some reason for stopping there."

"And your theory," said Levin, "is that he was... what? Meeting the people who'd hired him to shoot Marden?"

"Pretty stupid place to meet them," observed Frank.

"Well, Bucholz wasn't a professional killer," explained Danny. "He couldn't have been. A professional would have picked a shopping mall food court, or a restaurant, or someplace like that, where he would be safe and anonymous."

"The Kane County Sheriff is leaning towards carjacking gone wrong," said Mike. "I didn't talk to them long, but it's clear they see it having something in common with the other carjacking nearby in recent weeks."

"Did you come across anything on those other crimes?" asked Danny.

"No. Didn't get time."

"Well, I did, and those aren't anything like this one." Danny pulled some more papers from his pocket and spread them out as their drinks arrived. Frank could see in a minute that Danny was on to something. He dumped three packets of sugar in his coffee and took a big sip as he reviewed the documents.

"Okay," Frank allowed, "I'll give you this one. These car jackings were all planned, at night, targeting cars that had been parked for hours. They couldn't have staked out Bucholz like they did these others."

Levin wasn't ready to concede the point. "So maybe they took a target of opportunity. Bucholz was driving a nice BMW. Could have broken their pattern for that. Maybe Bucholz put up a fight and it got out of hand. Santa's Village might have been the nearest place close by to park without being seen."

"Close to where?" asked Danny, triumphantly.

"OK, I see," said Frank. "That's your ace here, isn't it? Why did he exit the interstate where he did? Not on the way home. No particular shopping there, right?" Danny nodded. "Maybe he needed… oh, okay. Smart move checking that." He looked at Mike Levin.

"A little over half full."

"I know it's thin," said Danny, almost pleading for the detectives to agree with him. "But why else would he have gotten off the interstate *and* ended up parked at his old high school stomping grounds?"

"Everything else just doesn't make sense," added Carol, firmly. "He had opportunity – could see the street where Marden was killed. He had means – a rifle from someplace and training in one of Uncle Sam's endless war zones. And motive – the promise of money. *And* he was murdered himself less than two hours later. The coincidence is just too significant to ignore."

Frank smiled. Ah, the wonderful imagination of the amateur.

"What?" Danny protested. "I know it's pretty speculative, but it holds up. It's as good an idea as any."

Frank could see the appeal. But it only worked that way in detective stories. "You do what we do long enough, though, and you see the fallacy here. Any two people who get murdered, anyone, anywhere, and I'll bet you millions you can find things that show they are connected, even when they never really are."

Levin joined in. "If you only look at the two events it's always going to look like they have something in common. It's like the guy who goes to the casino to play roulette, and all of a sudden he's hit seven numbers in a row. After all, he says to himself, the odds of me hitting seven numbers in a row are ridiculous. No way it can be chance; he must genuinely be lucky. But he's only looking at himself. The odds of *any one* person hitting seven numbers in a row are abysmal, but, with all the millions and millions of games of roulette happening in a year, the odds of *somebody* getting seven in a row are for all practical purposes 100 percent. It would be crazy if it didn't happen, frankly."

Gaffney picked up the beat. "You've got to understand that what you have so far is pure coincidence. I guarantee that there are dozens of people who work in office buildings downtown. With military training, who had a view of the street where Marden was shot. Most would have no witnesses to corroborate an alibi to the time Marden was killed. More than a few will have criminal records, or ties to known criminals. I bet there's even a fair chance that one of them could be connected to the Stringfellow investigation, given how wide a net has been cast over that case."

"Heck," said Levin, "we could go through this restaurant right now, picking ten people at random, and I bet we could find some reason to suspect at least three of them for the murder. Your reason is more sensationalistic, because it's a carjacking turned murder, but the basic reality is still the same."

"I'm disappointed in you guys," said Danny, undeterred. "How do *you* explain the coincidence?"

"Your question answers itself," said Levin. "Coincidences have no explanation. That's what makes them coincidences."

Frank nodded. "Here's what I think. I think you're onto something with Bucholz's murder. It doesn't really look like the other car jackings, at least with what we've got on it. But your coincidences only really work for the couple of hours surrounding the murders. You're leaving the beginning and end completely wide open: for one, where's the rifle?"

"His killers could have taken it – or maybe Bucholz threw it a dumpster or something."

"OK, maybe, but that's a big question left hanging here, especially since you have zero proof that he even owned a rifle or knew how to shoot, and you don't have that built into your timetable or your best guess of his movements. The next one is bigger: who hired him to kill Marden?"

The server arrived with their food. Levin dug straight in. He chewed a big forkful of salad before piling on. "Of all the coincidences here, this is the most far-fetched." The alliteration sent little bits of green out of his mouth. "Bucholz – who we don't have any reason to think is a criminal of any sort – is hired to kill someone who just happens to walk down a street 500 feet from where he works? That's too hard to believe."

"It's more than that," said Danny. "Why kill Marden there? He walked six blocks to the train station every morning from his home in the leafy burbs. Would have been child's play to kill him then – few witnesses, plenty of getaway roads, no cameras. Waiting until he was in a crowd in downtown Chicago is incredibly counterintuitive."

Frank frowned. Danny was doing too good a job undermining his own case. He waited for the shoe to drop.

Levin also had a quizzical expression. "Truth is, this is the most interesting point you've made so far. Why wouldn't they hire someone to kill Marden in a more convenient location?"

"Oh, but they would have," said Danny.

"But…" said Frank and Mike together.

"Bucholz wasn't trying to kill Willis Marden."

Good Lord, the man is crazy, thought Frank, but with a charitable spirit of familial tolerance.

"Look," said Danny, "the only reason I'm still playing ball at my age is that I know about motion through space. Think about the physics of this. You were right before, Mike. Five hundred feet is a long distance for a shot. It's even more with what must have been something like a hunting rifle. It's not just the distance, though. There's the angle. Owens, Hampton, and Picard occupies floors four through nine, so he's shooting down. And, it's downtown Chicago. There's always at least a small breeze, and at that distance it will make a difference. And, if he did have a homemade silencer, that throws off the balance of the rifle and may interfere with the rotation of the bullet."

"Well, not to rise to the defense of your theory, but a good shooter knows how to adjust for those things," said Frank.

"Why are we supporting his idea, remind me?" asked Mike, amused.

"He's working up to a point. Never hurts to let him feel like we're engaging him," said Frank. It felt *good* to be a little patronizing to Danny.

"Go back to the physicality of this. Marden is walking down Jackson. He's shot, what about six, eight feet into the street? Add ten feet, fifteen, from the edge of the building on the corner to the street. That means he was shot after having been in Bucholz's line of sight for less than twenty-five feet – seven-eight yards. Marden's tall. Figure a little over a yard a step. How long does it take to walk eight steps quickly? Two seconds, three?

"Find me a shooter who can peer into his scope at hundreds of pedestrians, moving, shifting, who can pick out his target the instant he appears in view, confirm he's got the right guy, track him and shoot in less than three seconds. From five hundred feet. From an elevated angle. In a breezy downtown. Right in the side of the head. Nobody makes that shot. Nobody."

Both Frank and Mike were silent for a moment. Levin spoke first. "But, and yes, I appreciate the irony of bringing up coincidence, but are you really saying that Bucholz was hired by persons unknown, to kill person unknown, and he shoots, *misses*, and happens to hit a key witness in a major corruption investigation? Now there's coincidence."

Carol jumped in. "But that's it, isn't it? Was he killed because he was a key witness in the Stringfellow case..."

Danny hastened to finish. "Or did he *become* a key witness in the Stringfellow case *because* he was killed?"

Carol swallowed a French fry. "If Willis Marden had never been killed, would anyone think he was some pivotal figure in this Stringfellow case? Probably not. He would have been in front of the grand jury for maybe thirty minutes, and he would have been out the door, just another in a parade of useless witnesses."

"This is great and all, Danny," said Mike. "And we actually thought about the possibility of a missed shot. But you haven't actually addressed the big question we asked you. Who hired him?"

"People don't go around looking for hired killers at random," continued Frank, as his partner nodded vigorously beside him. "He'd have to have been connected already to get asked, and

Bucholz looks clean as a whistle. Why would he agree to do it? People don't kill lightly. He'd need a heck of a reason, and even then he'd need quite a lot of intestinal fortitude."

"People kill each other all the time for all kinds of reasons, and lots of them didn't know they had it in them until they did it," Carol argued weakly.

"It's one thing to kill suddenly, in a rage or high or drunk, or out of fear of imminent harm," said Levin, as Danny and Carol struggled for a comeback. "This took planning, time, and a steady hand. That's a different kind of killing. I don't want to play the veteran card here," he added, clearly more than happy to do just that, "but I'm the only one who's been there, and it's different."

"I hear you, I do," said Danny. "I get we don't have much, but this needs to be looked at, right?"

"I agree," said Frank, "the coincidence needs a little looking into. In fact, I wouldn't be surprised if we already did – someone on the team probably looked into all the murders done in days near the Marden murder. I'll see what's in our reports."

"You'll have to search his home and office, too, right?" asked Danny.

"And what about his bank accounts? They might have paid him some of the money up front," pointed out Carol.

"And get that car of his into the crime lab and go to town on it," added Danny.

Gaffney put up his hands. "Slow down there, you two. I get that you're convinced that this Bucholz guy is our killer. I'm not."

Danny broke in. "Come on, Frank! I agree – we don't have ironclad proof. I get it. But I've built a career seeing what doesn't fit. This isn't a normal homicide. You've got to look outside the box. I am, and I'm seeing Mark Bucholz. This is a strong lead that needs to be a priority." Frank almost expected to see Danny stamp his feet in petulance.

"Boy, oh boy, it's got to be fun being an amateur. I have at least fifteen priorities. I have a list from our Gang Unit of something like twelve guys who are believed to have killed someone or tried to kill someone for the promise of money in the last thirty-six months. I only have good alibis for six of them, and for two of the others I can play the Kevin Bacon game and get to Stringfellow in like three moves. It's the middle of a work day, my lawn needs mowing, I'm out of shirts, but I'll be working until seven today just to get caught up on my reports.

"To be honest," he added in a low tone, "if it wasn't from the two of you, what with your track record and all, I'd dismiss this out of hand."

"Ouch, Frank. That wounds my pride." But there was a smile on Danny's face.

"Look," Gaffney said, "I get that this situation sends your Spidey senses tingling, and God know your theories have a nasty habit of coming out true. But if I tell Lt. Halloran that I'm…"

"Yeah, I know," said Danny warmly. "You are the police: you're best at police stuff. You do your thing and we'll do ours."

"And what exactly do you all have planned?" Mike asked.

"Nothing illegal," Carol hastened to reassure them.

"Season's over for me," said his brother-in law. "What else are Carol and I supposed to do with our time?"

*   *   *

"Do you really think so?" Carol asked that evening, as they climbed into bed to watch TV before falling asleep.

"Think what?"

"Is the season over for you?"

Danny shrugged and looked intensely at his fingernails. "I don't know. Maybe."

Carol reached out and gently turned his chin so that he was looking at her. "Is it?"

"Yeah. It is." He let out a long sigh and his shoulders sagged slightly. "I really hoped Pittsburgh was going to take me, but Gerry said they haven't even returned his calls."

"Really? That's rude."

"Yeah, but whattya expect? Just another washed up middle reliever on the wrong side of forty, eh?"

She frowned and smacked his thigh playfully. "Don't go playing the self-pity card with me, honey. We've been cut before the end of the season before. You know it's less about you and more about letting the new kids get a shot."

"Yeah, I know. It is."

"And you'll find a spot next season, won't you?"

"Gerry thinks so. He says St Louis, Los Angeles and New York all are going to be looking for right-handed pitchers. I've got a good relationship with Don Zucker in New York. He knows I've still got innings left."

"New York? That could be nice. We haven't seen a Broadway show in years. I'm not on the roster for teaching next summer, so I can spend a lot of time out there with you."

"Yeah." He refused to make eye contact with her.

"Yeah?" She drew back.

"Yeah."

"I'm sorry. If you don't want me coming to New York, I don't have to." Carol kept her tone balanced between playful and angry. Just to make sure he couldn't tell for sure.

He turned. "Don't even."

"Well?"

He grimaced. "Sorry." He leaned in to kiss her cheek. She accepted it reluctantly. "I think that would be great, pumpkin, I really do."

"But?"

"But it sucks, honey. I know, I know, it's not about me. But I'm twice the pitcher … I'm tired of this happening. Three straight years now." He bit his lip and blinked rapidly.

She reached out her arms for him. "I know."

"It really sucks."

She held him close, relieved he was talking about it. She kissed him on the top of his head.

An hour later, he got out of bed to brush his teeth.

"Did you look at the photos yet, honey?"

She nodded. "They look good enough for what we need to do."

"You going in tomorrow?"

"Yeah. I'll give it to my 11am class. They're pretty bright. End of the week fast enough?"

"Oh, sure." Danny took the toothbrush out of his mouth. He caught Carol's eye and held it for a moment. "Our first murder. Big, huh?"

Carol bit her lip. "Very big. You all right?"

Danny stared into space for a moment, thinking. Then he nodded. "Yeah, I think I'm all right. You?"

She drummed her fingers on a pillow. "I think so." She looked up at him. "Does that make us... I don't know, something?"

Danny swished some water, spit it into the sink, then dragged the back of his hand across his mouth. "Good question." He looked back at her. "What do you think?"

"I asked you first."

"I think whatever you think, honey." He tried out his winning smile, but Carol felt her jaw tighten in response.

Danny walked back to the bed and sat down with one foot still on the floor. He screwed up his face in thought.

"OK," he began. "It definitely felt a little... slippery to crash the funeral like that."

Carol nodded vigorously, "I know, right? But also fun."

"Lots of fun. Like the time in Denver when I talked my way into that stockholders' meeting. White guy with a briefcase..."

Carol nodded in agreement. "White guy with a briefcase." She shook her head a little to get them back on track. "In Denver, it wasn't murder, and we weren't helping the cops. I kind of think we ought to feel worse, but I don't think I do."

"Well," said Danny, reaching out and taking her hand. "We didn't kill him, and if we can solve this thing, we can do some good, right?"

Carol nodded. "It feels good to me because we did it together."

"Yeah." He squeezed her hand and let it go.

"What are you going to do tomorrow while I'm at class?"

Danny shrugged. "I'm going to go look at the crime scene. Try to get a feel for how it went down."

"Which crime scene?"

"Oh… I'll call Gerry to help me out with the law office, but before he gets here I guess maybe I'll take a ride out to Santa's Village." She could tell he was getting caught up in his thoughts about the next day.

"Be careful, honey. Just take a look and be done. We go slow with our first murder."

He nodded. "I will." He paused. "Do you think we convinced Frank and Mike Levin today?"

She shrugged. "I doubt it. They have to think in terms of indictments and warrant affidavits and so on. They're right – we really have no solid evidence Bucholz did the shooting. But that's okay. We'll give them something to think about soon, I hope. I'll bet anything that when my students report back in a few days things will look a lot clearer."

"A few days is a long time in a murder investigation, honey."

"Yeah."

Chapter 7

No one appreciates the power of librarians.

What we see are Dewey Decimal systems and electronic card catalogs, glasses on chains and constant shushing. If we looked a little harder, it might occur to us that to be a librarian you have to know something about organizing information, and we might notice that when we ask questions librarians seem possessed of remarkable amounts of arcane knowledge. But even then, at most, we think that librarianship attracts those inclined to trivia, or people with enough free time on their hands to learn lots of otherwise useless things.

We would be wrong. At its heart, being a librarian is about understanding the myriad ways that information is collected, stored, transmitted and received. A chemist's medium is chemicals. A mathematician's medium is numbers. A librarian's medium is information.

Carol Alexander was late getting to campus, and as a result was later still to class, because she had to park nearly six blocks away, all the better spots having been taken. In contravention of the union contract, but the grievance would wait. Undergraduates are not patient, and the Five-Minute Rule had nearly expired before she arrived panting in front of her 9:00 Introduction to Library and Information Science class to deliver a decidedly distracted lecture. The students responded with an abnormally high level of torpor, and all present were more than happy to see the hour end.

After seeing off her truculent students, Carol made her way from the classroom building and walked over to the University Library, an imposing nine-story structure with all the grace and charm of a cement factory. Inside, she quickly navigated the maze of hallways and conference rooms behind the circulation desk until she arrived at her office.

Susana Melendez, a tall, dark-haired woman in fashionably tattered jeans, sat at her desk, grading papers. The university had little regard for the faculty status of librarians. Despite the rather impressive number of letters after Carol's last name, and the long list of journal articles and published papers she'd authored, she still had to share her office with her graduate teaching assistant. Thankfully, Susana was one of the brighter eggs Carol had seen in her years of teaching. She could count on her to help out.

"Morning, Carol," said Susana brightly. "How was class?"

Carol gave out a grunt and set her papers on her desk. She took off her coat, draped it over the side of a battered sofa in the corner of the office, and logged in to her computer.

"Did you get my email this morning?"

"I did," said Susana, swiveling in her chair to face Carol. "Sounds like fun! I like the idea of turning the class into junior G-Men."

"Now, now," admonished Carol with a grin. "Nothing of the sort. I don't think the University Ethics Office is going to approve us spending school resources on amateur detective-ing that's not in the syllabus. I am merely suggesting that nothing is better for students than practical applications of learning, and that a fascinating project is at hand to help with that."

Carol reached into her purse and pulled out her phone. She tapped carefully on the tiny keyboard. A moment later, Susana's computer beeped.

She clicked the file open and looked at the images. "You took these with a phone? Not bad." She clicked the zoom button, and the images got bigger and clearer. "Some of the handwriting is a little hard to see, but it should be easy enough to transcribe these onto a Word file." She began typing as Carol started putting her notes together for what was going to be a much different class than she'd previously planned. Susana was still working when Carol stepped into the hall. She needed to make an uncomfortable phone call about an appointment the next day and didn't need to be overheard.

Forty-five minutes later, MLS 391 met in a classroom deep in the living tomb that is the university library. Carol could tell by looking at the assembled group that it was indeed a pretty bright class of first-year graduate students. Their notebooks had a very low doodle-to-page ratio. Fifteen of the seventeen students had in fact done the assigned reading. And while most of them had tablets or laptops out and turned on, fewer than half were checking their email or surfing the internet when Carol and Susana walked into the classroom at the stroke of eleven.

"Good news, bad news, folks," Susana said. "The good news is Professor Alexander is going to cancel the first paper she was going to assign today."

There was no cheering. They knew enough to wait for the other shoe to drop.

"We've got a new project for you," said Carol, stepping up to the podium. "You'll have the rest of the week to work on it, but this is time sensitive and there will be no late projects accepted.

"This class is about synthesis," she began, hoping she sounded more authoritative than she felt. "Taking information from multiple sources, with different contexts, biases and languages, and finding ways to paint a full and complete picture. This is how the real world works, after all – things don't get handed to us on a plate. We have to look all over and glean what we need.

"Your project is to use every available information source you can find, in one week, to tell us about these people." She clicked the mouse, and a list of names and addresses appeared on the screen.

"This looks like the names from a wedding reception or something," said Greg Buhl, who in a fairly nerdy class was one of the nerdiest, a status he seemed to prize judging by his classic black-rimmed glasses.

"Pretty close. We got the list from a guest book in the suburbs, from the funeral of this man." She clicked again and a picture of Bucholz appeared.

"We're looking at the friends and family of a dead man?" said another of the students, Melody Kasson. She had a look of horror mixed with more than a tinge of exhilaration.

Carol had prepared for this moment. She didn't want the students telling the whole world about what they were doing, and she didn't want to keep them focused on the death itself. She had spent quite a long time trying to find the right balance. Now that she was at the moment, she began to feel more than a little bit of trepidation, but she plunged on.

"In regards to the funeral," she began. "Mark was a father, a veteran. He died a victim of a crime, violently. His loss hit a lot of people very hard." She paused, swallowed, and took a breath. If they drew the logical and incorrect conclusion that she was close to Bucholz, then fine. She adjusted her cardigan, took another breath and kept going.

"I want to do something to help remember the life that had passed. None of us knows the whole of anyone else. Each of these people knew some of Mark Bucholz, but none of them knew all of him. I want to be able to tell his story, and the best way to tell it is through the people who knew him. If we know the context of his life, we'll know him better as a person."

She paused, tried not to feel too guilty about what she was doing, and delivered her last big line. "The best way to preserve his memory is to tell his story. We know how to do that. We can tell his story."

The classroom was completely silent. Carol knew, in fact, that this *would* be an excellent project for her students, that they would all learn a great deal from it, but she sure hoped they found something, or she'd never get this icky feeling out of her system. Danny could handle this part better than her, though he never would have thought of this idea.

"These names are an excellent opportunity to practice synthesizing information. We have names and addresses for about sixty people or families. Susana's passing out assignments. You have until Friday to find out everything you can about these people. Post your data as you get it on the class wiki, because things you find out will help your classmates, too."

Greg Buhl's hand was in the air; he was the only one in the class who did that. "But there's so many things to look at. Where do we start?"
Carol spread her palms. "That's not for me to say. You've been preparing for this task for years. There are any number of routes you could take."

"Then what are we being graded on?" Only Greg was bold enough to ask, but every student in the room was suddenly paying complete attention.

Carol groaned inwardly, but knew it was a legitimate question. "Creativity. Persistence. Imagination. I don't expect you to be complete, but I expect you to be thorough. Do the best you can, and show me you were following the trail of the information."

Susana stepped forward. "Let's walk through a scenario. You're all going to start by Googling the names – don't pretend otherwise. What do you do if you find their name mentioned in a news story about a lawsuit?"

"Westlaw" several of them said at once.

"Right. And from Westlaw you might get other names, and you run a quick search on them, too, just to see if there are connections. Let's say the suit has something to do with repairs on a house. How do you find out when the person bought it, and what they paid?" She held up her hand. "And it's not always on Zillow, remember."

A moment's silence. "Remember," interjected Carol, "what we always tell you. The internet is a wonderful tool, but it's not the only tool."

Shirelle Eden clicked her pen on her chin. "I guess I'd go to the county building and ask at the Assessor's office."

"And the Recorder of Deeds," chimed in Scott Richfield.

Greg Buhl's hand was once again in the air. "One name on my list is in Wisconsin. I'm supposed to drive up there to look through a county records office?" He seemed baffled by the concept of an out-of-the-library learning experience.

Carol nodded firmly. "Yes, if you think there's something to find. We have a grant," (from the *My Husband is a Professional Baseball Player Foundation*, she didn't say), "and will cover mileage and expenses for travel if you need it. What if we find out this person knew Mark Bucholz from childhood? Where else might we look for information?"

They quickly came up with high school yearbooks, microfiched copies of the local newspaper which have not yet been digitized, and a handful of other ideas. The students were now, as she had expected, warming up to the task. Several of them were already tapping away on their laptops, doing the first Google searches on their names.

"What about people's politics?" asked another student.

"The Federal Election Commission shows national campaign contributions," jumped in Melody Kasson, before Carol could reply, "but you have to go to the State of Illinois for money given to state and local folks."

"And the County Clerk for their voting records," added Susana, approvingly.

"Hey!" called out Rhonda Dilworth from the back of the room, chuckling as she held up her iPad for everyone to see. "Check this out. One of the people on my list is in the Mob!"

"What the hell?" Carol said to herself, as she strode rapidly to the back of the classroom to read what Rhonda had found. This was unexpected.

Chapter 8

Around the same time as Carol was reading up on the organized crime connections of Mark Bucholz's funeral attendees, Danny exited the interstate. Two miles down he turned into the parking lot of Santa's Village Theme Park. For a park that had been closed for many years, it looked largely intact: small roller coaster to the left of the front gates, spinning rides to the right, a huge building in the back that had once doubled as an ice rink in the winter. The parking lot gave it away, however. Consecutive winters without care had potholed it thoroughly, and the grass growing in the cracks would have been nearly a foot high if it wasn't been doubling over from its own weight.

The parking lot was open and bare. In the northwest corner, though, the asphalt turned into a fence-lined grass driveway that went some seventy-five feet to a rusty gate that used to give access to a large picnic area. To the west side of the drive several rides and outbuildings were visible; to the east there were picnic tables stacked up on their sides, chained together, paint peeling. He stopped the car where the driveway met the parking lot and got out.

He walked slowly down the drive, his eyes sweeping left and right along the ground. He stopped for a moment and dropped quickly to the ground with the grace of a trained athlete, looking intently at the dirt for close to three whole minutes without moving. He rose, reached the gate and took the lock and chain into his hands, then dropped them and raised his eyes to the top of the fence, walking slowly back as he did. He approached the fence and peered through, then took his phone out of his pocket and started taking pictures.

He was jotting some notes on his phone when there was a crunch of tires and he turned. A police cruiser was rolling to a stop just behind his car. A sheriff's deputy stepped out warily. He'd clearly spent a lot of years behind the wheel but his uniform was crisp and sharp as he advanced towards Danny, one hand on his shoulder radio, the other very casually on his automatic in its holster.

"Really not supposed to be here, sir," he said, in a textbook tone of civility and firmness. "This is private property."

"And a crime scene," added Danny. "I'm going to get something out of my pocket here. It's just a letter. Do you mind?"

The deputy took a quick once-over, nodded, and took the piece of paper Danny withdrew. He read it twice, then looked up.

"I met Frank Gaffney once, at a seminar on managing informants. He's a good cop."

"Yes, he is."

"But you're... what? A private detective?"

Danny shook his head. "Not really. I mean, I'm not getting paid by anyone. I'm just looking into this case."

The deputy paused a moment. "You looking to write some sort of book, or....?"

"No, not at all," protested Danny. "I'm looking into things, is all. Anything I find I send to Frank and the departments heading the case, and no one else. Just like the letter says."

The deputy looked Danny over again. After another long moment, he shrugged his shoulders.

"Look, you seem a decent sort. We're done processing the scene, so you can look around while I'm here, but I'm not going to go into any kind of…"

Danny held up a palm. "Absolutely not. All I want is to look around a little bit." He held out his hand. "Nice to meet you, deputy."

"Dylan Connor." His face peered into Danny's. "Why is the CPD interested in this case, anyway?"

Danny shrugged as he turned to walk back down the asphalt drive towards the gates. "As of right now they mostly aren't. I think there's a link with a downtown murder last week."

"Opinion right now is that this is a carjacking gone wrong."

Danny peered at him. "That your opinion?"

"Not so sure."

"This your regular beat?" asked Danny in a casual tone. When Connor nodded, he added, softly and hesitantly, "Did you…?"

Connor tilted his head and his eyes narrowed. "Yeah, I was third or fourth on the scene."

"I read that there were some suspicious characters messing with the victim's car."

"Yeah. Two males. McKenzie was first on the scene. Thought they were in their twenties, one African-American, one white. They took off while he was still driving across the parking lot."

"He didn't chase them?"

"Well, at the time he didn't know what he was driving into. By the time he saw the body they probably got across the road to the Wal-Mart and blended in."

"Where was the car parked?"

Connor gestured. "Right there, 'bout halfway down the drive."

"Meaning no one from the road would have been able to see it. Which way was the car facing?"

"Head in."

Alexander shook his head. "Not bright. He meets 'em out of sight, and doesn't even give himself a chance to drive out in a hurry if he needed to."

"No, doesn't seem he was too sharp."

Danny tilted his head towards one of the buildings just on the other side of the fence. "And what about the security camera there?" There was a barely suppressed look of triumph on his face.

Connor chuckled and the look of triumph disappeared. "Yeah, we saw it. It's a dummy camera."

"Really? The red light is on and it's got cords and everything."

"Yeah, it's a pretty good fake. This property has seen its share of trouble."

Danny's head clicked to the side for a moment.

"Where was the body found?"

"Right up against the gate. He was actually sort of leaning against it."

"Any reason to think he'd found a way to open the gate?"

"No, because he tried to climb it."

"Really?" Danny's eyes opened wider. "How do you know that?"

"He had rust on his hands from the fence, on his fingers where they would have gripped the chain link. You can see there's a lot of rust here, even if the fence is pretty solid."

Danny tipped an invisible hat above his head. "Good catch, deputy. So, he tried to climb the fence. Huh."

"Yeah. But he didn't make it. One to the head and he was down."

"Right." Danny paused as another moment went by. "Papers say there was no gun found. That right?" Connor nodded. "And you checked the other side of the fence, in case it had been tossed?"

"We did. The owners came down with keys and opened the gates."

"You didn't climb it?"

The deputy gestured to the top of the fence line, then spread his palms over his ample midsection. "That's real concertina wire up there, and the fence is eight feet. No one volunteered to hop over it."

Danny walked over to the west side of the driveway and pointed at a spot of ground just on the other side of the fence. "Then it wasn't the police who climbed this tree and jumped down right there?"

"What?" Connor stepped quickly over to where Danny was standing and looked through the fencing.

"See there?" said Danny, gesturing. "A fair number of feet have landed in that soft patch of soil in recent days. This tree is the only one on our side of the fence that goes high enough, but none of the branches reach over, at least not for a person to reach. But you could climb up, go out on that branch there, and drop on to the other side."

The deputy whistled. "That's a big tree."

"Oh, yeah. You'd need to be in shape, or at least pretty fearless, though the ground looks soft."

Connor appraised Danny once more. "We weren't even looking for it."

Danny smiled. "Thanks."

"The prevailing theory is that he was killed by other people in his car or another one. You think his killers jumped the fence to get him?"

Danny shook his head. "Weird spot for an ambush – and if it was, he would have been shot from the other side of the fence. The papers said the car was rifled. Maybe some of it was done by whoever killed him, the rest by the men this McKenzie saw. There's been some trouble here, right?"

"Yeah, on and off. For a while people were stealing the copper piping, and there's been plenty of kids hanging around, but it's gone down since the concertina wire went up last year. We figure someone stumbled across the scene, decided they didn't care too much about the body, and went to work on the car. Whether it was those two guys McKenzie saw, or if someone else found it first and tipped them to it, we don't know."

"Well," said Danny, "surely it wasn't those two guys. If it was, they would have escaped the same way they came in. Those two guys ran across the parking lot, not over the fence."

"Makes sense." Connor turned his head back to the footprints on the other side. "I don't see how whoever it was could get out here from in there. No tree on that side. You got an idea on that, too?"

Danny pointed to one of the outbuildings on the other side of the fence. "See that big wooden board on the ground next to the building? The grass is growing underneath it, or at least it hasn't quite died yet. It's big enough to bear some weight. You could put that up against the wall on an angle, climb up onto the roof of that building, and jump across. The grass line along the driveway is soft enough to jump onto." He walked over. "Here... and here... there could be marks of people landing, but it's harder to tell."

"They'd have the whole length of the roof to jump from so they wouldn't all land in one spot."

"Right."

"So, we've got someone jumping back and forth from inside the park and stealing things from the body and the car. Cold-blooded folks."

"Just as likely scared, don't you think? Dared each other to search the body, that sort of thing. Not to sound like my parents, but you know, with all the cop shows showing dead bodies on TV..."

"I suppose." Connor stopped. "But where'd they come from? I somehow doubt there's a tribe of feral teenagers living on the grounds of the amusement park."

"Up for a little hike, deputy?"

Connor grimaced. "Over?"

Danny shook his head. "Around. There's got to be another entry point along the fence line. The place where they come into the park from the other side. Let's beat the bounds and try to find it."

He started off through the grass along the fence line, the deputy following. They walked quickly along the edge of the parking lot and turned so they were parallel to the road.

"Not likely to be here – too easy to be spotted jumping in from the road," observed Connor, shading his eyes with his hand, as his head slowly traversed the ground ahead.

"I agree. Up there the fence turns off the road. Looks like there some commercial property and things. Might make a better place to find a jump spot."

"Sounds good."

"Say, Deputy... you made it sound like you didn't think this was a carjacking."

"Yeah, I'm not so sure."

"Tell me why. Gut feeling, or something specific?"

"Nothing in particular." He walked a few more steps before continuing. "Well, take the shot. It was precise, right in the side of the head. Maybe some random punk did it, but my guess is that the shooter was some kind of pro."

"Sure, I'd buy that. You've got a clear head, deputy."

Connor nodded, and his speech quickened slightly as he continued. "And then I can't figure the chain of events. They jump him and try to get the car, right? Gas station or something else nearby. If he is putting up a fight, you'd think they would have shot him then and there. What did they do, take him hostage for ten minutes, drive over here and kill him, then just leave the car? I have a hard time seeing it."

"I agree."

"You obviously don't think it's a carjack, either."

"Nope."

"And how do you think it's connected to a murder downtown?"

"If I knew that, deputy, I wouldn't be here walking through the mud."

It was getting warmer. A swarm of gnats kept pace with the two as they trudged through the tall grass. They turned at the corner and found themselves along the back of a row of warehouses. Danny kept his head moving constantly, but didn't slow his pace as they pressed on.

The warehouses fell behind and the ground became more rugged. Deputy Connor stumbled on a rock and cursed. They slowed down a notch to be better prepared for the uneven ground invisible below the grass.

"How big is this park, anyway?"

"Lot of the land never got developed, but the perimeter is probably five or six miles."

"Great."

Danny stopped and leaned his head closer to the fence, looking down its length. "What is that? Hmmm... I think we have our entry point."

He pointed and they pushed ahead fifty yards until they stood in the shade of tall oak trees on the other side of the fence. The ground was stony on the other side, but a pair of old, battered, dingy mattresses lay there piled on top of each other, well within jumping distance.

"That looks good for going over to that side....", he looked down the line and kneeled down. "Yeah, look at these shoe marks. This is definitely the landing spot."

"Look pretty promising, but we don't have a friendly tree to boost us over. Those oaks are tall, but none of them stretches over the fence. How'd they do it?"

Danny looked carefully at two small indentations in the mud. The ground rose gradually towards some mid-sized buildings a couple of hundred yards away. "Is that a school?"

"Adlai Stevenson High," said Connor, nodding. "Source of our pilfering teenagers?"

Danny started in that direction. "Think that corrugated metal shed is for groundskeeping?"

"And groundskeepers sometimes need ladders," answered Connor. He followed.

They reached the shed. The door was wood, secured by a large lock to a firm but somewhat uneven frame.

"Wood shop class," muttered Danny.

"Wonder how they got the key," said the deputy.

Danny stepped closer to the door. He ran his hands along the frame. "Don't think they needed a key."

He reached into his pocket and pulled out a Swiss Army knife. He flipped open the screwdriver attachment. "The door may be locked, but the latch here is just attached to the frame with garden-variety screws." He put the screwdriver in the first screw and turned. "Takes no torque at all. This shed is at least four or five years old. They should be stuck in by friction. Someone takes these screws off on a regular basis."

"Well, we're not going to," said the deputy, placing a hand on the latch. "Let's go up and see the principal. This is getting kind of real."

Chapter 9

As they walked up to the school Connor called into his radio for two more patrol cars. His badge got them past the front desk quickly enough, and they went through to the office.

"Who do I say you are?" he asked Danny. "No one's going to believe you're a cop."

"Don't say anything," he replied. "She'll just assume I'm here in some kind of official capacity."

"All right, but let me do the talking. Remember, you're here at my sufferance." If he saw Danny's smirk he didn't acknowledge it. He opened the door to the principal's office.

Principal Sheila Lonsdale was a harried-looking woman with hair as unruly as the grotesquely cluttered desk from which she rose to greet them. "Good morning, gentlemen. I didn't know anyone had called you... did something happen with the field trip...?"

"No, ma'am," said Deputy Connor, "we're here to ask your help on another matter."

The principal took a step from around her desk, nearly upsetting a tall stack of file folders. "Ooops...," she muttered as she shoved the stack straight. "What's going on, then?"

Danny jumped in, ignoring Connor's look. "You've got a group of students who like to hang out in Santa's Village, right?"

Lonsdale rolled her eyes. "Not this again?" She looked at Danny. "You with the owners?"

Danny shook his head. "No ma'am. I'm helping the police."

Connor jumped in quickly. "Yes, ma'am. We've been looking into some things, and we have reason to believe some of your students have been on the property lately."

The principal rolled her eyes again, and palmed her forehead with an audible smack. "The last thing I need. What did they do?" she asked, sighing.

"Well, we really don't know, ma'am," said the deputy. "But we think that they might have…"

"Might have done some more damage to the Snowball ride," Danny interjected quickly.

"That's right," said Connor, hesitantly, with a glance. "Do you have any idea who regularly goes over there?"

She gestured around to the chaos of her room. "Do you know why my office looks like this?"

"The cluttered genius of a brilliant mind?" offered Danny, with a breezy smile.

"Hardly. Because I had to lay off my secretary three years ago and there hasn't been money for file cabinets since the Reagan Administration. Had to eliminate the two Deans' position this summer, too. Fourteen hundred students and fifteen fewer teaching positions than just ten years ago."

There was a low whistle from the deputy.

"So," Danny interrupted, "when the Santa's Village people came around and complained about…"

"Some *petty* vandalism on their property? I gave it the attention it deserved. I've got bigger fish to fry than some kids hopping the fence to vape and throw rocks at boarded-up windows."
Deputy Connor half-raised a finger, but gave up and let it drop.

"Wow," said Danny. "That's just depressing."

"What about the groundskeeping staff? Might they notice anything?"

Lonsdale gave a snort. "Staff? We have one guy to spends two mornings a week here, rotating around the other schools in the district. Don't think he pays much attention to what he sees."

The deputy muttered something under his breath. "In that case, can we borrow the key to the shed back there? We'd like to see inside."

It seemed the principal couldn't come up with a poverty-pled excuse to refuse the request, and soon the two men were heading back across the grassy lawn to the shed.

"I think we have a winner!" said Connor, as their eyes lit upon an extension ladder up against the inside wall of the shed.

Danny stepped into the shed and inspected the ladder. "Look at this rope attached to the center rung. Must be twenty feet. That's how they get the ladder from one side of the fence to the other. They climb over, and the last one pulls the ladder over for the return." He looked at Deputy Connor. "I don't know much about fingerprints… are we going to find any on this?"

Connor shook his head. "Really don't think so, given how dirty it is." He paused and looked at Danny's eager expression. "You want to hop the fence, don't you?"

Danny nodded in the affirmative.

Connor nodded his head up towards the parking lot. "Let's wait for the cavalry to come help us." Three deputies, summoned by his radio call, were getting out of patrol cars and headed their way.

One of the deputies carried the ladder over to the fence and propped it up. Danny put his foot on the lowest rung. Deputy Connor laid a hand on his shoulder. "You might tell me what you think we're looking for before we jump the fence."

Danny hoisted himself up another rung. "Not a clue. But aren't you curious?" He reached the top and leapt onto the mattresses on the other side. "Wow. That knocks the wind out of you."

The other deputies followed carefully, Connor going last, cursing loudly as he belly-flopped onto the mattresses. One of the deputies pulled the ladder over to their side of the fence. They stood there awkwardly while Connor dusted himself off.

"Okay," he began, pointing his arm in a southerly direction. "About that way through the park is the gate where the body was found. If high school kids did find the body and take any of the poor fella's stuff from his car, they came back this way. We need to sweep the area between here and there, looking to see if they dropped anything or left anything useful behind." He looked at Danny. "Son, you're not a police officer. Stay close to me. And if we find anything, don't touch it." The deputy looked younger than Danny, but Danny just nodded agreement.

They fanned out and started off. A little farther into the park there were some rusting children's rides, and silent paths that led through the former amusement park. There was a calm stillness about the place, as though it was resting after having experienced years of huge crowds and chaotic noise.

They found signs almost immediately. Cigarettes. Empty pop bottles, along with some especially inexpensive cans of beer, perhaps purchased from a convenience store with a lenient attitude towards the drinking age. Wrappers from chips and candy bars.

A deputy called out, and they all rushed over to look at a weather-stained blue hooded sweatshirt lying on the ground. Connor knelt down next to it.
"Too small to be the victim's, but it hasn't been here long." One of the other deputies handed him a small orange cone, which he placed next to it. "We'll take it in and look it over. Good find, Warren."

Danny pointed at a piece of clear plastic stuffed in the left pocket of the sweatshirt, with a hard plastic square attached to it. "What do you make of that?"

Deputy Warren peered down. "Looks like a wrapper."

"Yep, it's a wrapper. Notice anything else about it?"

"Nope."

"Really? OK."

Connor put his hat on the table. "Well, what do you see, Mr. Alexander?"

Danny looked at it closely. "Probably nothing." He knelt down beside the hoodie and looked at it, then took a couple of pictures with his phone.

They moved on, slowing down so as to be extra careful, stopping to place more cones besides an empty pizza box ("how did they get a pizza over the fence without totally ruining it?" mused Deputy Warren), a pair of sunglasses, beer bottles, and more than a few empty packs of cigarettes. Danny was carefully looking a pile of cigarette butts when Connor shouted his way.

Danny trotted over to a pair of grimy picnic tables on a flat piece of grass, about halfway between the two fence-crossing points. The area around the tables was littered with trash. The deputies quickly set to work, methodically sorting through the debris. A cry went up. Danny ran over and found himself looking at a discarded brown leather wallet. Deputy Connor stuck out his pen and opened the fold; inside was a driver's license in a plastic sleeve. Even from where he was standing, too far away to read the name, Mark Bucholz's photo was recognizable.

Connor looked up and regarded Danny for a moment with an expression akin to amusement. Then he stood. "Bagley, Kenyon – you two head up towards the main gate. I'm calling in the crime scene unit – they'll cut the chain to the gate and they can come in that way."

Deputy Warren began taking pictures of the area. Connor set himself heavily down on one of the picnic tables. He removed his hat and fanned some air on his face.

"I don't suppose you've got an idea why they left the wallet here, do you?"

Danny was crouched down, looking over the ground. He held up his hands and showed them to the deputy. "I'm not going to touch it, but it looks empty. The kids weren't completely dumb. They took what they could and left it. It's a nice wallet, but I can't see it appealing to seventeen-year-olds. This is a real find. More than I'd hoped for."

"I have to say, I appreciate your help. We never would have found it."

"Thanks. I hope you can trace the kids and find out what they saw."

"Me, too. This is a good find and all, but I'm not sure it tells us much about who did it."

"You find the kids," insisted Danny, "and they'll tell you something. I'm sure of it."

*   *   *

"You're lucky you didn't sprain your ankle jumping the fence," said Carol that evening, as they ate dinner on the couch, relaxing in front of the TV. "You aren't twenty-five anymore, honey," she added, giving him a sympathetic look.

"No, we're not," he said, with a rueful grin. "Maybe I didn't think it through. I think the wallet is the least of what I found today. I just wish I knew what the rest of it meant."

Carol stretched out on the couch and put her feet on his lap. "Tell me about it." Her brain clicked into receive mode.

"Well, the first thing is the security camera."

"It was a fake, right?"

"It was, but how did the killers know that?"

"Oh, right," she said with a start. "So that means..."

"Either they were really smart or really dumb," he mansplained. "If they were smart, then they'd investigated the place in advance and somehow discovered the camera was a dummy. I'm not sure how they did that; they wouldn't have wanted to draw attention themselves by talking to the property owners... I don't know. On the other hand, if they didn't even notice the camera at all, then they're pretty dumb. I'm having a hard time squaring that particular circle."

Danny paused. "Maybe the person who pulled the trigger works there, or used to, anyway." He shrugged.

"That would explain it, for sure, but the place closed so long it seems unlikely," Carol added.

"The whole thing is unlikely. I mean, the carjacker idea just can't hold water, right?" He looked at his wife. Carol nodded. "It has to be something else. The fact that he used to work there suggests he chose the place deliberately, though we can't absolutely prove that."

"Maybe someone else suggested it to him, to make him feel more at ease with a familiar location," Carol ventured.

"I suppose," Danny allowed, "but that seems just as unlikely, given that he hadn't worked there for years, either. And then there's Bucholz's behavior at the site. Would you believe he tried to climb the fence?"

"Really? You think he was trying to get away from them," she stated more than asked.

"Maybe." Danny rubbed his scalp, deep in concentration. She knew the look – he was trying to visualize the last actions of the victim.

"But then why not jump in his car, or run out towards the road, or…?"

"Exactly," Danny agreed, slapping a palm on his knee. "Even if he *had* been able to get over the fence, what difference would it have made with someone chasing him with a gun? They would have just shot him through the fence."

"Or shot him trying to climb it."

"Which is what I would have expected," he added. "But just one gunshot at close range. No struggle."

"So he tried to climb the fence, failed, and then waited there for the killer or killers to walk right up to him and shoot him?" Carol raised a skeptical eyebrow.

"He must have known them," Danny shrugged. "That's all I can figure. Maybe they were joshing around, and Bucholz was showing them how he used to climb the fence in the old days, and they took him by surprise. Maybe they had him covered and they were all trying to get over the fence, so they could shoot him deeper in the park, where no one would hear. I don't know. None of it really feels right."

"I agree," said Carol, "but I wouldn't be surprised if he did know his killer." She sat up with a mischievous look on her face.

"Honey? Do you know something I don't?"

"Me?" she protested. "Not at all, Mr. Big Shot Detective Man. After all, I'm just the little woman. What could I have found out?"

He grimaced. "OK, I didn't ask. I'm sorry. I got carried away. I had some good luck today. What about you, sweetie?"

She smiled. "I had a little luck today, too. Did you know that one of Mark's high school buddies is in the mob?"

"*The* mob?"

"*The* mob," answered Carol, eyes twinkling, as she picked up another piece of pizza. "Pretty nice find for the first day, eh?"

"I'll say," he said approvingly. "Show me what you got."

Carol opened a manila folder on the couch and turned the pages towards Danny, her index finger ticking off the critical items as she talked about them. "Max Litinov. Graduated high school with Bucholz. Can't tell how close they were, but he came to the funeral, so, you know." Danny nodded. "Two years after graduation, he was arrested in a police raid on an illegal gambling operation operating out of a store front in Skokie. Never charged, he was probably too unimportant to waste time on. No other arrests, but his name comes up in newspaper stories on his uncle, Dmitri Litinov." She showed a picture of a middle-aged, balding man with an elegant white mustache that looked like it might actually have been waxed. It had reminded Carol of a nineteenth-century aristocrat. All that was missing was the monocle and top hat.

"The uncle's definitely connected. Multiple indictments for running illegal poker games up in Evanston of all places, smuggling cigarettes from Canada, stolen cars shipped out of here to Eastern Europe, and the like. No convictions, yet, anyway."

"Russian mob types, I'm guessing by the name?"

"I mean, I'm not an organized crime expert. The Litinovs are US citizens, but maybe they built some bridges back to the old country."

"Frank will be able to find out, I guess. You said this Max Litinov is mentioned in connection with his uncle. How?"

Carol smiled. "The boy made good. He's a lawyer now, graduated from John Marshall. He's helped represent his uncle in his recent encounters with the law. I mean, he's barely out of his twenties, so he's not taking the lead, but he appears on lists of his defense teams. Maybe keeping an eye on the hired help."

"Anything else yet?"

"This wasn't enough, honey?"

Danny chuckled as he took a swig from his beer. "It's pretty good. Now we've just got to show that any of this had anything to do with Mark Bucholz."

"You sound like you have an idea how to do that," she said warily.

"Today I called Gerry Lundgren, like I said I would. Time to make use of my faded and minimal celebrity to get some results." He briefly explained.

"OK, honey, I can live with that one. And I did make that phone call today," she added, "so we have the appointment tomorrow, after class and my union stewards' meeting on campus. I checked with the archives, and they will take the recording, so we're not really lying to her."

"Sounds good," he nodded. "If Frank and Mike aren't willing to go talk to her, then we have to."

She gave him a look she normally reserved for a student's lengthy and ridiculous explanation of a late assignment. "We don't *have* to do any of this."

"It's just a conversation, really."

She rolled her eyes, but lovingly took his hand. "It's not. But you've got a bug in your ear about this case. I'm coming along because at least while I'm there I can keep an eye on you."

"And maybe you've got a little bug in your ear, too."

She winked. "Plus, I ask better questions."

"Maybe." He smiled contentedly.

It wasn't until after she had gone up to bed that Danny called Scott Brubaker and left a discreet voice mail message.

Chapter 10

Carol pressed the doorbell at precisely one o'clock. She was in full librarian mode, with a cardigan, slightly overdone hair and a chain on her glasses. Danny stood a step behind her to the side, fiddling uncomfortably with the long cord of the small microphone as the newly-widowed Janet Bucholz opened the door.

The University Archives had introduced its "Families of the Fallen" oral history project some years before. Carol Alexander had been on the faculty team that had developed it. Researchers (mostly unpaid community volunteers and the occasional graduate student) sat with family members of those who had died in Iraq and Afghanistan, asking them to reminisce, share stories, and discuss life after losing their loved ones. The collected audio file would provide, so the grant proposal read, "a peek into the lives of ordinary American families dealing personally with global events." In this case, it would help two very amateur detectives interrogate someone without her knowledge or, arguably, consent.

Danny had lobbied strenuously to take the lead part but Carol would have none of it. "It's more ethical this way," she'd said, in a tone she knew he had learned did not brook argument. "I work for the University, and I even got the okay from the Archives to do it. You get to run the recorder, that's it." He had truly done his best to change her mind, but Carol had planted herself firmly on the high ground.

Janet's blonde hair was tied back economically, her eyes spoke volumes about her lack of sleep in the last week, and she was in nothing more elaborate than jeans and a sweatshirt, but there was no hiding her toned physique and blemish-free skin. Carol's appreciation of Janet Bucholz's looks quickly disappeared as she took in the sad condition of the woman in front of her. If Janet recognized Carol and Danny from the funeral, she showed no sign.

"Mrs. Bucholz," Carol began. "Carol Alexander. I'm so sorry for your loss. I really appreciate you giving us the time to do this." Janet managed a smile. "Of course, Professor. I understand. Please come in." They walked in a large entry hall with a broad, straight stair running to the upper floors, and she led them to a sitting room to one side of the hall, decorated with two leather sofas and, in the corner, a baby grand piano in dazzling white.

Carol gestured to Danny. "This is Chet, one of our sound technicians." She had won the coin toss to choose his name. "Do you mind if we get set up with the microphones?" Janet nodded, and Carol made a show of looking around and they settled on the leather sofas. Chet busied himself plugging in the recorder and placing two microphones, one near each woman. "This is a beautiful home," said Carol, honestly. "How long have you lived here?"

"We moved in right after we got back from our honeymoon? Mark found it before we were even engaged, and he went ahead and bought it right away, but we waited until we were married to move in. It was nice, y'know?"

"Oh, I'll bet," agreed Carol. "Chet, are we ready?" Chet gave an affirmative grunt and tried to step on her foot behind the coffee table out of sight, but she slipped out of the way. "Let me just get the formal stuff out of the way." She spoke the date and time into the microphone. "Interview with Janet Bucholz, wife of the late Mark Bucholz, for the University's Families of the Fallen audio archive." She smiled sympathetically. "Maybe, Mrs. Bucholz, you could start by telling us about how the two of you met."

Slowly, with some helpful prompting from Carol, the widow began her story. She and Mark had grown up in the same neighborhood, and gone all through school together, but they were never very close.

"We moved in different circles, kind of, y'know?" she said.

Carol nodded. "How did it happen, finally?"

"When he came back from Iraq, he was a different man, I think?" Janet's tendency to end lots of sentences with question marks was distracting, and Carol struggled to suppress her teacher's instinct to advise and correct. "We were both at a party and he came right up to me. He was all clean-cut and everything? And, anyway, he said he'd been hoping to see me because he wanted to show me something, and out he pulls this *amazing* bracelet that he said he'd gotten because he thought of me, and he gave it to me *right there*."

She reached out her right hand, and Carol and Danny both let out involuntary gasps at the agglomeration of gemstones. "That's so adorable!" said Carol, genuinely.

"I know. It was such a great gift, and he was just so... confident, y'know? We started going out, and it was like a movie. Great restaurants, shopping in downtown Chicago? We used to take these weekend trips to this fantastic lodge up in Lake Geneva, and he'd always have champagne and strawberries waiting for us when we got to the room. He just swept me off my feet."

"Sounds so romantic!" said Carol with just the right mixture of excitement and sorrow. "Where was your honeymoon?"

Janet gestured to a framed photo on the wall of a younger her and Mark Bucholz standing on the deck of a ship, the sun setting behind them in a blaze of color. "We took a Mediterranean cruise. 17 days. It was really amazing. Europe is just so interesting, y'know?"

That led to a varied and at times less-than-charitable exchange between the two women about the habits and manners of non-Midwesterners, interrupted when Janet briefly went to the kitchen to bring coffee out for her and Carol. The conversation then segued to Janet retrieving a photo album from that very trip, which then, seemingly at random, led to Carol asking to see the photo album from Janet and Mark's wedding.

The pictures were extremely well done, doing much to hide Mark Bucholz's essential plainness, especially alongside his wife, who was in nearly every physical respect a strikingly beautiful woman, with natural golden hair and perfect teeth. Carol looked admiringly through the many shots of Janet Bucholz, and had the good grace to act fully interested in pictures of the bridesmaids and groomsmen as Janet listed their names. The whole experience fairly reeked of sisterly bonding, and Carol smoothly managed to get Janet Bucholz to identify Max Litinov as a groomsman alongside several of Mark's military friends. The picture was unrecognizable compared to the grainy newspaper pictures – Litinov cleaned up well.

Carol also noticed that Janet seemed to involuntarily shudder whenever a picture of Max Litinov was shown.

Having admired the engagement ring on Janet's finger (another stunning specimen: whatever his other faults – such as the occasional murder - Mark Bucholz could pick jewelry), Carol then brought the conversation back to Mark's service to his country.

"Did he ever talk much about his time in Iraq?"

"No. He said he spent all his time in Baghdad and never got shot at, but that sometimes he was near mortar attacks and stuff like that?"

"Did he ever have to shoot at anything?" asked Carol with something approaching a panicked curiosity.

"They made him practice, but I don't think he ever did anything real."

"He was in a supply unit, right?"

"Right. He said he mostly did paperwork and inventory and so on. That's why he went to accounting school nights when he got back?"

"Oh," said Carol, with far greater interest than the subject surely warranted. "I didn't know he was an accountant."

"Well, he never actually finished, y'know? He got the job in the city and settled down with that. It was the same kind of stuff he used to do in Iraq, he said."

"Did he like it?"

"It was okay, I guess? He took the train every day, because he'd play games on his phone or listen to music, and he could do the work easy enough, I guess? He liked to be home, though, with Jacob and me, more than he liked work." Her face transformed with a melancholy smile.

They continued. Carol walked her through Mark's social life – church on Sundays about half the time, friends he hung out with at the local sports bar, the occasional weekend driving trips. The name Max Litinov never again passed anyone's lips, despite doggedly roundabout persistence on Carol's part. She asked about the birth of their son, drawing some tears as she did, and then brought the subject up to the present.

"I hate to ask about that day, Janet," she said, quietly. "But I'd like to hear about it from your perspective."

Janet Bucholz took a sip of coffee. "He just had a couple hours' work at the office, y'know. I didn't ever think he should go in? He had the rest of the day off. We were going to paint the new bedroom we're going to move Jacob to when he gets a little bigger. He left around the usual time, and I thought he'd be back around ten or eleven."

"You said he liked to take the train. Did he drive to run errands on the way home?"

Janet paused, looked down into the mug in her hands. For the first time in the conversation chose her words with some care. "I don't know why he drove. He wasn't supposed to run any errands."

Carol did not appear to notice Janet's sudden discomfort. "When did you first start to get worried about him?"

She evidently felt on safer ground with the question, as she answered readily. "Not until after lunchtime. I texted him, and asked how much longer he was going to be. He didn't respond, but his office was on the inside of his building and he didn't get great reception so I wasn't too surprised right away? By like, 1:30, though, things were weird, so I called his office and they said he'd left like around 9:00. I called Paul and he said I should call the police."

"Paul is your brother?" Janet nodded. "When did you finally find out?"

"Around four, I think. Someone from the police pulled up and I saw them walk to the door. I knew then." She seemed oddly stoic about it.

Carol gave a delicate pause then moved on. "Can I ask what you think happened that day? The police say it was a carjacking, right?"

"I don't know what happened," she responded. Too firmly. Too definitive.

"What do you think happened?" repeated Carol, casually, placing no importance on it.

A note of something that might have been desperation crept into the very back of Janet Bucholz's voice. "I really don't know. I don't know."

Carol gave another sympathetic smile. "I'm sorry to pry, Janet. It must be so hard for you right now. Can I just finish up with a couple of questions about your... plans and so forth now?" Janet nodded distractedly.

"Where do you work, Janet?"

"I used to wait tables," she said, somewhat ashamedly. "But when Mark and I got married he told me I didn't need to work anymore, so I stopped, y'know? I have to get started on that again, I guess," she added, without conviction.

"Do you think you'll stay here in your house, or is it full of too many tough memories?"

"I'll stay," said Janet, with a note of defiance. "I worked hard to get here, and Jacob deserves to be raised in a good home."

"How will you remember your husband, Janet?" Carol asked in conclusion.

They could see her weighing her words. "He loved me and he loved Jacob. I'll remember that."

*   *   *

"She knows something, that's for sure," said Carol Alexander to her brother.

Danny and Carol had left Janet's interview and driven downtown to have a very late lunch with Frank Gaffney and Mike Levin. The two professionals quite properly expressed alarm and unease at their compatriots' usurpation of law enforcement functions, but nevertheless listened carefully and even took notes.

"Well," said Frank, "something sure doesn't seem right about it, I'll give you that."

"The first question, obviously," added Mike, "is where Mark Bucholz is getting his money."

"That bracelet was sapphires and diamonds," said Carol, with a hint of awe. "It was nicer than anything I've ever owned, and my husband makes big baseball dollars. I wouldn't be the slightest bit surprised if it was over ten thousand. The engagement ring, too. That stone had brilliant clarity, and was easily two carats, plus plenty of smaller diamonds around it."

"And a seventeen-day cruise as a honeymoon?" said Mike. "Where's he getting his money all these years?"

"Where *had* he gotten his money, you mean," corrected Danny. "You're speaking as though he had a constant source of extra money all these years. I don't think so."

"But all the things he bought?"

"Bought in the past tense. As in way in the past. He gets back from Iraq and in the first year or so he spends money like water. The jewelry. A cruise. The housing market was wild back then, so he might have been able to get a home with not much down, but that house is a McMansion. Four thousand square feet, minimum, thousand more if there's a basement.

"Also cars," Carol added. "He had a BMW, and his wife had a Lexus parked in the front driveway. But both were from around 2010. If he had new money coming in, why haven't they gotten new cars? That's what people with lots of money do, at least if they've already shown their colors by splurging on jewelry and cruises."

Levin nodded thoughtfully. "What if he saved his money in the service? I didn't save much during my time in, but I know some who did."

Danny snorted. "I just don't buy it. A PFC today doesn't make more than $25,000 in a year. I looked it up online," he added, a touch defensively. "How much could he save? Heck, even if he'd managed to save $60,000 or so, the purchases he made would have run to north of $200,000 or more, plus whatever he put down on the house. Besides, it's the splurging that I think is most interesting. Maybe we'll look and find he inherited something or cleaned up at poker games or whatever, but the point is he got it and spent it."

"To win the affections of a woman," added Carol.

"Right," agreed Danny. "A not-too-bright woman who was probably the class hottie when he graduated high school. He threw money at her and it worked."

"I'm sorry," said Frank, "but you're belaboring the point. Let's accept that Mark Bucholz showed a lot of cash when he got back from Iraq. I presume, though you haven't yet said it, that this money has something to do with Max Litinov and his criminal uncle Dmitri. Or so you think."

"I know, it's still pretty thin, but there's one other thing."

"What's that?"

"Janet is scared of someone. And she's not a fan of Litinov."

Carol nodded agreement, "She got edgy whenever his name came up."

"There's more," added Danny. The Bucholzs live in Crystal Lake. City requires a tax sticker for your cars in your front windshield. Janet's car, parked in front of their house, had no sticker."

"So?"

"The side windows were tinted, but the passenger side window up front had a noticeably different tint than the others."

Frank tapped his watch. "I'm waiting."

"Both the front windshield and the passenger window were recently replaced," concluded Danny. "Janet Bucholz had her car windows broken sometime a few weeks before the murders. Probably by the Litinovs."

"Slow down there, Danny," said Frank, gently. "God love you two for your spunk and all that, but what you really have are a lot of imaginative speculations. Mike went over to St Charles and spoke to the Kane County Sheriff's office today, and Litinov never even appears in the Bucholz case file, right?" He looked over to his partner.

"Right," said Mike. "They've got no evidence linking Bucholz to anyone criminal. They searched his office at work and came up dry."

"Did they look at his phone records?"

"I didn't ask..." Mike paused. Frank's phone began vibrating. They exchanged a glance as Frank got up to answer it.

"Bucholz's office is in the interior of the building, right?" asked Danny. "Did they search any of the offices with window views overlooking the crime scene?"

"No. They had no reason to suspect anything happening in those rooms... hell, I'm still not suspecting it, either. Anyone else but you, Danny..." Mike went on, but Danny cut him off.

"I know, I know. I've got nothing yet that ties Bucholz to the Willis Marden shooting. Get a warrant and search the whole law office. I bet you'll find something. Also, search the Bucholz's house. She was way too calm about being able to support herself financially. Waiting tables doesn't support huge homes and a

Lexus. She should have been more worried about money. Also, someone needs to give me a reason why Bucholz drove to work that day, when he always took the train."

"Danny, I hate to break it to you, but we have nothing even remotely resembling cause for a warrant. Neither does the Kane County Sheriff, for that matter. I have no connection from my case to Bucholz at all. None."

Danny opened his mouth to reply, but Carol laid her hand softly on his arm, and he went quiet. "I know he did it. I know it," he said, more to himself than to them.

Frank came back to the table with a poker face. "And you still think Marden wasn't the intended target, don't you?" he asked.

Carol took a moment to answer. "We did, until you came over here. What is it?"

Frank looked at his sister. "Did any of your library sleuths come across the name Reggie Hayfield?"

"No, not yet."

"He works at the same bank Willis Marden did, and this morning on his way to his neighborhood train station he was shot in the chest."

Chapter 11

Sports agent Gerry Lundgren was fairly certain his client had
suffered mild to moderate brain damage. It was the only way to
explain why Danny Alexander was behaving the way he was.

Now in his late sixties, Lundgren had been a starter at Michigan in
a time when it was still normal for football players to be 5'7". His
hair had largely departed the top of his head. A reasonably sized
paunch failed to remain concealed under rather ill-fitting suits; his
wife of forty-three years had never insisted he dress to the nines,
so he didn't. There was a time when Gerry Lundgren was one of
the top up-and-comers in the country, a smart and tough
defensive lineman with lightning reflexes that left bigger
opponents flat on their face. He graduated from college glory to
the pros, where he had three highly inglorious years. Cut from
his team, he was quick to realize that professional sports were
becoming much *more* professional every day. He convinced a few
former teammates to let him be their agent, and a new and
lucrative career was born.

Danny Alexander was usually an easy client, but as Gerry sat in
this random lawyer's office listening to Danny talk nonsense
about making instructional videos about pitching, he wondered if
that was about to change. Some clients got early signs of
dementia late in their careers. Usually the football players, but
still. Gerry knew better than to say anything, though. He nodded
encouragingly as Danny told his story, about his lifelong passion
for passing his knowledge of the game on to the next generations,
with an earnestness that could not have been genuine.

Lundgren was used to quirks in his clients. Professional athletes
exist in a more rarefied atmosphere than the rest of us. Gerry had
become resigned to Danny's unerring but slightly eerie practice
telling fellow players that he knew they were cheating on their

wives, which led to more than one locker room altercation. His teammates were even less enamored of the rare but disturbing occasions when Alexander would predict aloud, to the bench, that their colleague at the plate would strike out in however-many pitches. Those events meant more than a few phone calls, and, eventually, specific clauses in Danny's contracts. Unusual, yes, but nothing Gerry wasn't prepared to handle in the interests of his business.

But, for all of that, Gerry was having a hard time figuring out what Danny was up to today.

The phone call had been bizarre. Without any sincerity at all, Danny talked about making and marketing an instructional video about pitching techniques, and how he wanted to be able to use footage of his own play as part of the video. Gerry patiently walked him through the numerous levels of permission that would be required to get Major League Baseball to consent to such an enterprise only to have Danny declare that he was sure there was a way around the copyright laws to let him do it. He knew a law firm, he claimed, that specialized in copyright law. They were brilliant, located right there in Chicago. He insisted that only this law firm, Owens, Hampton and Picard, could help them. Gerry knew when clients needed to be pampered.

For business meetings away from the ball park, Gerry had never seen Danny Alexander in anything more casual than an open-necked shirt and sport coat, so he was surprised to see him wearing blue jeans and a jersey from the two seasons he spent playing for a Chicago team more than ten years previously. He even had the team's cap on his head, and carried a large duffel bag, from which, once they reached Owens, Hampton and Picard's offices, he produced baseballs signed by his old Chicago teammates and extravagantly presented them to every paralegal and assistant he met as they were escorted to the lawyer's office.

Stan McCrory was a polite, perfectly average lawyer of fifty-some years old. He had drawn the meeting because he was one of the few people in the office to remember Danny Alexander's time playing for Chicago, and instinctively understood that this meeting was going to be about flattering the ego of a past-his-prime ballplayer. He took patient notes as they sat around a small table in his office, made warm by the sunlight coming through floor-to-ceiling windows.

Lundgren sat in mute confusion as his watched Danny tell story after story about his days playing in Chicago, to McCrory's polite and unbored amusement. Gerry's confusion increased as he realized the tales Danny told were not remotely true, but all calculated to make Danny appear to be little more than a blundering fool with the IQ of a birthday cake, one step above a simpleton, in a voice that seemed borrowed from a surfing pothead.

Gerry had to jump in time and again to try to bring the subject back to copyright law. It was a difficult challenge for Gerry, because had an instinctive tendency to answer anyone's amusing story with one of his own. Still, after more than forty-five minutes of this bizarre act of theatre, Gerry was able to get the meeting nearly to a conclusion. McCrory (whose firm, Gerry had discovered on the internet the night before, did not in fact specialize in copyright law at all) gave the expected answer to Danny's questions, the same answer that nearly all lawyers give nearly all the time: "Maybe, but it depends."

They were all shaking hands and saying their farewells when Danny turned to the lawyer and asked, in the tone of nothing more than a joke, "Everyone looks kind of down around this place, you know? Who died?"

McCrory struggled to hide his mortification. "Actually, last week one of our staff was killed in a robbery."

Danny looked horrified. "Holy crap. I'm so sorry, Stan, man. Wow. I had no idea. Jesus. What an asshat I am today."

The contrition was deep and profound, and yet Gerry felt a sharp kick to his ankle, out of sight of the lawyer, and understood he was to play a part in this, too. "That *is* just tragic. Who was it?"

Danny sat back down, so Gerry did, too, and Stan had to follow. "His name was Mark Bucholz, and he was one of our human resources staff."

"And he was murdered in a robbery? How awful!" emoted Gerry, quite genuinely. "Did they catch who did it?"
"Not yet," said the attorney, gravely.

"Did you know him well?" asked Gerry, with solemn concern. Now that he had caught up, he reacted gamely. Clients always come first.

"A little bit," responded McCrory, looking slightly uncomfortable that he did not know the deceased better. "He handled our health insurance and things like that. Quiet guy. He had a really nice family, I heard, but he kept to himself a lot."

"Was he robbed on the street out there?" asked Danny, craning his neck and peering out onto the crowded avenue below.

"No. He was carjacked on his way home from work, and I guess he fought back because they killed him."

"Well, that's just horrible," said Gerry, shaking his head sadly, stalling while he tried to think of another question. "Did you see him that day?"

"I don't think so. He was only in for a while in the morning. He had scheduled an all-office meeting that day at 9:30 to go over changes in our insurance carrier, but he emailed a cancellation about 8:45 or so. Too bad," said Stan, wistfully. "No one likes those kinds of meetings, but I would have preferred sitting in that meeting to what happened."

"Well, you can't do anything about that," commiserated Gerry.

"How are the people here taking it?" asked Danny. McCrory did not notice that he had ceased doing a stoner impression and returned to normal, but Gerry did.

"The people in his department are having a hard time still, and it's kind of bringing us all down." McCrory shrugged his shoulders.

"I bet," said Danny. "Look, I've got all these baseballs and stuff" - he gestured to his duffel bag - "maybe I could go around and pass some of these things out. I know people don't really remember me all that well, but I bet some of the autographs I have would mean something to folks."

If McCrory found the offer a tad weird, he evidently recognized that it was delivered in a good spirit. "Sure, that'd be great. I hope you don't mind if I let you do it on your own. I've just got a lot of..."

"Oh, sure, I understand," said Danny quickly, rising. He reached his hand over for one more handshake and then quickly began backing towards the door, all but pulling Gerry with him.

"Thanks so much for meeting with us today. Your advice was very helpful." He was out before Stan McCrory even had time to respond.

Danny shut the door to the lawyer's office and stood for a moment, looking each way up and down the long hallway. He picked a direction and started walking with determination. Gerry Lundgren composed himself and caught up to his client.

"What in the heck are you...?" he began, but Danny wasn't listening, and began talking over him. He grabbed his agent by the elbow and pulled him into a little nook with a pair of drinking fountains.

"Why do you call an all-staff meeting and then cancel it at the last minute? What was he thinking?"

"Why are you so interested in this guy's murder?" interjected Gerry as Danny took a breath. "Did you know this guy?".

Danny stopped and did a double take as if his mind hadn't quite realized he'd been asked a question. "Well, yes and no. I think I know how he died. What I'm trying to figure out is why *he* killed a guy."

"Wait! What?" Gerry raised a hand to his brow in a gesture of confusion.

"Yeah, I think on the day he died he was up here with a high-powered rifle and..." he stopped. His eyes widened. "Ohhhh... of course!" He suddenly took off again with great speed and purpose.

"What of course?" hissed Gerry in a forced whisper as he chased after his client.

"Why do you call an all-staff meeting and then cancel it?" asked Danny, triumphantly.

"I give up," said Gerry, looking up and down the hall, trying to see if anyone had noticed their out-of-place behavior.

"Excuse me, miss?" Danny stopped a young woman carrying a stack of manila folders. "I'm supposed to be meeting someone in the 'big' conference room?" He made air quotes with his hands.

The woman smiled, unable to hide her amusement at Danny's apparent desperation. "You're on the wrong floor. The large conference room is downstairs, then at the northwest corner," she pointed, "that way."

There were elevators at the end of the hall, but Danny saw the fire door was closer, and all but ran to the stairway. He rushed down the steps, his duffel bag bouncing loudly into him as he descended. He exited from the sterile concrete staircase, Gerry puffing behind him. The hallway they were in was nearly identical to the one above, with the same thick carpeting, but down at the end of the hallway was a large double door. He smiled at Gerry as he practically ran to it. "When you call meetings in a place like this you reserve the conference room."

He pointed. A piece of paper was in a plastic holder in the wall. It was a weekly calendar, broken down by day and hour, with names scrawled illegibly in about half the vacant spaces. "And, when you cancel the meeting with just an hour's advance notice, you know the room will be empty, so you will be undisturbed." He practically giggled in excitement, and opened the door. "In we go." He pulled Gerry after him and closed the door.

In the center of the conference room sat a long mahogany table – suitably grand for a downtown law firm - and plenty of extra chairs around the outside so that close to forty people could be packed in. It had the usual fluorescent lights, but they were largely unnecessary since six-foot-high windows ran all along the two outside walls of this corner room, ensuring good lighting any time the sun was up.

Gerry took a couple of steps in and looked around. "You think that guy Mark *killed* someone in here?" He was so incredulous his voice almost squeaked.

"*From* here," said Danny, who was already moving around the table, his eyes scanning the bottoms of the windows facing down the street. He gave a small cry of triumph and dived into his duffle bag, from which he extracted a small digital video camera.

He handed it to Gerry. "Probably a good idea to get this on tape. It'll make it easier for Frank to get the warrant. Here," he indicated on the camera, "just press this and try to keep it pointed at me. Go for a medium shot, that'll be fine." Gerry just stared at him. Danny took the camera, adjusted the zoom to an appropriate level, and handed it back. "Just point it."

Gerry held the camera down at his side. "So, those stories I occasionally hear about you. They're true, aren't they?"

Danny was slowly walking along the windows, looking at each one carefully and slowly. "Which stories?" he asked, not really listening.

"The ones where you spend your off days looking at crime scenes and calling in tips to the police. The ones where you practice taking fingerprints from the bats in the dugout. Those stories."

"Some of them might be true," Danny allowed, stopping next to a window near the corner. "Bring the camera over here."

Gerry stood closer as Danny pointed at the bottom of the glass. "Make sure the camera sees this. These windows are built to go up about eight inches – enough to let in some air but not enough to let some crazy jump. You can tell most of these haven't been opened in some time – but this one has a clear line at the bottom. It was opened and closed recently, within the last few weeks, and there's a hole in the screen. This is where he was." Danny looked around. "Makes sense. The far corner of the room from the door, so if someone did come in, he'd have a few seconds to hide what he was doing."

He reached into the duffel bag and pulled out a small bottle, a roll of tape and a plastic baggie with Q-tips.

"You think this guy Bucholz fired a rifle from here and shot someone." Gerry was now fully up to speed. It was a statement, not a question.

"Willis Marden, to be precise."

"Who's Willis Marden?"

"Who's Willis Marden?" Danny turned to Gerry, incredulously. "Have you been living under a rock the past week?"

Gerry gave him a sour look. "Not under a rock. Under a roof in my house in Brooklyn. We have our own crimes in New York you know."

"Oh. Right," said Danny. "Sorry."

He tore off a strip of tape and pressed it to the metal frame of the window. "My guess is the cleaning crew vacuums and dusts the table, but doesn't do the windows very often. I think we have a good chance." He placed the strip of tape on the table, opened the bottle and dipped the Q-tip in it and spread the liquid over the tape. "Keep the camera on that strip for the next five minutes."

"On TV, they can test for gunshot residue instantly," Gerry observed.

Danny rolled his eyes. "I got this off the internet. It's an instant shooter identification kit. If the strip turns blue, it indicates nitrocellulose, which is a component of gunpowder. It's not a perfect test, but if it comes out positive I think it'll be enough for my brother-in-law to come back here with a warrant and a forensics team. They'll be able to prove it."

He stared at the strip, willing it to change color.

*   *   *

Frank Gaffney stared at the report on his desk, willing it to yield more information. He knew it was a lost cause, but there was nothing more he could do.

Reggie Hayfield was a loan officer at City Guaranty and Trust. He took the elevated train every morning from his apartment to the stop nearest the bank's south side branch. He was regular as clockwork: 7:57 train, arriving at 8:16, giving him fourteen minutes to cross the street and start his shift at 8:30. He was thirty-one and ambitious, a semester short of finishing his MBA at Roosevelt University. He paid his rent on time. He was unmarried but with a steady girlfriend who managed a women's fashion boutique on State Street. He had forty-five hundred dollars in his checking account, a small 401(k) invested somewhat adventurously, and no debts aside from student loans and three payments left on a Chevy. He had one speeding ticket from four years earlier but had never been arrested, suspected, questioned or had any other encounters with police, until a few days previously when Detective Mueller had done a routine interview with him as part of the canvass of all of Willis Marden's co-workers, an interview that had raised no red flags of any kind.

Now he was recuperating in a city hospital from a gunshot wound to the chest, and Detective Gaffney's faith in the power of coincidences was wearing thin.

It was only a trifecta, but bad enough. No weapon, no immediate suspect, outdoor crime scene. Only this time, unlike with Marden, no one had claimed to be a witness.

They had recovered shell casings from four shots, fired from the end of the alley Hayfield walked through every morning to cut over to the El tracks. Hayfield had been halfway down the alley when the shooter had fired from behind a dumpster. One round had struck him in the right side of his chest, hitting too high to penetrate a lung but still doing a lot of damage. The others had gone wide. Shell casings were nice. If they found the gun, they could match them. But they hadn't found the gun yet.

As best Gaffney could tell, the shots were fired to coincide with the loud arrival of the train on the elevated tracks just a half block away. No one remembered hearing them. There were no security cameras around except at the train station, and they were of a far lower quality than what Gaffney's team had watched in Union Station, essentially useless. No one had seen, heard, or suspected anything until Reggie Hayfield, bleeding badly and a hair's breadth away from going into shock, had managed to dial 911.

Gaffney had spoken to the resilient Hayfield earlier in the morning; an operation the previous evening had repaired the critical injuries and he was expected to make a full recovery. He had seen a figure in a ball cap hat and dark jacket firing at him. The shooter was probably white, but Hayfield couldn't be sure, probably male, but again he wouldn't swear to it, of undetermined height and a medium build, but that was all. The shooter had been sixty feet away, the alley had been dark, and he'd only had a moment's look before the whole experience of getting shot distracted him. He was lucky that the train had arrived when it did; if it had been ten seconds later, he would have been that much closer to the shooter, and the other three rounds might have done the job.

And that was all that Detective Gaffney had to work with. The sum total of his useful evidence was four shell casings from a widely-available handgun and a physical description that matched just under two million people in the city of Chicago alone.

At times like this, Gaffney tried to avoid (usually failed to avoid) moving his attention to the stale chestnut that launched a thousand mediocre mystery novels: motive.

It's not that motive didn't matter. It did. It's just that of the well-worn triumvirate of means, motive, and opportunity, motive was the perennial winner of the bronze medal. If faced with a choice, he always suspected those with means or opportunity before those with motive. Sure, a jury always likes a juicy motive to help push them over the line to a guilty verdict. But, officially, motive doesn't matter that much. Gaffney had long discovered that in many of the violent crimes he had investigated that the person with the strongest motive was not always the perpetrator. Indeed, in a surprising number of cases, he was never able to figure out a reasonable motive to explain the criminal's actions. Gaffney slept more easily because of this fact: it eased his mind to recognize that the people who committed violent crimes didn't do so because of logic or reason. Murder wasn't the rational answer to any question.

But what else did he have here? There was no way that the murder of Willis Marden wasn't connected to the Hayfield shooting, but absolutely no evidence that it was. None. Hayfield and Marden worked in the same branch, but no one described them as particularly close. They'd never called each other. They didn't have offices near each other. They didn't go out to lunch together. Hayfield had never worked on anything related to Alderman Stringfellow. No connections at all.

The clock kept ticking. Marden had been killed a week and a day ago – an infinity in murder investigations. They were no closer to anything on that case, or the shots fired outside Phil Swigert's office, and now they had this case, too. And every day, he lost more manpower to the competing needs of an overstretched police department.

So now: motive. Who might have a motive to try to kill Willis Marden, Robinson Stringfellow (and/or Phil Swigert – no real way to be sure there) *and* Reggie Hayfield? Surely, surely, it had something to do with the Stringfellow investigation, but what? The feds – trying to find a way to get jurisdiction over the Marden case – had thrown every available agent into Stringfellow's finances and the City Trust Bank, and had come up with nothing new. Gaffney wondered if his brother-in-law was onto something; if Willis Marden and Reggie Hayfield hadn't been shot, would the feds would have given up on finding any criminal activity at City Trust? He couldn't be sure.

Was it someone else, trying to frame City Trust? Another bank, looking to cast suspicion in other directions? Would a bank really stoop to *murder* over something like that? Carol would say yes, but in Frank's experience corporations used lawyers and publicists to do their dirty work. Maybe it was another employee at the bank? That didn't make any more sense. And, whoever it was, Gaffney knew Danny Alexander was right about something: a long-range rifle shot at a moving target on a crowded city street was a really stupid way to try to kill someone. So, for that matter, was a handgun fired through a press conference, or a mediocre shot missing three out of four times from sixty feet in an alley.

None of this made much sense. He pulled up the report he was writing on his computer. He'd been given clear orders: a report every morning at ten, and another one every evening at seven. Gaffney wrote slowly, so no sooner had he finished one report than he had to begin the next. How could he package his big pot of nothing this time?

His self-pitying reverie was interrupted by a knock on his door. The desk sergeant peeked her head in. "Detective, someone's in the waiting area up front wants to see you. Think it's someone important. He has that kind of voice."

Gaffney shook his head to clear the cobwebs and walked out front. There stood a tall, magisterial African-American. Still dressed to the nines, still no flash. Gaffney thought, once again, how Robinson Stringfellow looked older than his years on purpose.

"Alderman?" Gaffney nodded his head and they took a few steps over to a quiet corner away from the main entrance. "What can I do for you?" he asked, with perfect and insincere civility.

"You're working Reginald Hayfield's shooting, aren't you?"

"I am, sir, but I'm not at liberty to discuss…"

Stringfellow raised a hand and nodded his head. "I just wanted to talk with you. Can we go to your office?"

Gaffney looked around. "Where's your attorney, Mr. Swigert?"

"I didn't tell him I was coming here."

"Well, then, Alderman, you need to get him or another attorney down here before we talk."

"I don't want him down here." Gone was the menacing snarl of the other day. Stringfellow towered over Frank, but today he looked meeker, more contrite.

Gaffney rolled his eyes. "Sir, I know this game. We talk without your lawyer, and the next thing I know it's coercion. Honestly, I can't believe you thought I might fall for…"

Stringfellow took a step closer to Gaffney and put his large but well-manicured hand gently on his shoulder. He looked into Gaffney's eyes.

"It's not about that. I'm not here playing some kind of game. *I need to talk to you.*" The Aldermen spoke quietly and urgently. He gazed steadily at Detective Gaffney, and Frank could have sworn there was a hint of desperation behind those eyes.

Gaffney stared back, judging the expression, then made his decision. "All right. This way."

As soon as Gaffney had closed the door to his office, Stringfellow spoke. "You think Reggie's mixed up in this thing with me and the bank and Willis Marden, right?"

"It would be a hell of a coincidence if he wasn't, dontcha think?"

"He's not." The tall man was firm.

"Well, glad we got that settled. Thanks for coming by, Alderman." Gaffney started back towards the door.

Stringfellow didn't move to block him, but his words and his steely voice stopped Frank in his tracks. "You're still not listening to me, detective. You need to learn to listen better. I'm telling you, Reggie's not into anything criminal. At all."

"Just like you're not, I'm sure."

Stringfellow shook his head, but his gaze never left Gaffney. It had an intensity that almost burned. "It's just you and me in here, detective. So here it is. Maybe you'll catch me, maybe you won't." He shrugged. "Fine. There that is. But even if I go down, I'm not taking people with me who don't deserve the trip."

Gaffney had long experience telling truth from falsehood, enough to know that you usually couldn't tell, but damn if Stringfellow didn't seem like the most honest man in the world right now. "And you're saying Hayfield's clean."

"Completely."

"And how can you be so sure? You don't know all the criminals in town, do you?"

"I know because I know his family. His parents, Walt and Shelley Hayfield, they're working folks. Walt's got thirty-four years teaching science for CPS. He's a union steward, deacon at All Praise Baptist. Shelley plays the organ on Sundays and teaches music. They got a nice little house with a tiny little backyard. I've had hot dogs over there. So has everyone else in the neighborhood.

"They raised a good boy. They took him to every Little League game, showed up for every school play. Never missed Sunday school. They raised him right. He goes over there two, three nights a week for dinner. He and his dad have season tickets for the White Sox, and they must go to sixty games a year. Terrible seats, because it's all they can afford.

"You're pretty sure I'm rotten, even if you'll never convince a jury. But don't dishonor that boy's family by putting him in with this. He's not like that. He's not like those folks... not like..." He didn't say the last word.

Gaffney mentally picked his jaw off the floor. A feeling that surely could not have been respect agitated inside him. Surely not respect. "OK, Alderman, let's say you're right. Why did someone shoot him then?"

"Was he robbed?" asked Stringfellow.

"No. Shooter never even got close to him."

"Then my guess is that someone's got the wrong guy," said the Alderman, though without much conviction. "It was in an alley, right?" Gaffney nodded. "Maybe they thought it was someone else."

"Hayfield took that same route every day. He says no one else was ever in the alley at that time. Maybe he surprised someone waiting for someone else, or doing something else, but what are the odds...?" Gaffney raised his eyebrows.

"Then the shooter knew it was him but thought he was dirty. Some kind of mistake. He's too honest," said Stringfellow, emphatically. "But Reggie might have been standing right next to something bad and never noticed. Maybe who shot him didn't know that. That's all I can figure."

"Someone at the bank?" Frank asked, cocking his head and looking at Stringfellow over the rims of his reading glasses.

"Look, detective, while we're being all close and cozy here, I'll throw you that one, too. Bank's clean. At least so far as I'm concerned."

"Is that so? Why do I get the hug-and-share about Hayfield, but stonewall about Willis Marden? He *was* in on the shenanigans, eh?" He immediately regretted the use of the word shenanigans.

"I don't know Willis Marden from a doorknob," said Stringfellow, simply. "I got no idea whether he was a good guy or a bad guy or whatever else. I don't know him; I don't know who he is or who he knows. I was telling you the truth about that. I came to you about Reggie because my family and his are friends, and I'm not getting him mixed up in this."

Stringfellow again stepped close, staring down at Gaffney, but there was no menace, no threat. Instead, he was almost pleading. "Do you believe me when I tell you Reggie Hayfield's no crook?"

Gaffney thought about it for a moment. "I do." He surprised himself by saying it.

To his surprise Stringfellow extended his hand, and with a politician's practiced skill gave him a powerful and intimate shake. "Good." He opened the door to leave. "Timeout's over. Good luck with the rest of it. You're a decent cop. Maybe not that swift, but decent. We should get a beer sometime." He grinned and walked out, leaving Frank unable to come up with a suitable riposte.

Huh. The Alderman Stringfellow he'd met the other day deserved nothing more than a life behind bars. This one was … different. Maybe he needed to recalibrate his opinions of the man a little bit. A *very* little bit.

His phone rang. He glanced at the number, sighed, and opened it.

"Be quick, Danny. I've got things to do here."

He could hear the smile on the other end of the line. "You sure do. First thing is to get over to Owens, Hampton and Picard with a forensic team. I've got real evidence now."

*   *   *

It turns out they didn't need a warrant. Robert Hampton, senior partner in the firm, happened to be in the building, and he agreed to let them search the conference room and Bucholz's office without protest. It occurred to Frank that whatever most people thought, silencers weren't actually all that silent, at least not to someone one floor away. Hampton's office was located right above that conference room, and he didn't seem all that surprised when the police arrived.

The initial test by the forensic team matched what Danny had found. The detective and his brother-in-law were drinking coffee in the squad room a few hours later when the lab - breaking all records in a bid to get some credit for success in such a high-profile case – confirmed that there was indeed gunshot residue around that window. They were even able to hazard a guess that it had been there about a week, though when pressed for the reasoning behind that conclusion they were more than a little vague.

"Don't gloat," said Frank, with a reproving glance at Danny's ear-to-ear grin.

"Come on," preened Danny, who was bouncing up and down on his toes again. "Admit you're impressed."

"It's good work," Frank allowed, "but you got lucky."

"The hell I did."

"You got lucky," Frank repeated. "Yes, it was inspired, and God help me, brilliant, but you got lucky. Don't mistake this for real police work. You took a flying leap of logic and it happened to end up being right."

"If I didn't know any better," said Danny, turning to face his brother-in-law, "I'd say you were jealous of my success."

"The hell I am."

"You're not?"

"Of course not," said Frank, standing. "I'm jealous that you make twenty times more than me to play baseball for a living, but not this." He rinsed his mug and set it on the draining board. He tilted his head in the direction of the coffee machine. "More?"

"No, thanks," said Danny, handing his mug over to Frank's outstretched hand. "So, search his house next?"

"And the whole law office. I doubt there's anything to find in the rest of the firm, but we'll run it down. I'll get typing on the warrants now, and we ought to be able to go to his house tomorrow."

Mike Levin swept in with purpose. He nodded to Danny, sat down at the table and opened a file folder. "You got a minute for this?"

Frank gave him a plaintive look. "Do we have to do it in front of him?"

"Am I right about something else?" Danny asked, with faux innocence.

Mike loyally ignored the interloper. "This is interesting. Ely and Cook checked all of Bucholz's phone records for the past two years..."

"I had nothing, eh?" crowed Danny in triumph. "Oh, no, it's just a flying leap of logic from your wacky brother-in-law. There's nothing at all to his crazy theories. Oh, no, nothing at all." He screwed up his face and blew a loud raspberry into the air. "Who's the man?"

Frank and Mike paused, looking anywhere but at Danny.

"Anyway," Levin continued, "Up until about three months ago he made regular calls to Max Litinov's personal phone, mostly evenings and weekends, and some calls to Litinov's law firm – presumably calling him at work."

"How regular?" asked Danny, leaning across the table on his elbows, trying to catch a look at Mike's papers.

Levin shifted quickly to block Danny's view. "Usually two or three calls a week, sometimes more, rarely less. Mostly like ten-minute conversations – looks like friends talking on the phone."

"What happened three months ago?" asked Frank.

"The calls stop. Not a single one from his mobile or his home phone since early June."

"Weird," said Frank.

"Oh, it gets weirder," said Mike.

"Ooh, let me guess," said Danny, eagerly. "He got a second phone, didn't he?"

"Sort of. He got three." He paused for effect. "They were burners – a thousand prepaid minutes and some texting." He looked at Danny, who had stopped moving around and was staring with his mouth open at the detectives. "You got an explanation for the third?"

"Not a thing," said Danny, with surprise in his voice. "Keep going."

"The whole point of burners," asked Frank, "is that they don't have registration information – how do we know he bought them?"

Detective Levin arched his eyebrows. "One of them called Litinov's law office three weeks or so ago. Ely and Cook couldn't find the number so they ran it down. That phone and two others were bought with Bucholz's credit card on June 4th."

"Pretty good work on their part," mused Frank.

"I told them you'd okay OT for them to look at it," Levin glanced up at Gaffney for *ex post facto* permission.

"Fair enough."

"What about the phones?" Danny interjected, fidgeting impatiently. "Who did they call?"

Mike pulled out several more sheets of paper. "It just gets more and more fun. With the exception of the call from Phone 1 to Litinov's office, they only called each other."

He spread the papers out. "Actually, it wasn't quite as simple as that. Phone 2 called Phone 1. Phone 3 called Phone 1. Phone 1 called Phone 2 and Phone 3. But 2 and 3 never communicated."

Gaffney leaned back against the counter and hitched up his pants. The slightly-too-large suit today. "This is making my migraines flare up. What the heck do we have going on here? Bucholz buys burner phones and sets up a comm network with one middleman for two others. Looks like somebody really wanted secrecy."

Danny turned and looked at him. "Right. Secrecy."

"Do you have something to add, civilian?"

"Only, once again it seems like we're dealing with a case of somebody being both too smart and too dumb. Bucholz wants to set up an untraceable phone network, but he pays for them with his credit card, AND calls a landline at Litinov's office, giving the whole game away."

"I agree, that doesn't really add up," said Frank.

"Oh, definitely," said Mike, without conviction, in a flat monotone. "Easily the strangest thing about this whole case."

Danny flashed his television-commercial grin, and nudged Levin in the shoulder. "Something tells me you saved the best for last, Mike."

"I did. There were about fifty phone calls in total, all in the last three months. And only one text." He pulled out one last sheet of paper. "One text. Sent the morning Willis Marden was killed, within a minute or two of the shooting. From Phone 1 to Phone 3. From someone we don't know to someone else we don't know, one of whom might be Mark Bucholz, Willis Marden or Max Litinov, but maybe someone else entirely. Phone company holds all texts for thirty days."

Danny and Frank looked uncomprehendingly at the sheet.

"You took the money and lied. Traitor. My family is in danger so long as you are alive, MAJOR. Bastard. You deserve to die"

They looked at each other in silence for a full minute. Finally, Danny spoke.

"Well, I have no idea what's going on here."

Chapter 12

The warrant for Bucholz's house came through in no time. Because of the multiple jurisdictions – Marden shot in Chicago, Bucholz dead in Kane County but living in McHenry County – officers from five different police forces were there, just in case there was something juicy to find and credit to take. There was.

By any rights a good search of a house that size should have taken hours. They found they gym bag under the Bucholz's bed about ten minutes in. It was almost anticlimactic.

The widow Bucholz sat at her kitchen table, trembling.

"Now, Mrs. Bucholz," Mike Levin began, standing at the granite kitchen island, "The lab guys are going to be looking at it more closely, but my guess is that there must be fifty thousand dollars in there" (the lab guys – which in this case meant two uniforms counting away in the back seat of a squad car – would in fact come up with exactly $50,000, as it turned out.) "Gotta tell you, it looks mighty suspicious." He took a sip of his gas station coffee, casting a brief, envious glance at the stainless-steel cappuccino maker on the kitchen counter.

Now, Janet Bucholz wasn't under arrest, nor had she been read a Miranda warning. She was entirely within her rights to keep her trap shut and refuse to talk. Moreover, if she did offer anything up, any reasonably bright lawyer would make sure it couldn't be used against her. All police officers – especially those experienced enough to have attained the position of a homicide detective – are intimately acquainted with those rules.

However, one also doesn't get the experience to be a homicide detective without realizing that nine times out of ten, people being interviewed by the police don't realize their rights. Even more surprising, and this never ceased to astound Levin, of those nine, at least seven will fail to exercise them when properly informed.

"See, Mrs. Bucholz," he continued, settling into a chair at the kitchen table across from Janet, "not a lot of people have that much money in a gym bag under their bed. And, when one of the people who slept in that bed was murdered just over a week ago, it really gets us in a place where we have to be suspicious. Now, I can do this two ways." He took another sip of his coffee, and pretended to savor the flavor (there was none) as Janet Bucholz grew paler.

"What I really ought to do," he began, talking more to himself than to her, "is take you into custody on suspicion of either larceny or" – in his most casual tone of voice – "murder, and go through the process of..."

He kept going, but Janet Bucholz had gone into a complete panic at the mention of murder charges, and she missed his deliberately boring recital of the process of arresting and charging her. Mike knew this, of course, and so ended his monologue by pushing back his chair, standing up, and leaning forward with his hands on the table to stare her down.

"But you know and I know that if I do that a lot of bad things can happen. So, I think we should try option two, which is we sit here like normal people, and you tell me what's going on. No tricks, no holding things back, just tell me what happened." He saw her visibly relax as he offered her an out, and he changed to a gentler tone. "Where did this money come from?"

"I don't know," she replied, earnestly, with a bewildered face. "I just found it under the bed Monday morning? I have no idea how it got there."

"When's the last time you looked under your bed?"

"Huh?"

"I want to know how long it's been there," Levin explained, patiently. "Do you look under the bed every day, every week, every month?"

"Oh. It's been weeks, I'm sure. We don't keep things under the bed, usually, so I never look down there?" He noted her tendency to make declarative sentences sound like questions.

Levin gestured to the gym bag, contents removed, sitting on the island in a large plastic evidence bag. "Do you recognize the bag?"

She nodded. "It's Mark's gym bag? He used it all the time." She gave him the name of Mark's health club in town, and the detective handed the bag to a uniform who headed out the door.

"Why didn't you inform the police about the bag when you found it?" he asked, without any judgment in his voice, a helpful expression on his face.

"Why? Oh… I just… I didn't really think about it, is all?" It was a lie, but her eyes were unfocused, almost tearing up. She was every bit as confused as everyone else was.

Levin looked at her for a moment. "Do you have any idea where this money could have come from?" She shook her head. "Closed any bank accounts lately? Cashed out an IRA or 401(k) account?" Again no.

He sat back down and leaned across the table, speaking in a confidential stage whisper. "You'dve been lucky to be able to hold onto this money, wouldn't you?"

"What do you mean?" she replied, but he could see Janet knew what he meant.

"I mean, you're kind of running on fumes, am I right?" he asked, like a doctor to a patient.

"We're doing okay," she said, defensively.

Mike popped open his tablet on the table and clicked through to what he needed. "House bought right near the top of the boom for $687,500. Ten percent cash down, the rest at six percent… a little high, but it was a lot of house. Six months later and you would have needed twenty percent down at least. Also, you got a *fifty-year* mortgage. I didn't even know you could do that. Had to look it up on the internet." He paused, having lost his spot in the dense paperwork. "Oh, wait, and there's a second mortgage as well? Sixty-five thousand dollars financed at fourteen percent? Gosh, people did a lot of crazy things like that back in the day."

He looked up. "What's this house worth now, Mrs. Bucholz?"

"I don't know," she said, defensively. Her left knee began bouncing, a fidget.

"Real estate agent I called yesterday said something in the ballpark of $450,000, maybe $500,000. You still owe…" – he flipped another page - "$560,000 or so. Your husband had a $25,000 life insurance policy through his job, but even if you used that, you'd need $100,000 or more to be able to afford selling off this house and paying the mortgage."

"I don't know anything about the mortgage. Mark handled all of that for both of us?" She was becoming overwhelmed by the numbers, he could see, biting her lip as she tried to keep up with the data.

"Well, ma'am, I call 'em like I see 'em, and here's what I see." He put the notebook down, laid his palms flat on the table and stared straight into her eyes. "Guy who never made more than seventy thou a year in his life is paying four grand a *month* in mortgage payments, and still finds the money to buy you all that fancy jewelry we found upstairs, plus the luxury sedans. He was even paying nearly six hundred a week to a place that must be the Ritz-Carlton of day care facilities, despite the fact that you don't have a job."

"So?" She crossed her arms in a defensive posture and avoided his gaze. Her left knee was bouncing up and down faster than a jackhammer, her heel making tiny impact sounds on each downstroke.

Levin raised his voice, not shouting but getting closer. "Where'd the money come from, Janet? We checked his credit cards. He owes north of seventy thousand, but that doesn't come close to the money he spent on you. Who gave it to him? Why?"

"I don't know!" she protested, too loudly, but with a convincing degree of panic in her voice.

"Are you saying you have *never* thought about how your husband could afford all of this?"

Her knee stopped bouncing. He was beginning to make Janet angry. She finally returned his stare. "Of course I did. I even asked him a couple of times, but he would just say he knew how to be frugal, and that I was worth it?"

"How do you think he got the money?"

"I told you, I don't know."

"Then guess," Mike said, slowly. "When you thought about how he paid for everything, what did you think?"

She furrowed her brow, half pretending to think, half thinking. He gave her a few extra moments before he threw down his ace.

"It was Max Litinov, wasn't it?"

Her body reacted. It only took her a moment to regain a semblance of composure, but in that moment, Mike had seen what he expected to see. "Don't try to hide it, Janet. You know Max is associated with some shady people, right?"

"I suppose so?" she replied, meekly. He stared at her and she rolled her eyes and continued. "I watch the news. I know his family is like, the Russian Mafia?"

"And Max was close to Mark, wasn't he?"

"But Mark wasn't in the Mafia? He did human resources for a law firm. He and Max were friends but that was it," protested Janet.

"That brings us back to my question, Mrs. Bucholz. Where did your law-firm-working husband get all his money?"

Her expression hardened and she spoke quietly. "I don't know. All I know is there's none left."

"Besides the..."

"Besides the money in the bag, yeah." She was looking at her hands on the kitchen table, the defiance draining away.

"When did you figure out you were running out of money?"

Janet shrugged. "Mark had been acting funny for the last few months. He was anxious, like something was up."

"Did he start cutting down on the spending?" Levin asked, glancing up to make sure the uniformed officer by the mammoth refrigerator was taking notes.

She nodded. "We were going to go to Crete for a ten-day vacation. We were actually on our way but we ended up turning around at the airport? He said it wasn't a good time to make the trip. He wouldn't tell me the reason why, but I knew he was upset."

"But he never said you were broke?"

"No. He even told me he was going to take me on a Caribbean cruise in the spring to make up for Crete. He said he was going to sell some of our stocks to pay for it."

"Your husband has no stocks. No bonds. No certificates of deposit. Not even a savings account. We've checked. There might be something hidden away, but I don't think so."
She looked uncomprehending for a moment. "Nothing?" And that was that. She wasn't pretending. She didn't know, and the realization that she was soon to lose everything was settling in.

The search went on for more than two hours after that. They found a rifle missing from a gun safe, a Remington registered to Janet's deceased father, which added another layer of confirmation to what was turning into a pretty solid case against the also-deceased Mark Bucholz.

———

Chapter 13

It was Friday, the end of a long week. Frank Gaffney sat at his desk going through the same set of papers for the third time. And it was only 8:00 in the morning. He'd had a precious ninety minutes last night to work in his garage, playing with disc brakes, which was the only reason he was still sane.

The duty officer interrupted his reverie with a quick rap on his open door. "Detective? The FBI is here looking to talk to you."

"The whole agency?" asked Gaffney, not bothering to look up. "Not sure we have the space for them." His morning coffee had yet to have its desired effect, which weakened his sense of humor. The FBI got up earlier than him.

It was only one FBI, as it turned out. Special Agent Cooper Stapley was long and lean, with a neatly trimmed graying mustache. His charcoal suit was immaculate, his tie restrained and professional. The only concessions to humanity were cowboy boots. Not that you noticed any of those things once he looked at you. His steely blue eyes took over, rendering even the strongest of men a little weak. The intensity and directness of his gaze made most people immediately add a ten-gallon hat, a brace of shooting irons, and a tin star to the outfit.

After what seemed to Gaffney to be the most masculine handshake he'd ever experienced, he led Stapley into the conference room and grabbed Mike Levin on the way. They sat down, Stapley keeping ramrod straight without looking forced. "We've mostly been working with Agent Forest on the Marden shooting. Are you taking over?"

An imperceptible shake of the head. "I flew in from Washington this morning." Gaffney tried to work out how early his visitor would have had to awaken to be here by 8:00. Two-and-a-half-hour flight… an hour to get here from the airport in rush hour traffic, the usual hullabaloo at both airports… he must have risen before three in the morning, even with the time change. How does his suit still look so good? "Last night I got a call from someone who thought I might be interested in the connection between Mark Bucholz and the Litinov crime family. It was suggested I come here and talk to you two."

"Who called you…?" Gaffney began, and then he rolled his eyes. "You're kidding. Please tell me he didn't. Please."

Stapley's eyes and mouth moved just enough to suggest a smile. "Your brother-in-law helped me on a case in Arizona a few years ago. Counterfeit baseball memorabilia. Seems to know his stuff."

Gaffney's face was now red with embarrassment. "Yeah, yeah. I know. I just don't like him showing off to the whole world. Could get him into trouble." Stapley acknowledged this with a nod that felt like a benediction. "Why did he happen to call you about this?"

"FBI-DHS task force. Targeting smuggling from Iraq, Syria, Afghanistan and other war zones, by service members and civilian contractors, that sort of thing. That's how I met Mr. Alexander," added Agent Stapley, "the counterfeits I was tracking were made in Pakistan."

"I think I remember that the Litinovs do a lot of black-market smuggling," Gaffney said, and then the light bulb went on. "And Mark Bucholz served in Iraq. So, this might be interesting."

"I should say. To us, Mark Bucholz is a name in a file. Nothing more. But now it looks like he was doing hits for the Litinovs, I hear?"

Gaffney nodded. "I mean, we don't know for sure, but it looks something like that." He briefly went through the evidence of the burner phones, the gunshot residue, and the gym bag stuffed with cash. "Hard not to think that maybe the fifty thousand dollars was a fee to kill Marden, except that the improbability of the shot means maybe Marden wasn't the actual target, and the text message makes it seems like someone else from the military – perhaps a major he served with."

"Also, regardless of the target, fifty thousand is above market for a hit," added Levin. "And, if they paid him in advance, why did they kill him after?"

"But it's the best theory we've got so far," finished Gaffney. "Happy to add anything you have to the party. Something from your case work overseas?"

"Right." Stapley reached down to his briefcase on the floor beside him, pulled out a file folder and passed around copies. "Let me lay it out for you:

"Mark Bucholz was part of a supply and logistics battalion that operated out of the Green Zone in Baghdad. In late 2007, ICE agents raided a warehouse in northern New Jersey and found a dozen Mercedes SUVs and Jaguars that belonged to wealthy Iraqis."

"They were stealing cars in Iraq and shipping them here? Kinda seems backwards to me," said Gaffney.

"Not stolen. Smuggled. Lots of Iraqis wanted to get out as the insurgency gathered strength, you know. Weren't a lot of safe routes out of the country. To get your family out required money, also money to get set up overseas. Even the Iraqis at the top of the scale didn't have a lot of ready cash, at least not ready cash that a mule would accept. What they had were cars, jewelry, works of art, and lots of other valuable stuff."

"Not likely to get a good price in Iraq for things, not at that time, I suppose," observed Levin.

"Right. And to sell things legally was difficult for lots of practical reasons. The primary one being there was no way to get their stuff out of the country without it being stolen along the way. So, they needed a way to get these things past the bureaucracy and the thieves and in the hands of buyers. After ICE found the cars, they brought us in and we worked the case both here and in Iraq for a few years. The Litinovs came into play distributing the goods once they got over to American soil."

"And you think Bucholz's unit helped smuggle the stuff out of Iraq?"

Stapley shook his head. "Nothing so concrete as that. There were some cases back in 2003, right after the invasion, groups of individuals getting payoffs from Iraqis to smuggle out their possessions and sell them on the black market. Mostly civilian contractors with, shall we say, less than ethical standards.

"You have to realize how much chaos there was over there, not just in the beginning but throughout the war. Thousands of troops coming in and out every month from multiple countries, endless supply convoys and cargo flights. Mercenaries, construction crews, truck drivers, NGO personnel.

"We ran a pretty hard investigation, but we were hampered by a lack of cooperation from the Iraqis and the security situation." The detectives could tell Agent Stapley was reluctant to report something other than success. "Lots of secondhand information pointed to the battalion Bucholz was in, but that's still several hundred suspects and we could only go so far into any particular person. As part of that investigation, Bucholz was interviewed, and the agent who handled that interrogation felt his behavior was suspicious."

"Did you happen to talk to any majors?" asked Frank, rising and heading over to the coffee machine. He looked quizzically in Stapley's direction.

Stapley nodded in the affirmative. "Black is fine. I checked into majors last night after I talked to Danny." How long did this guy sleep last night? "During his time in training and deployed overseas, there were fourteen different majors who at some point in time were in his chain of command or elsewhere in his battalion. Nine of them are still active duty; two of those are colonels now working at the Pentagon, three in South Korea, two are in Afghanistan, and two others stateside are based in Fort Benning. Neither have been granted leaves in the last two weeks."

"And the five no longer in the service?"

Stapley took a drink of the coffee Gaffney had brought over, and gave an appreciative nod. "Three retired. Still running them down. The fourth became a civilian contractor and is now based in Qatar. The fifth was killed in a drunk driving accident in 2014."

"Any particular connections between any of them and Bucholz?"

"Nothing noteworthy. Bucholz was an enlisted man. He didn't spend his free time with majors."

"Wait," interjected Levin, putting up his left hand as he jotted notes furiously on the papers Stapley had given him. "What about lieutenants and captains who served with Bucholz who became majors afterwards?"

Stapley shook his head. "Four of them, all still active duty and accounted for as best as the Pentagon can tell."

Gaffney nodded. "This 'Major' business means something, I'm sure. But we're getting sidetracked. Let's back up a step. What about the Litinovs? Did you get any prosecutions?"

"Not a one. The chain of evidence from Iraq to here was just too tenuous. We're pretty darn sure the Litinovs handled the smuggling on this end, but we couldn't prove it."

Levin interjected. "Did you know that Mark Bucholz went to high school with Max Litinov?"

"Really..." Stapley nodded in Frank's direction. A small gesture, but Frank beamed, then quickly muted his expression self-consciously.

"And Max was a groomsman at Bucholz's wedding," added Levin, as if eager to impress the teacher, too.

Stapley sighed, deeply. Frank could almost swear he saw Stapley tip his hat. If he'd been wearing a hat.

"Danny didn't get around to mentioning that," said the lean FBI agent, eyes lost in thought. "What does Max Litinov say about all this?"

"We don't know," admitted Frank, reaching up to straighten his tie nervously. "We didn't have any good reason to bring him in for questioning yet, and we don't want to spook him before we have some kind of leverage. Did Max appear in your casework at all?"

"His name was there but nothing else. He was still in college and law school at the time, so we didn't treat him as a person of interest."

"If I can ask, Agent Stapley," Frank began, carefully. "Seems to me you're speaking in the past tense a lot. Is this case closed?"

"Not closed. Shelved. FBI is stretched every bit as thin as the rest of law enforcement, and, besides, no one really wanted to be charging 'the troops' with conduct unbecoming while over in Iraq. I suppose you know how it is."

Frank did.

"Hey," Mike broke in, "the last page here has a bunch of references to something called BLACK HOLE. What was that?"

"Maybe complete bullshit, maybe crime of the century. We never could tell."

Both the homicide detectives leaned in simultaneously.

"During our investigation, we read a lot of emails coming in and out of Iraq. Lots of them referred to some kind of a big score – a theft. The references were always vague, more like passing on rumors than sharing facts. Never enough detail. Never enough corroboration to justify a change in our investigative protocols, but we gave it the name BLACK HOLE." He paused, thinking, and apparently decided to keep going.

"In the early years of the occupation – in both Iraq and Afghanistan – the military used massive amounts of cash. Massive. Good ol' American greenbacks. Pallets full of $100 bills were shipped in on C-130 cargo planes. Right into two war zones where a lot was going on. For years. Generally Accepted Accounting Principles were hardly near the top of anyone's list. Millions are still unaccounted for. Maybe billions."

Gaffney wanted to snort in disbelief, but was too awestruck by the Agent Stapley to go through with it. "Oh, come on. With respect, that sounds like a plotline from *CSI:Iraq*. Next you'll tell me Bucholz stopped off in London on his way back to the States and stole the crown jewels."

Stapley put up his hands, which was the biggest gesture he'd made so far, immediately silencing Gaffney. "I know. Like I said, it's probably ridiculous. We know some light fingers tried to grab handfuls of cash and sneak it out in their pockets, but we caught those people, and that sort of thing would never add up to millions. The thieves we caught usually didn't even make it out of the room. It seems impossible to believe some low-echelon clerks pulled off something this big."

Levin was speculative. "Absolutely. Bucholz was living above his means when he died, and he had money when he came back from Iraq. But it was money in the tens of thousands, not millions. I'd buy that he was helping smuggle cars and things out of Iraq, but, well, not to put too fine a point on it, he hardly seems bright enough to mastermind a big score."

"I'd buy it, too," said Frank, "but let's not forget that we still don't even know that Bucholz did anything like that. We have no criminal link, or suspicious link of any kind between Bucholz and the crime-lord side of the Litinov family. And I don't know how we're going to get one."

"Detective?" A uniform appeared at the door. "Someone waiting to talk to you and Agent Stapley. Says he's expected." He nodded out to the hallway, where Danny Alexander was hopping energetically on two feet.

"Yeah, all right," Gaffney sighed, gesturing to his brother-in-law to enter.

"Did he tell you about BLACK HOLE yet?" he asked Frank excitedly, walking over to shake Agent Stapley by the hand.

Gaffney gave Stapley an amused look. "Fella's got a persuasive way about him," Stapley drawled. "Knows how to ask the right questions."

"Isn't it amazing?" gushed Danny. "Bucholz helps the Litinovs steal millions from Iraq, under the nose of the entire US military? I mean, I knew this was big, but not this big."

Danny's brother-in-law looked at him skeptically. "And how, pray tell, do you imagine this happened? A million dollars, even in hundred-dollar bills, weighs quite a bit and takes up plenty of space. How do you suppose Bucholz snuck it out? In his duffel bag?"

"Get ready to call me brilliant," he effused. "You're gonna love this."

"He's going to say they took it out in the cars," said Stapley, simply.

Danny was too excited to care about his thunder being stolen. "They took it out in the cars! The same cars they were smuggling out of Iraq. Stick the loot in the trunk, smuggle the car out of Iraq, and take the money out on the other side."

He plopped into a chair, as if worn out from his genius deductions, and smiled triumphantly at the three lawmen. They stared back for a long moment. Gaffney was the first to lose his composure and start chuckling. Levin followed, and even Agent Cooper Stapley exhibited a small smile.

"What?" Danny asked. "Why is that so crazy?"

Detective Levin walked over to Danny and draped an arm around his shoulders. "Tell me, Sage of the Pitcher's Mound, how exactly do you think those cars got smuggled out of Iraq? Assuming Bucholz was part of smuggling them, how did they get out?"

Danny shrugged. "I don't know. Driven across the desert at night? Clandestine airplane pick-ups? Sneaking them down to the docks and hiding them on a freighter?"

"See, kid" said Mike, who was perhaps five years older than Danny, "this is why it helps to let real police do some of the work. If you'd tried to drive one of those cars out across the desert, you would have run out of gas *and* had the car stolen by bandits, *and*, you know, murdered. If you tried to get them on a plane, the plane would have been forced down or shot down by the Air Force. And you can't slip a Mercedes into your pocket and stick it inside an air vent on a merchant vessel."

"So, how did they sneak those cars out?" asked Danny, making a show of appearing chastened.

"In plain sight," said Agent Stapley, simply. "The trick isn't keeping the car out of sight. The trick is coming up with a way to get the US military or a contractor or NGO to take it out of the country for you."

"Huh?" Frank was pleased to see Danny at a loss for words. Such a rare occurrence.

"There were dozens of cargo planes and ships going back and forth between the US and Iraq in those years. Every piece of equipment, every person, who went in or out had to have paperwork with them. All kinds of paperwork." Agent Stapley shared a quick, knowing look with Frank, who knew from paperwork.

"The smuggling is in the paperwork," Stapley continued. "They created false documents – or finessed the bureaucracy to generate legitimate documents, more likely. The documents would state, for example, that the car was bought by a State Department employee and needed to be transported back to America. The car would have been put on a truck for Kuwait and a container ship here. Along the way there would have been several different inspections points. Looking for drugs, guns, explosives, anything. No way anything big could have been hidden in it. A roll of quarters would have been found. When the car arrived here someone showed up at the port with the right paperwork and drove it off.

"In fact," Stapley added, "under certain circumstances you could even smuggle it out without breaking the law, just disguising the real purpose of the transportation."

"You're thinking that every kind of smuggling is like sneaking a downed RAF pilot out of Nazi-occupied France," Gaffney said to Danny. "The art of smuggling from an American military occupation overseas is to find a way to get the military to do the job for you. You need to understand that difference." Was Gaffney piling on a little for fun? Probably. The crestfallen look on Danny's face was priceless.

"Shoot," sputtered Danny. "Now I have to rethink the whole thing. I need to figure out how they stole all that money and got it out of Iraq. Then we'll know why Bucholz was playing sniper."

"Sorry, friend," said Stapley. "I don't think such a crime ever even happened."

"I think we need to move away from missing millions and focus on finding a way to connect the Litinovs' smuggling operations with Mark Bucholz," added Gaffney.

Danny pivoted to Frank, his confident-just-this-side-of-pompous smile back on his face. "I've been working on that. You need some kind of leverage, right? Some sort of way to get a Litinov or one of their associates in a room with some leverage to make them talk, right?" Gaffney nodded. "Well, here's my plan. I called Scott Brubaker on Tuesday, you see, and…"

He went on for another minute until Frank finally exploded. "Are you fucking insane?" he fumed. "That is just about the stupidest idea I have ever heard."

"No, it's not," shot Danny back, talking not to a detective but to his brother-in-law. "You need something to get a Litinov in a chair with a reason to talk to you. This will do it. Guaranteed."

Gaffney threw up his hands in dismay. "Special Agent Stapley, tell him how crazy this is."

"Might not be so crazy," said Stapley, simply.

"What?!?!" Gaffney spun on the FBI man, feeling irrationally betrayed.

"Really might not be," echoed Mike Levin, quietly and meekly.

Gaffney glared at his partner. "Carol is going to have a fit when she hears about this plan."

"I know," said Danny, "but it's easier to ask forgiveness than permission." He spoke like a man with a lot of practice.

"How do you even know there will be a Litinov in the room?" asked Gaffney. "You might go through all this risk and come up with nobody."

"Then I walk away and nothing bad happens."

"Look, Frank," said Mike, walking over and placing an arm around his partner. "Come get some coffee with me." He guided Frank out into the hall.

"Look," said Mike, his arm still on Frank's shoulder, "this is no different than what we've done dozens of times with an informant. I get it. I do. But even if we both know there's no missing millions in reconstruction money here, this guy Bucholz was up to something dirty, and it has to have been with the Litinovs." He looked up at a junior officer standing nearby with a printout of an email and waved him into the conference room with his free hand.

Gaffney waited until the officer was out of earshot. "She will *kill* me when she finds out about this."

"Maybe," said Levin, "but maybe there's something else going on here. Right?"

"What do you mean?"

"I don't like it either," said Levin. "He's not a cop, he hasn't put in the time or done the training. He just waltzes in with one harebrained theory after another, and some of them turn out to be true. But you can't let it get to you."

"Carol already looks down at me because I didn't go to graduate school or make the Dean's List. And, gosh, when Mom and Dad hear his stories…" he paused. Levin knew when to keep his mouth shut. Gaffney nodded and sighed. "OK. OK. I get the point. Let's get back in there."

He opened the door of the conference room. "So, let's just pretend we decided to do this crazy thing," he began, but stopped when he saw Stapley and Alexander studying the piece of paper that the officer had brought in.

"They found the gun," said Stapley, looking up. "The gun that killed Bucholz."

"Really? Where?"

"Locker of a high school kid. End of the day yesterday. The principal got a tip from a student and they went in. County police lab ran ballistics and it came up as a match to the gun that killed our guy."

"Was it the high school next to the amusement park?" asked Levin.

"No...." said Alexander, slowly. "Harry D. Jacobs High in Algonquin. Five, ten miles away..." he drifted off, deep in thought.

Stapley handed the sheet over to the detectives. "Kid claimed his girlfriend gave it to him as a present, but he won't give a name, and his parents got a him a lawyer now so he's incommunicado. Goes to school, works at the food court at the mall..."

"Oh... wow..." said Danny, wonderment in his voice. "I think... I think I got something here..."

The other three looked at him, expectantly.

Alexander nodded repeatedly, mumbling aloud to himself. "Finds it... scared off... never would leave it..."

He straightened up and looked at the others. "Frank, I know you don't like my little scheme. I'll make you a deal. I've got an idea about the gun. If I'm wrong about it, I won't go ahead with Brubaker, but if I'm right, you'll want me to do it. Meet me at Spring Hill Mall in Carpentersville around 4:00. I'll be in the food court eating a Cinnabon."

"Do you even know that they have a Cinnabon there?"

"I sure hope so, because now I'm thinking about it. Either way, I promise you that by six I'll have solid proof for you, or else no go on the Brubaker game."

"Proof of what?"

"Who killed Mark Bucholz."

Gaffney groaned.

Chapter 14

Carol Alexander looked upon the pile of papers in front of her with unfeigned excitement. "Looks like they took to the task," she said to her assistant, Susana Melendez. "Can't wait to see what they found."

"The highlights the class posted to the Wiki this week are certainly thorough," said Susana, ticking them off one by one as she looked through a stack of printouts. "Sixty-three names total. About two-thirds probable relations of the deceased, including parents, cousins, two aunts and an uncle. For most of them we have addresses, occupations, the usual. No criminal history to speak of. Most work in blue collar jobs near where Bucholz lived."

"What about the non-relatives?"

"Twenty or so. Five ex-military, looks like they served with Bucholz..."

"Hand me those files," said Carol, remembering what Danny told her last night after talking to his friend from the FBI. She rolled her desk chair over a few feet to Susana's desk and grabbed the proffered files. She paged through them as Susana went on.

"There were also at least two guys who, judging by comments the students found on Facebook, used to date Janet Bucholz but had no other relationship to her husband, so far as we can tell."

"She's an attractive woman, no doubt about it," said Carol absently. "The sharks get the scent and they circle."

"Could be a motive to kill him, maybe?"

Carol put down the papers and pondered that suggestion. "I suppose. But searching for a new sugar daddy seems kind of cold of her, though. She cared about him more than that."

Susana moved a finger down the list. "Half a dozen co-workers of Bucholz's, living all over the Chicago Metro. Three families of neighbors. Pastor from their church. Not a ton of information on any of them."

"Look at this," said Carol, holding up the papers she was holding. "Who had the soldiers?"

"Greg Buhl. He really dug into it, didn't he?" she said, with a touch of pride.

"He's trying to impress someone," said the voice of experience.

Susana rolled her eyes. "What is it you found?"

"Well, look at this and tell me what you think. Glenn Beatty: grows up in Austin, Texas, moved here after he comes home from Iraq. Andrew Ernst, same thing, from Oregon. Lars Gilbert moved to Chicagoland after having spent his entire youth in Virginia. Dwayne Tracy was in Los Angeles. Only Marcus Kryevsky already lived here."

"And, check this out. Lars Gilbert's family owns a chain of auto parts retailers. He could easily have joined the family business, made a good living. Instead he moved here and drives a truck for the grocery store. Dwayne Tracy got an Honors degree in Chemical Engineering from UCLA, and was publicly awarded a graduate fellowship to take effect after his service, but is working as an ordinary lab tech here. Andrew Ernst could have gotten a full ride through school on the GI Bill, but he works for the Post Office in a sorting facility."

"So…" Susana began, then paused as if she could think of nothing else to say. "I'm not sure what that means."

"Well, neither am I," said Carol. "But think about this. You had six guys serve in the military together. After their service is up, they all move to the greater Chicagoland area, even though for at least a few of them it cost them a chance at better things. Also…" she flipped back and forth through the pages. "Counting Bucholz, four of the six bought houses in 2009 or 2010, all of them pretty fancy."

"Hmmm. Wonder how that happened."

"Somehow, I suspect we're going to find it's nothing good." She grabbed the next files and was glancing through them when her phone beeped with an incoming text message.

*   *   *

Frank Gaffney and Mike Levin pulled into the mall parking lot a little after 4:00, both grumpy from the road. They had been working outrageous hours since Willis Marden was killed, and it was starting to wear on them. The pre-rush-hour traffic had been worse than they'd hoped, and it occurred to Frank more than once that even if he'd never drawn his service weapon on the job, he might very well do so on the Kennedy Expressway.

Danny (smelling of cinnamon) and Carol were waiting for them in the food court with a uniformed, slightly rotund police officer, who Danny introduced as Dylan Connor of the Kane County Sheriff's office. Frank attempted to tuck his shirt in straight as they stood in a circle. "All right, Danny. You dragged Mike and me all the way out here. It's Friday, so it'll take two hours to get

162

back into the precinct tonight. Let's move as fast as we can. I might actually have a chance at a weekend."

Alexander smiled and turned to the deputy. "I don't know this mall at all. Is there a video game store here, or something like it?"

Dylan Connor nodded. "This way." As they walked, Levin turned to Danny.

"Are we going to find our killer at a video game place?"

"No, we won't, but I think there's a pretty good chance we'll figure out who killed him."

"Should I be putting some uniforms on standby tonight?" asked Gaffney. "If whoever we talk to lets the murderer know we were here…"

"I really don't think that's going to be a problem," said Danny nonchalantly, strolling a few steps ahead of the others.

"He's pretty confident, isn't he?" observed Deputy Connor to Frank, raising his eyebrows and nodding in Danny's direction.

"Kind of makes you want to punch him in the neck, doesn't it?"
"Now that you mentioned it."

Carol stifled a laugh.

A few more storefronts and they stood outside Video Palace, a small shop lined floor-to-ceiling with video games and equipment. "Look," said Danny, pointing at the displays. "Each of the games has a security tag on the plastic wrapping. Familiar?" he said to Deputy Connor.

"Sure, we found one like that on the grounds of Santa's Village."

Frank was skeptical. "You're suggesting the package you found where Bucholz died means someone who worked at this store was there? You can't prove..."

"Not one hundred percent, no, but more than you think. Check this out." Danny stepped into the store and took one of the video games off the wall. He showed it to the others as they followed him in. "All kinds of security tags out there. Some the cashier just swipes them across a demagnetizer or something to deactivate the alarm. Others they actually have to take the tag off with a special device. This is one of those kinds."

"Ahhh...," said the deputy, nodding. "The one we found still had the tag on."

Danny laid his finger alongside his nose and nodded conspiratorially. He looked at the three staff people, all teenagers by the look of them, standing behind the register engaged in desultory conversation. "Officer Connor, if you would, please ask the red-headed teenage girl behind the register to come to the back of the shop and talk with us. Be commanding but non-threatening."

"Hold on," interrupted Carol. "You want to corner a teenage girl in the back of a store with three guys carrying guns?" She rolled her eyes. "I really wonder what it must feel like not to have to think about the consequences of your actions. You all stay here."

Carol walked up to the girl, spoke a few words and nodded towards the rest of them. The girl looked at the men, especially the uniformed Connor, and visibly swallowed a huge lump in her throat. She walked with Carol as she led them all back to the food

164

court, where Mike squished a couple of tables together and they sat down. Her name tag read, "Amelia."

"Amelia," began Danny, in a voice an octave deeper than usual. "You know why we want to talk to you, don't you?"

Law & Order had been on the air for a decade before Amelia was even born. She knew enough not to say anything.

"Where did you find the gun, Amelia?" Danny asked, with a tone of gravitas tinged with disappointment. He watched her eyes widen and her body stiffen. The others all read the body language as well as Danny did.

"We're not here to get you in trouble, Amelia. We've got bigger things at stake. Someone was killed with a gun, and I know you found it and gave it to your boyfriend who works in the food court – not at the Cinnabon," he added hastily to the officers, ignoring the puzzled expression on Amelia's face.

"Let me tell you what we know, Amelia" said Carol. She scooted next to her, keeping her tone serious but conversational. "Last Thursday you and your pals took the ladder from the storage shed behind your school and climbed into the Santa's Village property, like you do all the time. It must have been sometime in the late morning, right? You hung out at the picnic tables, smoked, and you showed off the video game you'd swiped from here the previous day after work." Again, her eyes widened, but she kept silent.

Danny continued "You'd unwrapped the game and slipped the plastic wrap in the pocket of your hoodie, which is the same size and a similar design to the one that is hanging on the hook behind the cash register at Video Palace." The policemen started in surprise, but Amelia's expression told them Danny had hit the mark. That had been a lucky shot on his part, thought Gaffney.

"Don't worry. We could care less about shoplifted video games. You took off your sweatshirt because it was a warm day, and you all wandered around the grounds a little, until one of you spotted something unusual on the other side of the park. A car, and a body. I bet you know his name by now. He wasn't really much older than you, you know." Danny paused, looking away from Amelia, whose eyes were boring a hole in the table in front of her.

"You got over that fence using the board like you usually do. We know that by the time his body was discovered by police the crime scene had been looted by all kinds of people, but I'm betting you and your friends were the first to find it. I bet a lot of your friends took off right away, too freaked out by a dead body. But not you. You looked all over. You or one of your friends got his wallet. I'm betting it was in his car. Then you found the gun and took it with you." He spoke the last sentence in almost a whisper, and succeeded in getting Amelia to briefly glance up and make eye contact with him, after which she resumed her downward stare.

"It wasn't until you got to the other side of the fence that it all got too much for you. Suddenly you all realized the trouble you could be in. Maybe you heard a noise. You grabbed the cash out of the wallet, tossed it, and headed back to school in a hurry. So much of a hurry that you left your sweatshirt behind."
"Amelia, when we found that sweatshirt it had a fair number of red hairs in it; that's why I know it was yours. I think you know that all we need to do is compare the DNA in the hair from the sweatshirt we found to your hair, and we can place you right at the crime scene, and this can get a lot more serious." Gaffney held back a snicker; neither the CPD nor the Kane County Sheriff

would spend the money on a DNA test based on evidence as slim as this. But he saw the girl twitch again, and he knew Danny was getting to her.

Carol took over, placing her hand right next to the girl's on the table but not touching her. "Amelia, we don't care that you found the body. We don't even care that you found the gun. Other police might come and talk to you about it, but if you tell us the truth right now, I promise that the five of us will stand up for you if it becomes necessary. You're not a bad kid. I can see that, but you've got to tell us."

"Where was the gun, Amelia?" she asked, softly and slowly. "We think we know, but I need you to tell us so I know I didn't plant the suggestion on you. Get this off your conscience, Amelia. Tell us where you found the gun."

She turned, and Carol looked into her eyes for a long moment as she stared back. Then Amelia closed her eyes and exhaled deeply. She clenched her fists, then released them. One hand slid over and grasped Carol's.

"It was in his hand," she whispered, and began to tremble and cry.

"In his hand?" said Gaffney in disbelief. "Then, that means..."

"That you'll never arrest the murderer," said Carol, sadly, as she reached out to hug the scared girl. "Mark Bucholz killed himself, overcome with the knowledge that he had taken an innocent life."

*   *   *

"I had my suspicions all along," sighed Danny, as he sat next to Frank's desk while the detectives typed their reports. Carol sat next to him as he told his tale of triumph. "The rust on the hands got me started. Why would he climb the fence? Or, to put it another way, why would any killer *allow him* to climb the fence? If he'd broken away and bolted for the fence, then they would have shot him in the back and then finished him off with the headshot. But he had only one bullet wound, to the head.

"Imagine Bucholz firing his shot from the conference room onto the street below. The street was crawling with people, and when he fired I'm sure the scope moved a little bit, so there was no way for him to see exactly what happened. He had to close the window, pack up his gun, and get out of there in a hurry."

"On the way home he listens to a news station," continued Carol, with a nod from Danny, "which began reporting Marden's death very quickly after it happened. They didn't use his name, but he would have heard that the victim was connected to the Stringfellow case, and he knew that wasn't his target, wasn't the Major, whoever that is."

"Still not completely sold on that point," interjected Detective Gaffney, furrowing his brow, "but I agree that Bucholz's suicide makes your theory more likely." He turned and continued typing his report, one ear still tuned to the conversation.

"Exactly," agreed Danny. "We had been trying to figure out how a mild-mannered benefits administrator could be a secret assassin, but I think he wasn't. I think he was a man who had walls closing in on him. He was running out of money, and something this Major did to him was putting his whole family at risk. He was desperate."

"He must have lured the Major to the street below," suggested Carol, "sent him the text but then missed when he tried to shoot him." Danny nodded vigorously.

"Unless Willis Marden is the major," threw in Gaffney, stubbornly.

"In which case..." Danny and Carol both began. Danny bowed his head slightly. "In which case," Carol said...

"Marden would have had a prepaid phone with the text message on it," finished Levin, with a sly grin on his face.

"This is what they mean when they talk about success having a thousand fathers," groused Danny, displeased at the interruption.

"Sorry, Sherlock," said Mike, good-naturedly. "Please continue."

"Having failed to hit his target, he now hears on the radio in his car that it was someone else. He knows not only did he miss his one-and-only chance to kill the Major, but the Major knows that he knows... well, whatever it is that he knows, we still have to work on that... and that the police will be looking for a murderer. He is at the end of his rope. He pulls off the highway and drives to familiar ground, Santa's Village, where he parks the car and tried to climb the fence so he can sit down at a picnic table and think things through.

"He'd brought a pistol with him, too, perhaps because he thought he might need it somehow, and he is overwhelmed with dread, fear and sadness, and so he takes his own life. Sad." There was silence.

Gaffney stopped typing and looked at his brother-in-law and sister over the top of his reading glasses. "You know what's going to happen now? Get ready for disappointment. We've just cracked open something huge: who is the Major? What did he do to make Bucholz so mad? If Bucholz didn't get that $50,000 for assassinating someone, why did he get it, and from whom? What role do the Litinov's play? His ex-military buddies, who moved here to be near him?" He spread his hands wide. "Big case now. Sprawling. Could lead us anywhere."

"And you know what's going to happen on Monday?" he went on, looking not at them but at the pile of papers scattered on his desk. "They're going to take away all my manpower, because the case – the original case - is closed. The murderer of Willis Marden has been found, and that murderer's death ends the investigation. No time, no resources, for rooting around in the rest of this morass. That's what Halloran will say." He threw up his hands and crumpled a little as he contemplated the inevitable.

"Maybe something will come up this weekend to give some more life to the case," said Danny innocently, flashing a wicked grin when he saw that Carol's back was turned.

Frank opened his mouth to tell Carol about Scott Brubaker and Danny's stupid plan, but he remembered what he'd promised and said nothing.

Chapter 15

Scott Brubaker had had an entirely undistinguished but reasonably long professional baseball career. He had somehow, despite mediocre talent, frequent injuries, and disreputable off-the-field behavior, contrived to stay in the Majors for nine full seasons. When you spend most of nine seasons riding the bench, as Brubaker did, you can either let your own sense of mediocrity get to you, or you can find other ways to keep yourself occupied. Some benchwarmers become prodigious readers of books or connoisseurs of music. Others spend most of a game in the weight room or batting cage, trying to push their performance just a little. Others become obsessed with game tape, watching and re-watching every pitch, every at-bat, trying to find that edge.

Not Scott Brubaker. He learned to get people things. With discretion.

Baseball players spend half their year on the road. When they got into town, and wanted to find a nice place to get a steak for dinner, who arranged a private back room for them? Scott Brubaker did. When they wanted to find a nice club with lots of cute girls but no paparazzi? Scott Brubaker took care of it. When they missed their wives or girlfriends, and needed some (extremely discreet) company for the evening without the hassle of finding one at a club, all they had to do was take Scott aside before the fourth inning, and by the seventh he would show them his laptop, which would have pictures and vitals of five or six acceptable options. He got his percentage from the club owners and escort agencies, and lived well. He was, truth be told, extremely content with his life.

As such, when Danny Alexander had called him out of the blue earlier this week, he had treated it just as he would any other call. The aging players, those past their prime and looking forward only to a slow, sputtering end to their career, often made the best customers. So, if it was poker Danny Alexander wanted, it was poker that Scott Brubaker would get. If Danny wanted to play on the North Side, Skokie or Wilmette or Evanston, Scott Brubaker knew a guy who could make that happen.

Brubaker had made his phone calls, and after picking up Alexander at a nice hotel, made another call, and that call sent them to a parking lot outside a supermarket, where a black Cadillac carried the two of them to the back parking lot of a family-run German restaurant and inside. Some small talk and snacking, and then they were off.

Brubaker had reminded Danny that no one was to use names, but he could tell several of the players knew each other, and most were well known by the guy who was running the game, a sallow, rat-faced man in his fifties, wearing a cream-colored sport coat over a blue turtleneck and jeans. He gave Scott and Danny a good, long look when he came in, but after that it was all smiles and free drinks. He obviously liked players who showed up with $5,000 in cash.

After an hour or so, Danny had considerably less than that left. Brubaker (who himself played an extremely conservative game, since his payoff came from the finders' fee of roping in someone new) noted that Alexander liked to take a lot of risks, betting heavily on weak hands, and sometimes bluffing extravagantly, refusing to fold despite being caught out. He also carefully noted Danny's eyes, taking in all around him. On the other hand, he barely noticed the young, lawyerly-looking individual who entered from the restaurant side of the building and began conversation with the rat-faced man.

*   *   *

While Brubaker did that, Frank Gaffney sipped a beer in the bar of the same family-run German restaurant. He hated it when his brother-in-law's wild ideas worked, but so far it was working very well indeed. Half an hour after Danny arrived in the back, Frank came in the front door, looking as un-cop-like as possible, sat himself at the bar, and began nursing some kind of excellent German beer.

He had to be patient, and passed the time watching the baseball game on the bar television. Danny's old team, as it happened, doing just fine without him. He had to assume the Litinovs had a lookout in the restaurant, maybe a bartender or waitress paid to alert the back room if anything looked suspicious. So, time to be interested in the ball game.

He found himself studying the pitchers intently. Danny Alexander was right around six feet tall, and he was in pretty good shape, Frank knew, but these guys seemed to be superhuman by comparison. They were tall and strong, with muscles that rippled even through their uniforms. Made him think about how hard someone like Danny had to work to stay even in that game.

Gaffney's plans for a restful weekend had definitely been ruined. A belated examination of the report on Mark Bucholz's death found that the coroner had in fact noted the presence of possible gunshot residue on Bucholz's hand, but it had been buried in the middle of several dense paragraphs of minute anatomical detail, and no one had really noticed it. That helped confirm the teenager's story.

He had spent most of his Saturday with Cooper Stapley and the organized crime unit of the federal prosecutor's office, getting briefed on the Litinovs in greater detail. Like most successful crime families, it was metastasizing, with new growth opportunities popping up all over, and with success came the need for more personnel.

The Peter Principle, Gaffney knew, was that an individual rises to the level of his own incompetence, and that was true in the mob as well as in corporate America. When the rat-faced man in the *Miami Vice* sport coat emerged briefly from the back room to call for more food and beer for the back room, he saw this principle was at work in the Litinov's expanding empire.

Gaffney was a homicide cop in Chicago. He had never worked organized crime. He had never worked outside of the city, either, so he'd never heard of Dmitry Litinov until Carol had drawn his attention to the name. Prior to that day, Gaffney had never heard of any of Litinov's lieutenants, either, but he had paid attention this afternoon at the briefing from the feds, and looked closely at the pictures. Harry "The Fireman" Fiero.

The nickname, contrary to what Gaffney had initially assumed, did not mean Harry was an arsonist. It was, to the best of the US Attorney's knowledge, simply a play on his last name. Harry Fiero's job was the Mob's equivalent of middle management: enough responsibility to be blamed if things went wrong, but not enough power to do things on his own. What made him valuable to the Litinovs was that despite his minimal competence, Harry had somehow made it more than thirty years in the business without being convicted of a single crime. He could be the name on liquor licenses, permit applications, and much else. From Gaffney's perspective, watching the man return to the back room, that was also an opportunity. Fiero had no experience with prison. That would make him scared.

The younger man who entered through the front door of the restaurant and headed to the back also had no experience of prison, Gaffney knew. He watched Max Litinov out of the corner of his eye, careful to not let him see his face – Litinov might remember him from the funeral. Litinov gave a nod to the maitre'd – the lookout, Gaffney concluded, and headed back.

Gaffney looked at his watch and waited ten minutes. Time. He sauntered to the back of the bar to where a battered payphone still hung on the wall. He found the change in his pocket and dialed the number of the local FBI office, which anyone could learn was found in the phonebook attached to the pay phone. It was now 9:30 at night, and the FBI office would normally be closed, but by amazing coincidence someone was there to answer the call.

"FBI, this is Special Agent Stapley."

"Sorry to bother," said Gaffney, "but I'm over here at Albrecht's Restaurant on Cunningham Avenue, and I'm pretty sure I saw a poker game going on in the back. Isn't that illegal?"

"Yes, it is, sir," came the clipped reply. "What exactly did you see?"

If it ever became necessary to defend before a judge the FBI raid that was going to swoop in on the restaurant in approximately thirty minutes, it was this call (recorded as a matter of course by the FBI) which would allow them to claim probable cause without implicating Danny Alexander in any way. It was ethically very dubious. Based on Danny's information they had plenty of cause to raid the game. If it came down to it, if the only option was to fess up or have the case thrown out of court, then they would have to tell the whole story.

But the first line of defense would involve Agent Stapley describing an anonymous call from a bar patron who was shocked, shocked to find gambling going on. And the call was, of course, anonymous. Gaffney never gave his name, and Agent Stapley didn't ask it. Stapley could then point to other sources that had named Albrecht's as a possible site for some games, and hopefully the matter would be left there. Gaffney hoped to the heavens that none of this ever got near a trial.

On the phone with Stapley, Gaffney patiently described cards, chips, a table, and serious-looking players as if he had seen them. His description was specific enough to give Stapley (who had a judge on the other line, waiting to sign the warrant) cause, but not specific enough to make clear that Gaffney had not in fact seen a thing in the back room. Danny had earlier lobbied to be allowed to send out clandestine pictures from his phone, but had been instantly overruled by everyone else.

*   *   *

Danny's game was marginally improving, thought Scott Brubaker. He was probably a little rusty, and as he settled into the rhythm of things he began to play a little smarter. Alexander was still losing, but not so quickly or so deeply. Brubaker began to let himself daydream about how else he might profit from Danny Alexander's needs. Maybe he'll want someone young and pretty to sympathize with his losses at poker. Maybe he's in the market for... and then the door crashed open.

*   *   *

Detective Gaffney cursed his luck. He had to play innocent patron as a swarm of FBI agents and local police charged in through every available entrance, converging on the back room. This would have been a great chance for him to have engaged in some policeman derring-do. He might have even been able to brandish his pistol. But, no, here he was, stuck at the bar looking innocent and surprised.

He watched as The Fireman was walked out the front door. His underlings would also be booked, but the actual players would be released after proving their identity to the FBI. Their names would be in the case files, but there was no real need to arrest or charge them at present. Danny's involvement would never see the light of day in a courtroom. Probably.

Litinov was next, looking more scared than Frank expected. Frank saw that it was over, and decided it was time. He pulled out his phone and dialed his sister's phone number.

*   *   *

Carol's stomach was in knots, her palms moist with sweat, her head spinning like a top. She could barely remember to breathe and was getting lightheaded as she shouted.

"What the hell... what on earth were you thinking, you idiot?" she yelled at Danny, her voice dripping with fury. She had driven out to the FBI office when Frank called her, her rage rising with every mile, and now the three of them were in a small office, and she was venting half an hours' drive worth of anger and fear.

Looking like a whipped puppy, Danny said nothing, just turned his head away in shame.

"Oh no, you don't get to pull that bullshit today, you dumbass. Do you realize how fucking dangerous this was?"

She grabbed his shoulders and looked him the eye from up close. "Answer me. Do you realize how dangerous that was?"

"I guess it was…"

"Damn right it was! What if someone there had had a gun and tried to use it?"

"No one had a…." but she was having none of that.

"Did you KNOW that? You didn't. And what if they figure out you were the stool pigeon, huh? What are you going to do then?" Righteous anger flowed through her arteries.

"Carol, I don't think they will find out…" began her brother, gamely.

She swiveled in an instant. "Don't you even. Don't." The quiet, cold fury in her voice was even more terrifying than her shouted rage a moment ago.

She paused to breathe for a moment and stared at her brother. "How many cops have seen Danny coming in and out of the police station in the past week? How many of them might have said something about it to their family or friends? How many of them might not be above selling that kind of information to interested parties? Copy the incident report and send it to that pretty crime reporter?"

"I thought about that, Carol," said Danny, acting a little resentful at the tongue lashing. "But there was something bigger at stake. The cause of justice demands that I do what I can…"

"Oh, no. No!" It took all her willpower not to slap him upside the head. "Do NOT try to pull that moral high ground bullshit on me. No. Do NOT try to fool me with your self-serving sanctimony.

Do not pretend that this is about anything else than you having a puzzle to solve and showing how fucking smart you are."

Danny went silent.

She stood tall, glared down at him, and dropped the hammer. "Did you even think about what is going to happen to *your career* if Scott Brubaker tells someone he took you to a poker game?"

Danny's eyes opened wide unexpectedly.

So did Frank's.

They hadn't.

She laughed, the sound caustic. "Too damn excited about your little plan to remember, like, the *only* rule the baseball players can never break. You somehow *forgot* what happened to Pete Fucking Rose? Banned for life. No team reunion dinners. No chance to play, no chance to manage. No anything. Did you even think about that!?"

Her eyes soared heavenward in frustration. "Maybe you haven't been paying attention, but if I don't strangle you tonight then we've both got forty or fifty more years, and I am NOT going to spend the rest of my life as the shamed spouse of a washed-up has-been who blew his career because he decided to play Sherlock Holmes without checking in with his partner."

She looked at him glowering, and she kicked his foot to make him look back up at her. "Don't go sitting there, thinking you've got a shrew of a wife who never lets you have any fun. I had no problem crashing a funeral with you. I *enjoyed* our trip to see Janet Bucholz. Hell, I *thought* of it." She spoke the words slowly, emphasizing each word. "Because you're not the only smart person in this relationship. In fact, I'm smarter than you and you damn well know it." There was a loud silence. It was the first time in their whole relationship she'd ever said it.

She wheeled on Frank. "What do you think I would have said if you'd told me about this?" She didn't wait for him to answer. "Do you think I would have said no? Told you not to pursue a lead that might bring bad guys to justice? Do you really think I would have done that?"

Her anger was still going strong, but she began to speak in a more normal tone of voice as she worked through everything she was trying to say. "If you had talked to me, you might have remembered what happened to Buck Weaver. I could have gone in to the poker game instead of Danny. Brubaker wouldn't have been surprised by that, and baseball isn't going to ban Danny because of what his wife does."

"But..." began Frank, putting up a hand.

"But what?" she retorted. "But I couldn't do it because I'm the little lady? Get with the twenty-first century, boys," she said, looking back and forth between the two of them, daring one of them to argue with her.

"If that wouldn't have worked, we could have found something else. Instead," she said to Frank, "you let yourself get bowled over by that damn boyish enthusiasm of his, and you," turning to her husband, "got so proud of your idea that you *kept it from me* instead of sharing the credit."

She reached for Danny's arm and jerked him up towards the door. "I'm taking my husband home now. He's done playing policeman for the night." She opened the door and shushed him out, turning only to give Frank one more angry look as the door slammed closed behind her.

Chapter 16

Frank Gaffney left the room after Danny and Carol had gone. He stood in the hallway, leaning against a wall breathing softly, for five minutes. Then he headed down the hall to his second, but by no means the last, argument of the evening

Everyone wanted a piece of the action. There were now at least six different law enforcement agencies trying to get involved in exploring the Litinov-Bucholz connection. Each of them had sent representatives to the Evanston jail, and as Saturday night turned into Sunday morning, they gathered to try to figure out who was going to interrogate Harry Fiero and Max Litinov, and, moreover, what exactly it was they were investigating.

The second question turned out to be the real bone of contention. For the FBI, this was about the Litinov family's smuggling operations, and they wanted to offer Fiero immunity to roll on Max Litinov. The Evanston police, however, argued strongly against that idea; they had caught a gambler red-handed in their jurisdiction. His conviction would mean lots of credit with the City Council, as well as the civil forfeiture of the more than $70,000 found at the crime scene. The Evanston police needed more than a new pair of shoes. They wanted a confession from Fiero to the gambling, and no extraneous clutter to mess up a clean case. Plus, with the gambling bust taking place on their turf, they felt they had the right to lead the interrogation.

With Bucholz's death now a suicide, the Kane County Sheriff and the East Dundee police really didn't have much of a dog in this fight, so it seemed to Gaffney, but there they were. They both smelled blood in the water and wanted to be associated with a big gangland bust. They supported the FBI – the higher this case got, the greater their glory.

The Crystal Lake police cared nothing about the bigger picture. They wanted to know if the Litinovs had anything to do with the $50,000 found during the search of the Bucholz home, and if that meant Janet Bucholz might still be charged with a crime of some kind. No one was listening to them at all.

The US Attorney's office was all about the big game, too, but they had stubbornly refused to go along with the Litinov bandwagon and continued to insist that the case was all about Bucholz and the Robinson Stringfellow case. Gaffney thought it would be a total waste of time to interrogate Fiero about Stringfellow, but you didn't want the US Attorney on your bad side so, like everyone else, he lacked the guts to say so out loud.

Gaffney and Levin were running out of string. Their claim to the center ring was getting thinner. There was definitely a big case here, but it was a big case that had by and large moved beyond city limits. They would be back in the regular homicide rotation by the end of the week unless something spectacular happened. On the plus side, Gaffney and Levin they had the deeply-held police maxim that the first detective on the scene of a crime owns the case. The Marden murder had started this ball rolling, and the others knew it.

All told, there were seventeen people in the conference room at Cook County Jail, all men (a fact which none of the men in the room noticed), all trying to get their point across. These were seasoned professionals and everyone behaved with (relative) decorum, but when the first hour had passed with no consensus on approach or interrogators, it was safe to say that some tempers were rising and fuses were being cut short.

Stapley held up his hand, and the fragmented conversations in the room drew to a close. "All right. Everyone sit down. Let's take this one step at a time."

He walked to a white board and uncorked a marker. It was particularly fragrant, and half the room shuddered in displeasure. He wrote a series of headings across the top of the board: Marden, Bucholz, Stringfellow, Litinov, $50,000, Phones, Major, Smuggling, Gambling, Hayfield.

"OK, let's focus on the critical facts here," Stapley went on. Gaffney nodded in agreement as Stapley ticked off the points.

"Willis Marden was killed ten days ago in Chicago. We now are all pretty sure he was killed by Mark Bucholz, who subsequently killed himself, perhaps because he had killed the wrong person, but we can't prove that yet. Marden was going to be questioned in the Stringfellow corruption case. A few days after Marden and Bucholz died, shots were fired at or near Stringfellow, his lawyer, and a bunch of reporters. We don't know if those shots are connected to this case or not. We don't know if Stringfellow is directly connected with this case. Some of us here think so." Everyone glanced in the direction of the two men from the US Attorney's office, and then hastily looked away when the two noticed what was going on.

"Some of us don't, and in either case the CPD ran down that angle pretty thoroughly, so it seems like if there is something to find it's buried deep. Moving on..."

"Bucholz was close friends with Max Litinov, who may have provided him with $50,000 in cash. At least Janet Bucholz thought it was likely. Litinov is also connected to Bucholz through three burner phones, one of which called Litinov's law office. That same phone was used, presumably by Bucholz, to send a text message to another of the burners, with a threatening message to someone named, nicknamed, or with the military rank of Major; the last of those seems most likely, but *again* we don't know."

"This suggests a possible link between the Litinov family and wartime smuggling out of Iraq, which is probably where Bucholz and his other Army buddies got the cash they were flashing when they were discharged, although, *again*, we have no real proof on that. We *do* know the Litinovs run poker games up here, one of which we raided tonight in the hopes of getting a good reason to get Litinov or a Litinov associate in an interrogation room, which we have. We now need to figure out what to talk to this guy about."

Voices bubbled up immediately, but Stapley raised his hand again and they quieted down. "Last thing. A man named Reggie Hayfield was shot on Wednesday morning. He worked at the same bank as Willis Marden. Hayfield's going to be okay, but, gentlemen," Stapley added with a grim expression, "he may just be the one-and-only truly honest taxpaying citizen in this whole mess. He deserves justice, and if his shooting is in any way connected to this case, we should be the ones to handle it."

"Now, let's look at this list. We've got Fiero and Litinov waiting in interrogation rooms. Litinov has a lawyer on the way; Fiero seems to have forgotten to ask so far. Where do we begin?"

Captain Worthington of the Evanston police stood up. "If we only have so much time, we should make sure we get something worthwhile right away. Let's roll them on the gambling. Get them to give us a list of regular players, the accounts. We've got 'em cold on this. It's a good collar. Let's take it and congratulate ourselves on a job well done." He sat back down with an air of finality, convinced all would see the wisdom of his point.

Amid murmurs of approval and disapproval, Assistant US Attorney Cal Burns rose to respond. "We've already got them on the illegal gambling charge. We don't need a confession to convict, and given that Fiero and Max Litinov have clean records, they might not even do prison time. We need to push them on Stringfellow, and fast." If he noticed everyone suddenly looking away he imperiously ignored it.

Lieutenant Nicollet of the Kane County Sheriff's office stood up. "I don't agree. This guy Fiero is soft. I think we go in with the big scare, right away, and get him to give up the Litinovs. I've met guys like him before, I could push him over the line in five minutes."

Worthington snorted loudly. "Don't give us that fucking horseshit, Jake." The rest of what he said was drowned out in the wave of voices that now crested beyond anyone's control. Unexpected usage of swear words can do that.

Things degenerated rapidly. Gaffney was arguing a little too loudly with a Crystal Lake cop when he felt his phone vibrate in his pocket. It was, to his great surprise, the fingerprint lab. He had no idea anyone there worked weekends, let alone 2:00 on a Sunday morning. "Yeah. Gaffney. What's up?"

"Frank, is that you?" came a scratchy voice over the other end of the line. "Are you at a bar or something?"

Gaffney moved towards the hall to get some quiet, and saw a wall of solid bodies between himself and the door. "Just make it quick," he shouted into the phone. "What have you got?"

The voice made it quick, and Gaffney's face dissolved into a look of pure delight and unbridled glee. He grabbed Levin and whispered in his ear, and the two of them danced through the room and had a quick conversation with Agent Stapley. Stapley listened, then motioned to a younger FBI agent next to him. "OK, shut these people up."

The young agent put two fingers in his mouth and let out the loudest, most piercing sound *not* from a teenager that anyone in the room had ever heard. They stopped arguing, more out of wonder than anything else.

"OK, folks, here's how it's going to be," said Agent Stapley, in a voice that brooked no interruption. "CPD has found something new." He expanded on that theme for another minute while everyone shook their heads at the power of dumb luck. "We're transferring Fiero and Litinov down to Chicago, where they are going to be held on suspicion of conspiracy to commit murder. CPD will handle the interrogations." No one objected.

Chapter 17

Sunday was the eleventh day in the investigation of the Marden killing. It was going to be a busy day for everyone.

Carol let herself sleep in a little later than usual. She had barely spoken to Danny on the drive home. Her fury had faded a minute amount, but she was still angry and fearful in equal quantities. She could tell he was angry right back at her, that he felt himself justified, but she also knew that what she had said was gnawing at him inside. He'd come around. However slowly.

*   *   *

Carol was one of the few people who had the opportunity to sleep in that morning. Greg Buhl, for example, was up before dawn.

They all said it, but it wasn't true. Greg Buhl did not go into the Library and Information Science Masters' Degree program at the university to meet women. He said it to anyone who asked, and it was the truth. He was dimly aware when he applied that women outnumbered men by something like four to one, but if it had any impact on him it was mostly to make him nervous. Greg's admiration of the fairer sex was, in general, a distant one.

For Greg was, in appearance, demeanor and behavior, the classic nerd. Thankfully, Greg had grown up in a generational cohort that did not regard being a nerd as an inherently negative trait and he was spared much – not all - of the mocking and bullying that previous age brackets had. He did, however, spend most of his time in a social and cultural circle that included only other nerds, and this meant that if he wasn't in the presence of other nerds his social anxiety kicked up a notch or two. Or, if he was near Susana Melendez, five notches (up to eleven, he would tell himself, as a nerd would).

The hope he hung his hat on was to show Susana how good a
student he was by producing amazingly detailed and thorough
assignments. Of the seventy-two-or-so hours from when Prof.
Alexander's funeral list assignment was handed out to when it he
had turned it in, Greg Buhl spent no less than forty-nine of them
working on it. He wanted to show Susana that he could produce
amazing work in a hurry.

Having turned in his assignment that Friday, he returned to his
studio apartment and crashed. He slept until dawn on Saturday,
when he realized he had three other classes that needed his
attention, and so he worked all that day until he once again had to
crash, this time around midnight.

He shot bolt upright in bed at just after five in the morning on
Sunday. He would never – when he looked back on it - be able to
say precisely what had caused him to do that, as he was still
exhausted and worn out, but he was also awake, and he was
thinking (surprise!) about Susana Melendez, and he'd had an idea.
It was to him a brilliant idea, if not to anyone else. Why end the
assignment so soon? After all, he'd been researching these five
Army buddies of Mark Bucholz for just three days. He had tons
of leads left to track down, to look into, to explore. He could find
out so much about these five guys that Susana would be unable to
hide her admiration for his dogged persistence and analytical
genius.

It was very early and Greg had not slept much.

He padded over to his desk and awoke his computer. Opening
his email, he was surprised that there were Google News Alerts in
his inbox. He had set up alerts for each of his five research
subjects, just in case they made the news while he was working on
the assignment, but nothing had come up, and he had assumed

nothing would. Here, though, were a whole bunch of emails with links to news stories. This was great. He'd find something awesome, and Susana would smile at him, and the world would…

He clicked open the first link and his stomach collapsed. "Veteran, father of two, killed during home invasion." He scanned it and opened the next one. Same story, different website. Clicked on the third. "Area man shot dead in Spruce Creek Park."

Two of his five subjects had been brutally murdered in the past 24 hours.

*   *   *

Frank also had not had the chance to sleep in. In fact, he hadn't had a chance to sleep at all. About the same time Greg Buhl suddenly got out of bed, he sat down across a table from Harry "The Fireman" Fiero.

The decision to move Fiero and Litinov from Evanston down to Chicago had occasioned a delay in the commencement of the interrogation, and Fiero had apparently used that opportunity to remember some of his basic Constitutional rights.

"I think I need to talk to my lawyer," he said, his (now-obvious) toupee losing its shape with all the sweat pouring down his head. It was hot in the room. His perspiration had a distinctive and unpleasant aroma that Frank tried hard to ignore.

"If you don't want to talk to us without a lawyer, that's fine with me," said Frank, confidently. "I'm good either way. But before you make that official, just sit back and listen to me for a minute." Gaffney put a paper bag on the table, from which he extracted a delicious-smelling Italian beef sandwich from an all-night hot dog joint. "I'm going to eat while I talk. You know how it is," he added, with a conspiratorial wink.

"I'm not listening without..." but Frank cut him off quickly. He was skating on thin ice here with Fiero's Miranda rights, which had been formally read to him back up in Evanston. Once the suspect requested to speak to an attorney, the interview was supposed to end immediately. "I think I need to talk to my lawyer" was legally ambiguous enough that Frank could keep going (Carol not being here to remind him of the relevant Supreme Court cases, he told himself), but if Fiero ever got out a flat "no talk at all without a lawyer present," then Gaffney had to stop.

"No, no, no, Harry. This isn't an interrogation. Always two cops for an interrogation, right? Just me here. I just want to tell you a story. You sit there and keep your mouth shut, and if by the time I finish you still want your lawyer, I'll lend you my phone right here." He fished the phone out of his suit and put it on the table.

"You see, Harry, I could give a shit about the gambling. I don't care what happens in Evanston. I care about Chicago. As do my bosses, for that matter." He paused to savor another bite of his sandwich. He wasn't faking that. It was *good*.

"We care about this guy." He grabbed a clean napkin and used it to pull out an autopsy photo out of the file folder and put it on the table. "He got shot last Thursday morning. Willis Marden. I'm sure you've heard of him," Frank held up his hand, "but don't say anything now – not without your lawyer."

Another bite of the beef sandwich, then another photo, and this time a twitch from Fiero. "We just figured out a couple of days ago that this guy killed Marden. High-powered rifle from an office building. 500 feet away. Hell of a shot. But Mark Bucholz didn't have long to celebrate his kill, since he was dead an hour later." The name of the shooter caused The Fireman to twitch involuntarily a second time.

"Maybe you heard the news yesterday that the Kane County sheriff is calling this a suicide." It was the day before yesterday, actually, but Gaffney was understandably treating Sunday morning as an extension of Saturday night. "Sometimes we have to fake out the media to give criminals a reason to let their guard down. This was no suicide," Gaffney lied, "it was murder." Fiero was a lifelong criminal but a rookie when it came to interrogation. His sharp intake of breath told Frank this was working.

"One thing we haven't made public yet is this," and Gaffney tossed another photo on the table. "Cash. Lots of it, in a gym bag under his bed."

Gaffney put down his sandwich, wiped his hand on a napkin, leaned back from the table and put his hands in his lap, relaxed and conversational. "Now, I gotta tell you, between you and me, if we ran as many DNA tests and fiber sample comparisons as the people on TV, the department would be bankrupt in about a month. So, when we handed that bag of money to forensics, we didn't expect much." Fiero didn't know how to hide his growing anxiety, Gaffney noted with some pride.

"Now, with this much cash, you can't test every bill. Just can't. Too much time, too much manpower. The lab tech took a random sampling of twenty-five bills and looked for fingerprints. Know what he found?" asked Gaffney, with a raised eyebrow. He took another bite of his sandwich and let the question hang in the air for a long moment while The Fireman stewed.

"Nothing." A huge, visible exhale from the suspect. Interrogation wasn't rocket science. Build them up, knock them down, make them anxious, make them relaxed, keep it moving until they moved back.

"But here's the crazy thing. Turns out this lab tech is friends with someone who worked with Mark Bucholz at his law firm. The tech didn't know Bucholz, never met him, but he feels like a friend of his friend must be *his* friend too, you know? So even though he wasn't being paid overtime he decides to be thorough and do another twenty-five bills. Can you guess what he found?" He gave Fiero a knowing look, and took another big bite as the question lingered, lingered, lingered...

"Nothing again." And again, the exhale. Gaffney swallowed, took a sip of coffee casually, then put the mug down. "Well, actually, not nothing. Almost nothing. Just the tiniest part of a fingerprint. A partial of a partial." He paused again. "Too small to match to anyone."

Fiero had to know what was coming, Gaffney knew. Had to know. But the Fireman would cling desperately to any faint hopes he had.

"So the guy went home. It was Friday night and he was tired so he went home."

"But the strangest thing is, Harry, is on Saturday he comes back. No overtime, Harry. Who comes in on Saturday for free? Nobody does. Nobody. Except this guy. He decides, hell with the protocol, he's gonna test another twenty-five bills. Know what he finds?"

He held the question in the air, looking at Fiero expectantly, almost daring him to answer.

Fiero breathed in, and his shoulders rose, preparatory to speaking. Gaffney jumped in a moment ahead of him.

"Your thumbprint, Harry. Your thumbprint on a hundred-dollar bill. You're an accessory to murder."

*   *   *

Carol finally awoke to a tasty scent wafting upstairs. Danny was doing penance via breakfast, she guessed, making apology bacon. She put on her robe and headed downstairs, where her husband was blending cream cheese into scrambled eggs in a pan on the range. He put down the spatula and walked over, arms out. She allowed the hug but moved her head so that the kiss landed on her cheek instead of her lips. She sat down at the kitchen table and waited while he put a plate of food in front of her and poured her morning coffee.

"Thanks for the breakfast," she said, generously.

"Look, honey," he began.

She stopped him short. "I don't want to talk about it right now. You scared me to death last night..."

"I know I did, sweetheart, but..." Again, she interrupted.

"I'll say this now and then I need you to think about it. Not *talk* about it, but think." Her voice wavered a little as she spoke. She had hoped to have a quiet morning, and jumping right back into it so quickly was sending the adrenaline coursing through her veins again.

"You think this is about me being scared. It's not. It's about *you doing things that make me scared.* I can tell, you still think you can somehow convince me that what you did was all right, that it wasn't an incredible risk to your career, to your *life*, that it was okay not to talk to me about it beforehand. You can't.

"I know you, honey," her voice softened, and a tear rolled down her cheek. "You need to find a way to be happy with yourself. If you keep trying to prove your worth like this, it's going to blow up in your face, and then what will I do?" She gazed at him intently, took his hand and held it. He looked back at her, and tears began to well in his eyes.

*   *   *

Frank Gaffney was expecting something to happen when he finally revealed the discovery of the fingerprint to Fiero, but he didn't expect this. A grown man, more than ten years older than him, as a matter of fact, sobbing and crying uncontrollably.

To Frank's way of thinking, this was finally just karma coming back around the other way. Every once in a while, the fates grant you some real luck, and this fingerprint had been it. In his written reports, of course, he would paint it as an inevitable discovery given the thorough nature of the investigation that had preceded it, but he knew it was mostly luck. Once the print had been found, they had run all the other bills from Bucholz's gym bag – none of the rest had any usable prints besides Mr. and Mrs. Bucholz. The fact that this one had been found at all was the sort of serendipity that cops just didn't really get that much of.

For Harry Fiero to break down in tears was icing on the cake. He knew long before he had dropped the bomb on Fiero that the crook would waive his right to a lawyer and talk. Gaffney knew that Fiero was in no way part of the muscle in the Litinov family;

indeed, Harry was the kind of guy who probably was able to convince himself that the Litinovs didn't even use muscle, since he never would have come across it. Harry would never have thought that his involvement with the money - whatever it was - would be related to violence of any kind, let alone murder.

"I didn't kill anyone," Fiero pleaded, through gasps and sobs. "I swear I didn't."

"Of course you didn't, Harry," said Frank, reasonably. "No one thinks you did. But we've got two dead bodies on one end, and a bag full of cash on the other end, and the thing that ties them together is your thumbprint. What am I supposed to do?"

Frank leaned in and rolled his eyes towards the ceiling in frustration. "Look, Harry, you and me are in the same kind of boat here. We both sit in the middle. The bosses upstairs tell us what they want done, and no matter how impossible it is we're supposed to do it anyway. My boss may be the law and your boss may be the crooks, but bosses are bosses, right? They don't care how; they just want it done. It's not like they ever worry about giving us the *tools* to do the job right, or the manpower, or the time. They just want it done. My guess, Harry, is that you know exactly what I mean." It helped Frank's performance that his frustration was wholly genuine.

"Now, here's what I've got. I've got a big open hole in this case – how did that money end up with Bucholz, and who gave it to him? Whoever did that, we figure, must have been the one who sent Bucholz out to kill Willis Marden. You can't begin to understand, Harry," continued Frank, with great sincerity, "how important it is to my bosses to be able to close this case. They want to close it quick. And so, they'll take a sure thing that might not be the whole truth before they take a risk on going for the bigger picture."

"Do you follow me, Harry?" Fiero actually did look a little confused – it's hard to sob and listen carefully at the same time. Frank decided to simplify. "If we can't find anyone else, we'll pin this on you. We won't be able to get murder, but manslaughter for sure. You're what, fifty-three, fifty-four? If we want to, we can keep you in prison until you're eligible for Medicare. And we don't need a word from you. We don't have to interrogate you for a second. The fingerprint is all we need."

Gaffney went back to his sandwich and let Fiero process for three solid minutes. Then he eased himself forward to the edge of his seat.

"So, you'd best decide. You want that lawyer, here's my cell." Frank slid his phone across the table towards The Fireman. "Just know that that fingerprint guarantees you ten years, no matter what the lawyer may tell you."

"The other option, Harry, is to tell me how your fingerprint got on that money, and tell me how you are innocent of murder. To do that, you'll need to waive your right to an attorney." A form to that effect magically appeared on the desk, along with a pen. "I'm going to go get some more coffee. Call your lawyer if you want, or sign the paper and I'll bring in witnesses for it. Either way I'll be back in fifteen minutes."

He hadn't yet closed the door when he heard the scratching of pen against paper, and Frank Gaffney allowed himself a satisfied smile.

*　　　*　　　*

Greg Buhl sat at his computer, working on the eleventh draft of his email:

Hi, Susana! Greg Buhl here from MLS 391. How's your weekend going? Hope it's going well. I was just sitting here and I got this email, and I thought, 'I bet Susana would just LOVE to hear this.'

He backspaced to the beginning. Too desperate. Have to seem more relaxed.

Susana – this is Greg Buhl from MLS 391. You probably don't care about this at all, but two people from my research project this week were killed this weekend. Really sad, isn't it?

Again he backspaced. He had to have some kind of build-up to the main point. Had to make sure that Susana not only knew what happened, but that she understood that he had discovered it.

Susana – Hi! This is Greg from MLS 391. I was following up on our research project of this week, because, well, I guess because I just LOVE research, and...

He deleted again, and his struggle went on as the morning sun climbed higher into the sky.

*   *   *

Danny had finally stopped trying to argue, and Carol calmed down enough to get on with a normal day. He got out his tools and put some coat hooks up on the wall underneath a shelf in the kitchen, something she'd asked him to do several weeks before. He carried laundry downstairs. He worked out in the basement. He vacuumed the living room and the den, without being asked.

This was Carol's favorite part of the year. Baseball season was over, and training camp was months and months away. Danny would be home while she taught, and they would have plenty of time to go out to nice dinners, see friends, and sneak away on weekends. She began mentally planning a trip to a nice resort on the North Shore of Minnesota for next week. Fitger's, maybe. He could use the rest, too. As soon as he was done with this case, he'd want some time to recharge just like her.

*   *   *

> *Hi, Susana! Are you having a nice day? I came across some new stuff from my research project for MLS 391... maybe I could meet you at The Coffee Club and we could talk it over. I think you'd find it very interesting.*

Delete.

*   *   *

Frank Gaffney practically floated down the hallway to Lt. Halloran's office, Mike Levin and Cooper Stapley walking more sedately behind him. He had waited until 8:00 in the morning to call her in, reasoning (sensibly) that the Lieutenant would be more likely to be in a listening mood if she'd gotten some sleep. It had taken him another few hours to get the paperwork in order for the warrants he was going to ask Halloran to endorse. Now it was time to act.

"Fiero cracked," he said simply.

"Yes, you told me on the phone," grumbled back Halloran. "Gimme some details quick, so we can go in and talk to Max Litinov."

A full two hours later Halloran, Gaffney and Levin walked into an interrogation room. Max Litinov looked much better than he had some hours before. His lawyer was persistent, and he had been allowed a shower and a change of clothes, as well as some breakfast. He was going to be a completely different kettle of fish than The Fireman.

Gaffney didn't exactly love it that Lt. Halloran was in the room with him and Mike, but she was the boss and got to insist on being part of things like this. They'd at least agreed on a plan.

The lawyer, a suit of some kind whose name was eminently forgettable, got things rolling. "We have nothing to say to you, so either take us to a judge and charge him or my colleagues will be filing a writ of *habeas corpus* within the hour."

"We can charge him if you want," said Lt. Halloran. "But maybe you might want to know *what* he's being charged with."

The lawyer was in no mood for interrogation-room trash talk. "Not really."

"Well, just for fun, here's the list. Illegal gambling, conspiracy to engage in illegal gambling, and failure to report illegal earnings on your taxes." She made it seem like she was done, and Gaffney admitted to himself that she was handling it well.

He'd hoped the lawyer would help out with a spirited defense of Litinov against the charges, but he wasn't that cooperative. "Shall we head over to the courthouse now, then?" he asked. Litinov didn't seem to love that idea, but he was keeping his trap shut nonetheless.

Halloran opened her mouth as if to reply but then, right on cue, there was a knock on the door and Cooper Stapley – his collar still stiff and clean, his suit jacket entirely unwrinkled – walked in with a manila folder and flash drive in his hand.

"Agent Stapley," said Frank, brightly, "did you finally finish up with Harry Fiero?"

Stapley nodded. "Sure did. He gave us everything we need."

Finally, the lawyer began doing what they'd hoped he would. "You had no right interrogating Mr. Fiero without an attorney present."

Stapley opened the manila folder and extracted a piece of paper, which he laid out in front of the lawyer. "He waived his right to an attorney on this form, and then," setting down flash drive "repeated that waiver on camera as we began his formal interrogation. Here," said Stapley, handing over a small laptop that Gaffney just assumed had been conjured up by magic from within Stapley's suit pocket, "feel free to watch the whole thing."

That threw the lawyer for a curve, to say the least.

Agent Stapley continued. "We have in our possession search warrants for your client's home and office, which we are executing as we speak."

The lawyer's arrogance was still there, but fading rapidly, Frank thought. Stapley went on, his voice never showing excitement of any kind. Gaffney was in awe. "The money referred to in Fiero's confession was in consecutively-numbered bills. I'm willing to bet that in the safe in your law office, Mr. Litinov, are more bills with serial numbers that are next in the sequence. That alone will be evidence sufficient to verify The Fireman's story that three months ago you gave him $450,000 from your office safe to deliver to Mark Bucholz."

Max Litinov's breathing was becoming more shallow and rapid, and his face had taken on an unpleasant grey color.

"But there will be more, I'm sure. I have little doubt that we will find an old-school flip phone, a burner, somewhere amongst Mr. Litinov's possessions. We know who bought that phone, along with two others, and one of those other two is directly tied to a murder. You know which one, Mr. Litinov. It's tied to a suicide, too, which I know you know about since your name is on the guest book at the funeral. And with that phone, Mr. Litinov, we have conspiracy. A clear chain of evidence connecting you to Mark Bucholz's special phones and the $50,000 still hidden in his house."

"Also, Mr. Litinov, I hope you're thinking about what else you may have in your house or in your office. Items unrelated to this case that might be found in the course of our investigation."

The detectives and Lt. Halloran rose, on cue. They all started for the door, but Gaffney hung back. He'd begged to be able to have something to say, and so they let him have this.

"Think it all over. I'll be honest; $450,000 is way too far above the going rate for murder, and Bucholz was no hit man, so I'd be open to believing that you didn't give him the money to kill Willis Marden or anyone else. But it's conspiracy even if you didn't explicitly talk about killing someone, if the killing was incidental to the larger crime being committed. Watch the tape, think it over. We'll be back in a few more hours to talk."

Frank felt very proud of himself as he walked out. Fool.

*   *   *

Greg's eighty-second draft, around noon, finally captured what he wanted to say. It had taken the first thirty drafts to clear from his mind the idea that he could both provide the information to Susana *and* ask her out at the same time. Murder was just too heavy a subject to tack onto flirting. Twenty more drafts had been required to get him to ease up on the self-congratulation and excessive ego, twenty additional drafts to realize he needed to keep it simple and short, and another dozen drafts to decide he had to include all the relevant details in the first email rather than hoping for a reply.

Two other factors made it possible for Greg Buhl to finally write a decent email. First, his natural caution and low self-esteem began to re-assert themselves, reminding him he didn't have a shot at Susana Melendez, that TAs did not date students even if he'd had a shot.

The second reason Greg was finally able to write the email was the picture of the kids. In between drafts, Greg kept going back to the Web, looking for the latest info on the two killings. Around nine in the morning the *Sun-Times* website posted a photograph of one of the victims. A church directory photo, and there were two small kids. Smiling, happy, innocent kids. Just looking at Greg through the screen. Not names on a sheet of paper, not a class assignment. Little, adorable kids, in their ridiculously cute Sunday best. Now without a dad.

> *Susana, this is Greg Buhl. I thought you and Prof. Alexander ought to know that two of the people in my MLS 391 research assignment were murdered on Saturday. Glenn Beatty was home alone Saturday afternoon while his wife took their kids to a birthday party. Someone came into the house and shot him several times in the chest. Marcus Kryevsky was walking his dog through a park near his home just after sunset Saturday and he was shot in the back. No one has been arrested for either crime. So far, I don't think anyone in the police thinks the two murders are related, because the crimes were in different cities,*

but since you and Prof. Alexander seemed so interested in the case I thought I'd let you know. If it was up to me to say I'd think the two killings WERE related.

I've pasted some links below to news stories if you want more info. Sorry to bother on a Sunday. If you need anything else just email or call.

Sincerely, Greg Buhl

The *"or call"* was his one concession to his romantic imagination, and a well-deserved one.

*   *   *

The object of Greg's desire got out of late Mass around the same time as he hit send. Susana Melendez went to Mass most Sundays with her mother, and, being a dutiful daughter, endured her mother's sniping about Aunt Rosa's latest perfidies. This Sunday, it was over to Aunt Maria's for Sunday brunch with the whole extended family, followed by quiet conversation and naps by at least two of her uncles. She helped her mother into the car and went around the other side. She had a standing deal: no looking at her phone when she was with family on Sunday. It was in her purse, and she didn't even notice it vibrate.

*   *   *

It was about one in the afternoon when Danny plopped down on the couch next to Carol. "OK," he began. "You're right."

She scanned his expression, checking to see if he was just going through the motions of apology. He looked sincere. She nodded and he continued.

"I know I don't always think things through."

"That's the understatement of the year." But she smiled just a tiny bit, with the corners of her eyes.

"It was a mistake not to tell you about my idea to call Scot Brubaker."

"Not just not tell me. You deceived me. You deceived your *wife*."
"Yeah." A pause. "If I had come to you ahead of time, what would you have said?"

She shook her head, but gently. "That's not what matters right now. What I do know is that even if I had told you the idea was crazy, I would I have felt like your partner, not your parole officer."

"OK." He thought it through a little longer.

"I really like playing detective, honey," he said simply. "And I'm good at it."

She nodded. "Yes, you are. And I want you to be able to pursue things that you like, but…"

This time he finished her sentence. "But you worry about me being safe, and I make *you* feel unsafe when I hide what I'm doing from you."

She saw the question in his words, and she relaxed just a little bit. "That's exactly what happens, honey. Exactly." She saw his smile, and smiled back. A quiet, knowing, exasperated, loving and tolerant smile.

*   *   *

Frank's smile wasn't exasperated; it was incandescent. He kept shifting his weight back and forth on his feet, wired from lack of sleep and too much caffeine and the thrill of the chase. Max Litinov and his attorney had been holed up for several hours now, probably watching the tape of Fiero's statement again and again. They had to be breaking down. Litinov was going to give a statement. He was going to break this case wide open.

He and Stapley knocked on the door of the interrogation room and heard an answering call. They walked in. It took everything Frank had to keep a dopey grin off of his face. Litinov was ready to crack. He knew it.

"This tape proves nothing," the lawyer said, coldly and firmly. "We welcome your search of Mr. Litinov's office and home. You will find nothing at all of relevance to this case or any other criminal activity. If you want to charge my client based on the word of one lowlife who was kept up all night before being interrogated and is desperately trying to avoid the gambling charges, please do so now. Otherwise you need to let him go or explain yourself before a judge." He stood and put his hand on the shoulder of Max Litinov, who no longer looked scared or worried.

Gaffney cursed under his breath. *So close.*

*   *   *

It was close to three in the afternoon before Susana Melendez finally glanced at the email on her phone. Seeing who it was from made her roll her eyes. She almost clicked past it, but the word "murdered" caught her eye just long enough to make her pause and read the rest of the message. Then she clicked on one of the web links. She went back to the message and started to forward it, then thought better of it and dialed Carol Alexander directly.

*   *   *

"Both killed?" cried Carol. "Jesus. Are you sure Greg isn't just making..." she listened. "OK. OK. Wow. OK. Thanks. No, I'll take care of it." She hung up and scrambled to the study, where her carrier bag was stuffed with the research assignments from the class.

Danny followed her in. "What's happened?" he asked as she pulled Greg Buhl's findings out of her bag.

"Remember those Army buddies of Bucholz's we met at the funeral?" He nodded. "Two of them were shot yesterday."

"Killed?"

"Killed."

*   *   *

"We got killed in there," muttered Gaffney.

"We took our best shot," said Lt. Halloran, consolingly. "The kid is ballsier than we thought."

"Any word yet from the warrants?"

Halloran shook her head. "So far, nothing. Litinov's office safe has only legal documents; no cash. Give them some time. They'll come up with something."

"No," Gaffney disagreed, "the reason Litinov and his lawyer were so damn cocky is that they know there isn't anything to find. We assumed there would be, but that was hubris on our part, wasn't it? This guy's a pro in his own line of work. He knows how to keep an office and house clean." He hung his head. "Dammit."

His partner, Mike Levin, thought aloud. "So, what have we really got? We got Fiero's fingerprints on the money, and we got a statement from him tying the money to Litinov. And we got a connection between Litinov and Bucholz that seems tied to the murder of Marden. It's still something, you know."

"Wish we had more."

*   *   *

Carol found the page in her bag that she was looking for. "Glenn Beatty. Lived in Kenosha, Wisconsin. Marcus Kryevsky. He's in Chicago on the west side. Good God. What's happening?"

"We need to call your brother, and fast."

"Yeah." Both she and Danny, still looking at the page of names, noticed the same thing at the same time.
"He lives five minutes from here," he began. She didn't let him finish.

"I'll get the car started. Call Frank and fill him in."

*   *   *

Danny had barely gotten off the phone when Carol pulled up in front of Dwayne Tracy's upscale suburban home.

"Is he married? Kids?" he asked.

"No. He lives alone." Or, maybe *lived*, thought Carol. "Is this safe?"

"You're asking *me* if it's safe?" Danny almost smiled, then stopped and appeared lost in thought for a minute. "We don't go into the house. We stay out front until the police arrive. Then we're under the watchful eyes of the whole neighborhood. That keeps us safe, I think."

They got to the front door. Danny rang the bell. They waited.

Carol heard and saw nothing, but saw Danny cock his head. He rang the bell again, then knocked. He turned to Carol. "Do you have a home phone number for him?"

She pulled out the sheet and showed it to him as he dialed. Carol could hear the phone ringing inside. "How do you know he's home?"

"You know how you can walk into a room with your eyes closed and know that a TV is on, even when it's muted? That electronic sound you sense more than hear? A few seconds after we rang the bell, a TV was turned off inside this house. I'm sure of it."

The phone hit its fourth ring. Danny waited for the beep. "Dwayne, if I were you I wouldn't be opening the door to strangers either. You've heard about Marcus and Glenn, and you're wondering if whoever did it is after you, too."

He paused and Carol saw him bite his lip in deep thought. "Dwayne, we're not here to harm you, and I think I can prove it. Go to a computer or pull out your phone and google the name Danny Alexander. You'll get a lot of people, but one of them's me. I'm a professional baseball player. Lots of pictures of me on the Web. I'm here with my wife, Carol. Her brother is with the Chicago Police Department and has been working on Mark's death."

She caught his eye and jerked her head towards the lawn. He nodded. "We're going to take a few steps back onto the grass, so you can see us from any window you want, Dwayne. Once you're satisfied it's me, open the door so we can talk."

It took less than two minutes before they heard the bolt slide and the door cracked open. They waited a moment, and walked forward. The door opened wider and Dwayne Tracy stood in the doorway, an automatic pistol in his hand, pointed at the ground.

"I know who you are, but what are you doing here?" His eyes looked past them out to the street, searching, scared.

"We work with the police. Informally, kind of. We've been looking into Bucholz. We live nearby and when we heard about Marcus and Glenn we thought maybe someone should come check on you. You ok?"

"Yeah," he said, still wary.

"Is it the Litinovs, Dwayne? Are they pissed off about their fifty grand?"

To Carol's surprise, Dwayne Tracy shook his head in confusion. "No, not them. What fifty grand?"

"Who are you scared of, then, Dwayne?" Tracy shook his head again.

Carol thought it was her turn. Play the gentle one. "We work *with* the police, Dwayne. We're not the police. Neither of us cares about the smuggling stuff. What we do care about is who is trying to kill you, and why?"

Dwayne began to tremble. "It's the Major. It's got to be. He wants all the money for himself."

"The money from Iraq?" Danny said, excitedly. "The money you guys stole from the Green Zone?"

To Carol's complete surprise, Dwayne nodded. "Fifty-four million dollars. We thought we could trust him, but now he's trying to kill us all. I know it." He began trembling uncontrollably as the first police car pulled up and, suddenly, pitched over onto the ground and passed out.

*   *   *

It was late Sunday afternoon when Danny and Carol met up with Frank at the police station. Dwayne Tracy had been taken to the emergency room in a state of nervous exhaustion bordering on shock. It would be a few hours before they would be able to get anything useful out of him, but what he had already said made Frank's eyes roll.

"I still don't buy it!" he said, for the fourth or fifth time. "Fifty-four million dollars? Impossible."

"It's what the man said," began Danny, fidgeting in the high-backed conference room chair.

"…while on the edge of a complete breakdown," finished Frank. "Somehow, I bet when he's gotten fluids, some rest and a hot meal, he won't tell the same story."

"Well..." Danny began again, and then seemed to think better of it. "What did you get from Fiero and Litinov?"

"Scratch from Litinov. He didn't bite. But Fiero coughed up a bundle," he said, with a smile.

"How big a bundle?" asked Carol.

"Fifty thousand dollars?" asked Danny, with that perky, jerky, know-it-all grin on his face. If Gaffney hadn't been on the verge of falling asleep, he would have enjoyed popping Danny's balloon more.

"Four hundred and fifty thousand, actually."

"What?!" both Alexanders said at the same time, simultaneously slapping their palms down on the conference table.

"This is what Fiero says," said Frank, flipping through the pages in his notebook. "About three months ago – around the same time as Bucholz bought those burners, but he couldn't swear to the exact date – Max Litinov called Fiero to his law firm. In his private office, Litinov opens the safe and has Fiero put $450,000 in a couple of canvas grocery bags. He gives Fiero an address...." Gaffney paused. "Come on. You know you want to guess."

Danny stared blankly at his brother-in-law. Gaffney counted a full twenty seconds pass before suddenly Danny lit up in triumph. "The parking lot of Santa's Village Theme Park."

Gaffney nodded, beaming beatifically. "See, you've still got it." That felt good. He went on. "Fiero took the money there and handed it to a waiting stranger, who he identifies with certainty as

Bucholz. No one else was with him. Bucholz took the money, thanked him and shook his hand, and drove off."

"Did Litinov tell Fiero why he was delivering the money?"

"Nope, and The Fireman was too smart to ask."

"And he'd never seen Bucholz before, not at any secret mobster meetings or anything?"

"Nope."

"That would have been just too convenient, I suppose" mused Danny.

"Yeah."

"And what happened to the other $400,000?" asked Carol.

Gaffney shook his head. "Not a clue. There's no sign of it. If Bucholz got it three months ago, you have to think he'd have paid off some of his debts, or at least gone on a spending spree, but neither is the case."

"But we know he got it from Litinov, and three months later he kills Willis Marden, while trying to kill someone else..."

"...or trying to kill Marden."

"Not Marden," Danny was firm. "But there has to be a link between the money and the shooting, right?"

"If we could prove the money came from Litinov," said Frank.

"Fiero told you it did. He gave you a videotaped statement and everything."

"It's not proof," said Mike Levin, entering the room from the hall. "It's a statement from a man facing a major felony charge, meant to exculpate him. We want to believe him, because we want the Litinovs to be behind this, but the fact is, if he was looking to make up a story to save his own ass, this is exactly the story he would make up."

"Well," said Danny, "aren't you a ray of sunshine?" Danny's lower lip took on a slight pout.

"It gets worse," Levin said, with a mournful look in Frank's direction. "Fiero's lawyer showed up, and he just called the DA and told him that Fiero intends to recant his whole statement, that it was made under duress after a long night in custody in an attempt to escape blame for the gambling charge."

"Son of a bitch!" Gaffney stage-whispered so that all could hear. "The Litinovs got to him, didn't they? Fuck me."

"Looks like it. The DA says that Fiero is willing to plead to the gambling charges but denies any connection to the Litinov family." Levin shook his head.

"But you did it right," protested Danny, sounding just a little naive. "You got him to sign a waiver and everything, on camera. Surely that has to carry some weight with…"

"Some weight, sure," said Gaffney. "But it makes our life a whole hell of a lot more complicated, and it means we'll never be able to get any more warrants on the Litinovs off Fiero's statement alone."

"Hell," said Levin, looking skeptical. "For all we know he *did* make it up. Even an idiot like Fiero knows that the best way for him to duck prosecution is to make a deal and implicate the Litinovs. Then he's just a little fish who gets to swim away."

Levin sat down, and Gaffney picked up the thread. "Take away his statement, and what do you have? Fiero runs a gambling operation. He sees lots of cash coming through, and could have come up with $50,000 to give to Bucholz for some reason."

"Maybe Bucholz won it gambling," said Levin. "That would explain why he told his wife he was going to make it big soon."

"Then how can you explain what Dwayne Tracy told us about the fifty-four million? And why did someone kill Beatty and the other one... Kryevsky?" protested Danny.

"I agree," said Gaffney, and Levin nodded affirmatively. "All of this is connected somehow. We're just making sure you understand that there's a world of difference between knowing that there is a connection and *proving* it. As of right now, thanks to Fuckup Fiero finding a pair and backing down," Frank was swearing more than usual – it had been a long day, "we're out of good options for the Litinovs."

"What now?" asked Carol.

"Mueller and Wright are trying to find the other two Army buddies – Ernst and Gilbert. If they're not already running scared, they will be soon enough, and in that state of mind they'll be more likely to tell us the truth about whatever happened in Iraq. As to Litinov, I don't know, we'll think of something," said Frank. "But first, I haven't slept in two days. Some rest will do me good."

"You did good today, Danny, Carol," he added, as he shrugged on his coat and headed for the door. "If you hadn't connected these two murders to Bucholz, we wouldn't even be looking at them now. We'd have nothing. We'll pick these two Army guys up and see what they have to say. No excitement until we get them into an interrogation room."

Chapter 18

Of course, he was wrong.

When Frank heard the stories the next day, he couldn't help but kick himself. He was the lead detective on a case that was sprawled across seven counties, and yet whenever anything really exciting happened, he was either lying on the ground or out of the picture.

He talked to Detective Wright first, just after he got to the office the next morning. She'd been assigned to pick up Lars Gilbert, who lived in a near north suburb. Frank had assumed it wouldn't be any more complicated than when Danny and Carol picked up Dwayne Tracy, and had only sent one officer along with Marilyn. He could tell before she began that there was more. Dammit.

She'd gotten to Gilbert's home and knocked on his door, only to discover that the door slowly swung open as she knocked. This was the sort of thing that never actually happened, and Detective Wright was frozen for a moment before drawing her service weapon (*everyone gets to draw their gun but me,* whined Frank) and heading in. She and the officer did a room-by-room search and found no Lars Gilbert, but some signs that the bedroom had been disturbed – clothes scattered around and the like – and Gilbert had quite obviously taken his toothbrush, shaver, and other toiletries with him. There was also a small safe in the closet, the right size to hold a handgun. It stood open and empty.

Detective Wright sent the uniform to put out an alert for Gilbert's car, while she did a second, more thorough search of the house and hit paydirt. Gilbert had a desktop computer, and it booted up without needing a login. A quick search of the internet history showed that he'd been on a travel website and, like most people, his password was saved on the computer. It was child's play to figure out that he'd made a reservation at a hotel along the interstate nearby.

Frank wasn't green with envy, but that was only because he hadn't had enough coffee. He knew what got to happen next. Trying to pick up someone holed up in a hotel room, probably armed with a gun... it meant SWAT.

"It was pretty intense for a little while, there," said Detective Wright, with studied casualness, typing away at her report as she talked. God, Frank wanted a reason to affect that casualness.

"Did you have to break down the door?" he asked, trying to pretend he didn't care all that much.

"Thankfully, no. We got the people out from the rooms on either side, and then I called up from the house phone. It took a little while to talk him out, but in the end he came willingly." *She got to negotiate someone's surrender? Come on!*

"Good work, Marilyn," he said to her. "I'm sure you had a more exciting evening than Eric, right?" he said, turning to Detective Mueller, who was just coming in.

Mueller smiled as he slid his service weapon out of its holster and into a drawer at his desk. "Was it more exciting than a hot pursuit across state lines?"

Gaffney groaned in agony.

Detective Mueller, in his department-issue Ford, accompanied by a squad car, reached the townhouse complex in the far south suburbs to try to find Andrew Ernst. Mueller knocked on the door and then (this ALSO only happens in the movies, Frank thought, as his face grew red with jealousy) he actually heard a window opening. Lacking both a warrant and the fortitude to take down the heavy door, he and the two uniformed officers split up, running around either side of the multi-unit building, only to see Ernst pulling out in his own car from the back parking lot. Calling in the license number, they ran *back* around the building to their cars, one heading north on the interstate, the other south.

For an anxious ten minutes, maybe twelve, they heard nothing, but then a patrol car just a mile from the scene complex spotted Ernst headed east towards the Indiana border on a county road. Mueller was farther east on the highway, and got off to intercept him from the front while the patrol car turned on its lights and siren and began a chase.

"He pulled over as soon as the rollers came on. I think he was happy it was us looking for him, and not someone else."

"Yeah," said Wright. "Same with our guy. He was scared as all hell. Pretty fucked up, to tell the truth."

"Ernst lawyered up right away, but told me if they can make a deal he'll tell us everything."

"Any hints on what the everything was?"

Mueller shook his head. "I didn't ask."

"There's no way they actually took fifty million dollars…" began Wright, looking back and forth between the two detectives.

"Fifty-four" corrected Mueller.

"Fifty-four million dollars and no one noticed," she continued. "This whole story is horseshit."

"Then why are they sure someone is trying to kill them?" countered Mueller, jabbing his finger onto his desk to emphasize his point.

* * *

While the CPD was tracking down Gilbert and Ernst, FBI Special Agent Cooper Stapley was sitting down with the US Attorney – who would have the closest thing to jurisdiction over what happened in Iraq – preparing him to accept the idea of immunity in return for information on the Kryevsky and Beatty killings. In this, Agent Stapley was pushing on an open door. The odds of pulling off a successful prosecution for smuggling – or even grand theft – that took place years ago in the Green Zone in Iraq were, to say the least, daunting. Murder, on the other hand, was always worth some attention.

It took a few more hours of legal back-and-forth but it all worked itself out in the usual way. Gilbert and Ernst were taken to the hospital, where Dwayne Tracy was still under observation, and the three of them with their lawyer sat in a conference room with Frank, his partner Mike, and Cooper Stapley on the other side of the table, a digital voice recorder in the middle.

"So," Frank began with a smile, "who's trying to kill you?"

The three veterans looked at each other. Eventually Ernst looked back at the detective. "The Major." The others nodded.

"Sure would love a name," said Frank, pen poised above his notebook.

Ernst almost looked embarrassed. "We don't know his name."

"What?" cried Gaffney and Levin in unison. Stapley contented himself with a contemptuous snort.

"The first time I met him his uniform said 'Nelson'," said Andrew Ernst.

"When we all met him the second time it was 'Murray'," said Lars Gilbert, as Dwayne Tracy nodded next to him.

"And the last time it was 'Lewis'," finished Ernst.

"You're going to have to start over, boys," said Frank. "You're not making a lot of sense right now, and this whole thing is starting to smell funny."

"Start with the smuggling," suggested Stapley, gently.

"It was never drugs, or weapons," began Gilbert.

"Or terrorists or sex trafficking or anything like that," added Dwayne Tracy, who still looked drawn and haggard, his eyes darting about at the slightest sound.

"People – Iraqis, I mean – wanted to get their cars out, their jewelry out, their artwork. Valuable stuff," said Ernst, looking to the others, who nodded supportively. "They wanted to move it out of the country so that they could sell it for American dollars."

"How did you get into this particular line of work?" asked Mike Levin.

"A guy came in to our office – we handled routine stuff, you know, building supplies, vehicles for the civilian contractors, and so on. Anyway, a guy came into the office, and he wanted to know if we were able to help him ship an antique grandfather clock to his relatives in the States. He wasn't trying to be a smuggler," Ernst paused again for nods of affirmation from his comrades. "He just thought we would know how he could send something valuable out of the country."

"So you dummied up some forms and got it sent out of the country on a military cargo flight," finished Stapley, and Gilbert nodded in reply.

"Word got around, I guess, and soon we had a lot more people coming in. We didn't ask for any money at first, but most were offering it, and so we took what they offered."

"Some just wanted us to find a way to sell them abroad," said Ernst. We didn't have any idea how to do that."

"And that's where the Litinovs came in, I suppose," asked Stapley.

"Yeah. Mark had mentioned that Max Litinov was in some kind of a mob family, and so we decided to approach them." Once again, Ernst paused to make sure Tracy and Gilbert were ok with him going on. "He went home for a short leave and he came back with a set of email addresses and a simple code. We'd email Max who'd come back with a price. If it was acceptable, we'd arrange transportation."

"Where to, exactly?" asked Stapley.

Gaffney took a guess of his own, as nonchalantly as he could manage. "You used military flights, so I bet you were delivering to military bases. I have to imagine it was usually Great Lakes Naval Air Station, right? North of the city along the lake, right in the Litinovs' territory?"

Ernst nodded. "Sometimes a place out east, but usually there."

Dwayne Tracy suddenly lurched out of his chair and staggered over to the trash can, where he retched. Frank reached for the nurse call button on the wall but Tracy looked back and waved him off. "Just give me a minute, man."

Tracy sat on the floor, panting. He pushed himself back up and sat back down in his chair. Lars Gilbert reached over and patted him on the arm.

"Look," began Frank, "I don't want to make you sicker than you are, but this has gone on for a little while now and I've heard nothing about a Major or about any fifty-four million dollars."

"You told him about the money?!" Ernst shot a murderous glare at Tracy. "We still have a chance to…" and then he trailed off, briefly muttering to himself. Then he grimaced and spoke. "Yeah, we stole fifty-four million. Give or take." His voice was sullen and he was looking at the ground.

"How in the hell did you do that?" asked a skeptical Stapley.

"You guys came up with some kind of crazy plan to steal a pallet of cash worth tens of millions, sure," echoed Gaffney

"Two duffel bags' worth," said Tracy, weakly. "Each one with 108 bricks of a quarter-million dollars. Mark Bucholz had the idea. He'd thought it up a year before, for fun one night while we were playing video games in the barracks."

They sat in rapt silence for the next ten minutes as Ernst, Gilbert, and Tracy told their story.

"No way," said Frank, a full minute after they were done talking.

"Not possible," concurred Cooper Stapley. "There's no way the forgeries would have worked, the bags undiscovered. Not possible."

Ernst put up his hands and almost smirked. "We were there. It worked."

There was another long silence.

"OK, let's agree to disagree and pretend you did steal all this money," allowed Frank. "Tell us about the Major."

"I met him the first time," said Ernst. "I was delivering some cigars to another soldier at the British Embassy..."

"The Major is *British*?" Gaffney was so exasperated that the end of his sentence came out as little more than a squeak.

"Oh, right. Guess I hadn't brought that up. Yeah, he was British. And like I said, the first time I met him he called himself Nelson. He told me about these old vaults under this building in the British Embassy compound. Dozens of them. Maybe they were used to hold WMDs or some shit before the war..."

"Saddam didn't have any ..." began Levin, who then obviously realized the futility of arguing the point.

"Well, whatever. They had these big vaults, and the Brits weren't doing anything with them."

"You had a plan to steal this money," continued Frank, "but you couldn't just walk out of Iraq with a cubic yard of cash. You decided to stash it in the vaults."

"Right," agreed Ernst. "I told Nelson we needed to stash some goods – I made him think it was the business papers of an Iraqi oil official."

"And this Major Nelson bought it?"

Lars Gilbert nodded and took over the narrative. "Andy arranged for us all to meet him a week later in a bar in the Green Zone. We didn't talk about the business much, just sports and the war and girls. We said we had a delivery of 'paper' for him. He told us he'd be happy to protect it for us, but that was all we said."

"And then he was Murray?"

Gilbert nodded. "It was on his uniform. Ten days later we carried out the plan."

Gaffney was glad he was recording this. He still didn't want to believe them, but he was too engrossed in the story to take any notes.

"We loaded the duffels at night into a Humvee and drove it over to the vacant building on the British embassy grounds. There were two guards and a little office with the name Major Murray on the door," said Ernst. "I walked over and told the Major we were there with our paper delivery. The guards let us through, and we carried the duffels down to the vault rooms. We loaded them in and pulled the vault door closed.

"The idea was," continued Ernst, "we'd wait six weeks or so, and then start going back and taking a little of the money at a time. But then everything got fucked up."

Ernst looked around, then leaned over to their lawyer for a quick whispered conversation. The lawyer nodded. "When you guys picked me up, I had an iPad. If you get it for me, I'll show you." Levin went out to get a uniform to find the iPad while Ernst explained. "Nelson, or Murray, or whoever, he was supposed to stay in Iraq for another eight months, but he sent me an email like five days after we stashed the money. He was being sent to Afghanistan immediately. He told us he knew the guy who was being left in charge of the area, and that he would watch over the vaults for us, keeping everything undisturbed, but..."

"But his friend needed some money?" queried Stapley.

All three of them nodded. "A thousand dollars from each of us at first. We put it in an envelope and I walked it over to the embassy, addressed to a Major Lewis" said Ernst.

"His name was Lewis now?" asked Gaffney.

Ernst nodded. "That's what we were told to put on the envelope, anyway."

"The thing is," said Dwayne Tracy, who was once again breathing a little more heavily and showing flushed cheeks, "we only had four months left on our tour. And the new guy..."

"Ever get the new guy's name?"

"No."

"Too bad," sympathized Frank.
The door opened and Levin came back in with a tablet computer. He handed it to Ernst who unlocked it and opened his email.

"I put all the emails in their own folder," he said, "look." He tapped the screen a few times and scrolled down. "He said he could guarantee no one would disturb our stuff, but that it might be a long time before we could get access to the site again."

Gaffney was quickly scanning the emails. "You get back to America, and about six months later he sent you the first demand for cash."

"Five grand each," said Gilbert. "Every year or so he asked for it."

"How did you send it to him?"

"Cash in a box, sent to a general delivery post office address," said Ernst. "Usually the United Kingdom, one year New York."

Stapley gave the three men a quizzical yet paternal look. "You boys know he was just blackmailing you, right? That he was never going to let you get that money?"

Ernst sighed, and the other two flushed. "But what else were we going to do? We hadn't worn gloves or anything. Our prints were all over that money. If he dropped a dime on us…"

"Plus," added Lars Gilbert, "the fact that he was asking for cash told us he didn't know what was in the vault. If he'd realized it was cash, he would have just taken it and cut off all contact from us." The others nodded vigorously in support. "The money should still have been sitting down there, probably covered up by new construction," he finished, wistfully.

"You're speaking in the past tense," observed Frank. "What happened?"

"Here," said Ernst. He scrolled down the screen. "Back in 2013 we got this."

He handed the tablet back to Gaffney, who read aloud as he scanned it. *"Too much security... career rotation means I am unlikely to return to Iraq... can no longer guarantee the security of your papers."* Frank looked up. "So, he gave up trying to shake you down?"

"Mark always had faith in him," sighed Dwayne Tracy. "He said the Major was just using the money to buy off Brits to leave the vaults alone."

"You know, I sometimes have thought that Mark was getting his own messages from the Major, not just the emails he sent to all of us," said Ernst.

"Yeah..." said Gilbert, thinking. "He did sometimes seem like he knew stuff we didn't. Weird, because he never met the Major alone so he never had any kind of relationship with him."

"That we know of," said Ernst.

"That we know of," agreed Tracy.

Stapley broke in. "Six years with no word from the guy, and now you think the Major has started killing your friends because he finally found out about the money?"

Gaffney looked at the tablet. "But you haven't had any more emails from him. Why do you think this is him at all?"

Ernst looked puzzled. "Who the hell else would want to kill us?" Stapley threw his hands in the air. "OK, I've had it. This story is nine-tenths bullshit."

"We're telling the truth!" protested Ernst.

"First of all, you're going to need to convince me that that story you told us was true, that you grunts figured out a way to get fifty-four million dollars away from a secure facility under armed guard despite all the holes in your story. *If* you can do that, you can then convince me that, at the same time you were smart enough to figure that out, you were also dumb enough to think that paying all this cash to this guy was going to get you anything. And *then* you have to convince me that, if this Major exists, and if the stolen money exists, and if the Major has found the money, why he has the slightest reason to bother trying to kill you, when he could just take the money and leave you with nothing. You don't even know his name, for goodness' sake."

Before they could respond, there was a sharp knock and a uniformed officer came in with a folded piece of paper that he handed to Detective Gaffney.

He opened it. *Det. Gaffney,* it read in a hastily-scrawled script, *I'd like to talk to you about Danny Alexander and the gambling bust in Evanston this weekend. Samantha Richter, Chicago Sun-Times.*

"Shit," muttered Frank, out loud. "Carry on without me. I gotta go take care of this."

*   *   *

He knew he'd recognized the name. In case he'd forgotten, Richter extended her hand in greeting as he entered his office. "Detective, so nice to see you again. We met in the parking lot outside Mark Bucholz's funeral."

"Did we?" he tried, but it was immediately clear that playing dumb wouldn't fly. He sat behind his desk. "Yes, yes we did. What can I do for you?"

"I think you know why I'm here, detective," she said with a smile. "Do you want to tell me or should I tell you?"

"Tell me what, exactly?" he asked, trying to seem as calm as possible.

Sam waited a moment, but when Frank said nothing more she pulled out a battered reporter's notepad from her shoulder bag lying on the floor next to her chair.

"Thought you all used tablets and smart phones now," said Frank, trying to be conversational.

"I like the old school," The reporter seconded that by taking the cap off a real live fountain pen. "I go with the tried-and-true. Like a lot of teams go with tried-and-true Danny Alexander, even if he's a little worn around the edges. Reliable, you know. He's your brother-in-law, isn't that what your sister said that day in the parking lot?" Frank didn't bother acknowledging the question.

"Funny you three showing up there, supposedly friends of the family." Richter gazed at nothing in particular, reminiscing. "I remember a lot of stories about Danny when I did sports. Something made him a little different. A reporter from the *Plain Dealer*, Lee Krohn, told me Danny had... what was it?" She glanced back down at her notebook. "He'd sat next to Danny on the bench. Danny was just talking to himself, really, but for three batters in a row, before they even got to the plate, he described the exact order of the pitches and the outcome of each at-bat. How interesting, then, that he shows up at the funeral with his homicide detective brother-in-law." Richter looked up from her notebook, eyes twinkling with merriment. Frank's stomach was dropping, and he was pretty sure it showed.

"And then, who woulda thunk it, the police search a downtown law firm and find out that Bucholz shot Willis Marden. And do you know who happened to be there just before the cops showed up? Danny Alexander. Shocking coincidence, wouldn't you say?"

"I don't know anything about Danny being at the law firm," lied Frank, gamely. Frank was good enough at what he did to recognize good work, even if it was embarrassing.

"Sure," Sam said, airily, tossing back her hair, "no doubt you don't. But it sure is interesting that just a few more days later, a Litinov-run gambling operation is hit, and Danny Alexander is one of the people swept up. Odd that none of the actual gamblers were arrested. Just escorted out and let go. Almost like you were trying to protect one of them." She looked straight into his eyes with a surprising toughness. "Like an informant."

Frank had had enough. He sank into his chair and held his hands open. "What can you prove, and what are you speculating on?"

"I've got a young deputy sheriff in Kane County who says he searched the grounds of Santa's Village with someone named Danny who wasn't a cop and who looks just like our guy. I have two paralegals at the law firm with autographed baseballs. I have a retired engineer-turned-baseball-fanatic who was getting into his car after dinner at a nice a German restaurant and is sure he saw Danny Alexander being walked out by the police. I have two sources at the Evanston PD ready to confirm that it was a Litinov poker game. What I want to know from you is why." Jesus. No wonder the sports beat bored her.

"What's your deadline for publication?"

Richter looked at him carefully. "I haven't told my editor about this side of the story yet."

"You haven't?" A glimmer of hope.

"I can only imagine," she went on, playing with a button on her jacket, "the consequences to Danny Alexander if this were to come out. They'd ban him from the game, no doubt about it."

"He's a good guy who doesn't deserve that," Gaffney found himself saying. "He's rash and sometimes a bit of a jackass, but he's just trying to do the right thing in his own way."

"Then help me out here, Frank, if I can call you Frank?" said Richter, brushing a stray hair off her cheek. "Look, on the one hand here I have a career story. This thing writes itself. I could stretch it out to two or three parts. It'd get hundreds of thousands of hits, maybe more. I'd get to be on CNN, Fox News, ESPN, the whole thing. Do you get how big a deal that is for someone in my line of work?"

Frank nodded.

"And there's also the public interest angle of this. This is a story people probably ought to know. I've no doubt that you and your brother-in-law are trying to do the right thing, and I'm sure you're smart enough to have mostly stayed on the right side of the law. But it doesn't change the facts here."

"I just... I never thought..."

"That anyone would make the connection? Ninety-nine times out of a hundred, you would have. If you hadn't seen me in that parking lot…" she smiled. It was a kind smile.

"You can't publish this," he began, and then immediately softened his tone. "Please don't publish it."

"Why did you even let him get near this case?" Richter asked.

Her notebook was back in her bag.

"It's not really a question of 'let' with Danny," said Frank, with a grin. "He figured out Bucholz killed Marden in about an hour, and from then on there was no stopping him." Frank sighed. "He can be a lot of work. He did all of that himself, except the gambling thing."

"Trying to get leverage on Litinov?"

"Yeah."

Samantha leaned forward in her chair, resting her elbows on the other side of Gaffney's desk. "What's the bigger story here?" she asked, more conversationally than as a question.

"It might have to do with at least two other murders and fifty-four million dollars." He watched with satisfaction as her eyes widened.

"There's a good story there, too," Frank promised, straightening his tie. "Murder, international intrigue, the mob. We don't have it all yet, and there's a lot that doesn't make sense, but it'd be a heck of a story."

"Especially if a reporter had an exclusive and a head start," said Sam, finishing the thought.

"You could write the whole thing without a mention of Danny, you know, and it would still be a hell of a read."

She scrunched her face in thought for a moment. "OK. It's a deal. You give me access, and first crack at everything, and once you're ready to go public I get twenty-four hours over any other reporter. Deal?"

Frank swallowed and exhaled. "Deal. But you need to know that I want to do this, but I'm not authorized to..."

"It's all right," she replied, brightly, "I trust you."

She stood up and so did he, unconsciously smoothing down his hair as he did. "I'll let you know when we have things you can publish."

"Sounds good," she said. "I knew the Kryevsky and Beatly murders tied into this all somehow..."

Puzzlement. "I didn't mention their names. How did you know they were...?" He smiled sheepishly. "You didn't, did you? I just confirmed it for you, didn't I?"

"Both about the same age as Bucholz, both veterans. It was a reasonable guess, don't you think?" Samantha Richter's eyes twinkled with the delight of discovery.

Frank took her business card and handed over one of his. "Maybe, uh... maybe we could talk through the case over a drink after it's all over?"

She smiled again, and it was the brightest thing Frank had seen in quite a long time.

Chapter 19

"So," said Danny Alexander, excitedly, "they told you how they stole the fifty-four million, right?"

"Yep," answered Frank.

"How'd they do it?"

Frank shook his head. "Nope."

"Aw, c'mon!" protested Danny, who really could sound like a teenager when he was whining.

"That's not why I asked to meet you," said Gaffney. He turned his head to his sister. "You were right. The press figured out Danny was involved." He briefly recounted his meeting with Sam Richter. Carol's expression was familial but cold by the time he finished.

The Mercury Café was sparsely filled in this late afternoon hour, and their famous milkshakes were delivered with great speed by the waitstaff. Carol took another sip of her chocolate-strawberry. "Well, I guess this is the end of it, then."

"No, it's not..." began Danny. The Gaffney siblings both interrupted him, but Carol got it out first.

"We can't risk it anymore," she said. It wasn't an argument; it was a fact.

"This reporter is smart," said Frank, *and kinda cute*, he thought. "But even the dumber ones might get there eventually if you stay involved. You want to run ideas by me on the phone, I'm happy to listen, but from now on you can't be seen near this investigation. Your career, your life – for that matter – *and* the chances of a successful prosecution will be in jeopardy if the word gets out about what you've done." As a point of emphasis, he took the cherry from the top of his shake and popped it into his mouth.

Danny looked more than a little like a rat trapped in a corner, his eyes involuntarily glancing around as if searching for a way out. If Carol noticed it, she was studiously ignoring him. "This story these guys told: do you believe them?"

Frank shook his head. "No, at least not all the way. I mean, when we picked them up they were on the run, and they didn't have enough time to concoct something so elaborate before we sat down with them, so there's something to it, but I really can't believe the part about how they got the money." He looked at Danny. "It just doesn't add up."

"Look," said Danny, with something near to desperation in his voice, "can I do one more thing? Please?"

"No," said Frank, and he meant it.

Danny inhaled deeply, held it, and then exhaled. He took a drink of water, swallowed, and sighed. What Frank didn't expect – but should have - was the resilient cheeriness that almost immediately reappeared.

"OK, you guys may be smart, but you missed something. From Fiero's statement."

"If he was telling the truth," said Frank.

"Yeah, yeah, yeah," said Danny, quickly. "But let's just assume he was. Didn't you notice anything weird about his story?"

"Danny," said Frank, "just get on with it."

He gave him a sharp glance for just a moment, then softened. "Right, sorry. Two questions. First, why did Max Litinov use Fiero to make a money drop? That's not what The Fireman does. Not in his job description."

"Presumably no one else was available," answered Frank.

"Think about *why* that might have been while I ask question number two: why on earth would the Litinov crime family keep $450,000 in mob cash in the safe of an otherwise-legitimate law office?"

Frank paused mid-sip and looked up.

"Huh." He unconsciously turned away and bit the end of the straw as he thought about it.

"We keep saying this was a Litinov *family* operation, to give the money to Mark Bucholz. What if it wasn't? What if little Max Litinov – remember, to the best of our knowledge he's kept out of the serious stuff so he can be the legitimate lawyer – what if he was doing this on his own? That is to say…"

"What if the *paterfamilias* doesn't know his little nephew's given away almost half a million dollars to a man who's now dead?" finished Frank.

"Fiero wouldn't have squawked, and Maxie called his own lawyer on Sunday, right? Someone who maybe would keep his mouth shut and not tell Uncle Dmitry what his little boy was up to."

Frank paused to think it over. He allowed himself a smile. "I wonder how far little Maximillian will go to keep the rest of the family out of the loop on this…"

"Good one, honey," said Carol, patting Danny on the arm.

*   *   *

Carol walked back to the car with Danny. The Mercury sold wine as well as milkshakes, and Danny had helped himself to an extra four glasses, plus most of Carol's one glass. Since he rarely drank, Carol had to keep a good hold of him as he staggered into the passenger seat.

"Don't worry, honey," she said, sweetly, kissing him on the forehead. "We're not going to let Frank keep us from working on this. I'm having a little *soiree* tomorrow night, and you'll see that we can still do some good on this case *and* stay away from it."

Chapter 20

As the guests began arriving and he saw what was going on, Danny began involuntarily bouncing up and down on the balls of his feet.

"It's like my own Baker Street Irregulars," he crowed.

"Well," said Carol, coyly, "they're really *my* Baker Street Irregulars, but I'll let you use them for a while."

Susana Melendez was on the couch, chatting with two of Carol's students, Melody Kasson and Deniece Rogers. In chair on the other side of the coffee table, Greg Buhl was visibly sweating and practically shaking. He settled down, though, once Carol handed out the packets and began talking.

"You all don't know it yet," said Carol, tactfully if inaccurately grouping Susana in with the younger students, "but for the last couple of weeks you've been criminal investigators." She paused to let that sink in.

She went on for a brisk eight minutes, covering the Marden murder, the Bucholz suicide, the gunshots outside Swigert's law office, the Hayfield shooting, the deaths of Kryevsky and Beatty, and the recent revelations by Ernst, Gilbert and Tracy. By the time she was done, her students just stared back at her.

Melody Kasson managed to find the ability to speak first. "Wait... wait... huh? You mean you work for the police? You two are cops?" Deniece looked similarly vexed.

"No," said Carol, quickly. "But my brother is, and sometimes when he has a tough case he talks to Danny and me, and this time we got a little carried away in our investigating." It was charitable of her to use *we* in that phrase, and she saw him give her a thankful grin.

"We're keeping our distance from the crime now," she went on, "but people's lives are at stake, and we don't want to let it go. My brother has said that any ideas we can generate he'll use. We want to generate some. You four are the best researchers I know. Big case like this one, I think everyone's interest is to avoid a miscarriage of justice." She made eye contact with Deniece, who frowned but nodded assent.

She went over to a large sheet of paper she had taped to the wall of the living room and pulled out a marker. She wrote three headings across the top: "Soldiers", "Major" and "$$$".

"Three lines of inquiry," she said, crisply and seamlessly slipping into teaching mode. "First, what more can we find out about this group of soldiers – Bucholz, Beatty, Kryevsky, Ernst, Tracy, and Gilbert? Greg, you did some great digging on this already. Can you keep looking? Any fact you find might be helpful." Greg Buhl accepted the assignment with evident pride.

"Second, what's up with this Major? Who is he? How can we figure that out, when there must have been dozens or hundreds of British majors in Iraq? Deniece, you wrote that great paper on live-blogging by troops deployed overseas. Think you can go back to your sources and see what you can find out about the major?" Deniece looked a little more daunted than Greg, but nodded.

"Finally, Melody, get into this business of the fifty-four million. There are lots of rumors about stolen funds from Iraq, but it's all pretty vague. We were told there were emails from folks in Iraq to their families about it. Track down anything you can. Someone HAD to discover the missing money at some point, right?"

Melody raised a quizzical eyebrow, but was already tapping into her tablet.

"Susana and I will be working with all three of you," she concluded. Just to see the expression on his face she said, "Greg, you should fill Susana in on all your work so far, so that the two of you can brainstorm new leads." So much sweating.

"We will meet every other day at my office, at 5pm, to go over what we've got so far. Any more questions?"

There were a million questions to ask, but for the moment they were quiet.

Danny's phone beeped. He unlocked it and read a text. "Forensics on Beatty and Kryevsky. Same gun used in both shootings, and same gun used to shoot Reggie Hayfield. Huh. Hayfield?" He was silent.

"Why would a British Major want to shoot Reggie Hayfield?" asked Deniece Rogers.

"There has to be a connection," said Melody Kasson, jumping in, "between the Stringfellow investigation and the fifty-four million." She looked up quizzically at Danny. "Didn't you say you thought Willis Marden was the wrong guy, that Bucholz was trying to shoot someone else?"

"That's right. I...."

"Well, you're going to have to rethink *that*," declared Melody.

And off they went.

*   *   *

While Danny Alexander was having his precious theories subjected to merciless attack, Frank Gaffney was pulling his car into the parking lot of a small bar in an out-of-the-way neighborhood.

He'd made a phone call. The other party was happy to meet, and showed little concern about the implications. This did not surprise Frank.

Robinson Stringfellow sat in a corner table, back to the wall, nursing what Frank guessed was a non-alcoholic beer. Even seated, his bearing was erect and proud, and the casual orange polo top he was wearing did nothing to hide the air of... *dare Frank say it* ... nobility that hung about his shoulders. Crook or no crook, he was a leader.

Frank sat and ordered a real beer while the two men eyed each other.

"You told me you wanted to see Reggie Hayfield's shooter brought to justice."

"And I do. He's nobody's fool and nobody's crook. Just a young man trying to go on with his life."

Frank nodded. "And that's what we've got so far, too. No criminal record, no funny stuff, adoring girlfriend, clean books, everything."

His beer arrived and he paused to sip it before continuing.

"Which makes it all the stranger, don't you think, that the gun that shot him killed two other men over the weekend? Two men who just so happen to be close friends with the guy who shot Willis Marden?"

If Stringfellow knew any of this before now, he was the best actor Frank had ever met. "What?!" He lowered his voice. "What? There's no way..." Frank patted himself on the back. He had stunned the politician speechless.

"I agree," Frank said, casually. "It doesn't make any sense at all. Who would possibly have motive to shoot Reggie Hayfield, as well as two Army veterans living in the suburbs with no connection to Hayfield at all?" His phone buzzed once – incoming text – but he ignored it.

"It's possible," he continued, "that the link is you."

"Bullshit," came the reply, fast as lightning.

"Yeah, I don't buy it either. I'm just saying it's possible. The only other link is the guy who shot Marden, and of course now he's dead." If Robinson Stringfellow really did want to help find out who shot Reggie Hayfield, he'd have to bite at that.

He did. "Well, who put him up to it?"

"How do you know someone put him up to it?"

"No one shoots a rifle out of a window across Dearborn Street without being put up to it."

"I agree. We were starting to think Marden wasn't the target, but now it seems like he might have been."

"So? Why are you and I talking right now?"

By way of answer Frank got out of his seat and walked over to the jukebox. He inserted a five-dollar bill and selected everything he could find by the Rolling Stones and the Beatles. The jukebox was loud. His phone buzzed again as he went back. Still ignored it.

He sat back down. He spoke slowly but quietly, so that Stringfellow could understand him above the music. Just in case either of them was worried about that. "We don't know exactly who put him up to it, but we know who gave the shooter almost half a million dollars."

Stringfellow raised his eyebrows, asking.

"Tell me, Alderman, you ever do business with the Litinovs up in Evanston?"

"Name rings a bell," he replied, not showing any cards.

"The nephew of Dmitry, Max. He's friends with the guy who shot Willis Marden, Bucholz. Close friends. Stood up at his wedding, even. Also, he was friends with the other two guys killed by the gun that shot Hayfield." He paused, making Stringfellow wait for it.

"And the Litinovs gave Bucholz $450,000 a few weeks before Marden was killed."

Stringfellow's eyes hardened. Frank could see him pondering, calculating the angles.

"I can't know what you're thinking, Alderman," he said, carefully, "but if I was involved in… the kind of things you're involved in, and I heard that a crime family from north of town was maybe targeting people from my part of the world, even if they were innocent, I'd be figuring out how to stay alive long enough to take the fight to them.

"But then," continued Frank, "if I were that man, I'd also be trying to think about why a homicide detective was telling me this. He's not trying to start a gang war, so he must have some other reason."

Stringfellow snapped out of his reverie and fixed his gaze on Frank. "And what would that reason be?"

"I don't *think* the Litinovs are behind this, at least not in the way you might think. You see, little Max Litinov was doing what he was doing on his own. Without Uncle Dmitry being on board. And we have enough evidence to *suspect* that Max Litinov's dealings were primarily directed towards criminal enterprises *unrelated* to the city of Chicago. Enterprises in no way associated with... anyone you'd have an interest in looking out for."

"Suspect? No proof?" This was easier than he expected, Frank reflected. Robinson Stringfellow was a smart man.

"Well, you see, our best proof is dead. Mark Bucholz. Now, we tried talking to Max Litinov, but oddly enough he is reluctant to cooperate. It was only later that we realized that he was acting without the family's knowledge."

"Sounds to me like that's leverage of some kind," observed Stringfellow.

"Well, yeah, but not as much as I'd like." Frank took another big drink of beer and had to turn his head while he discreetly burped. This was getting pretty real. "You see, if I were to haul in Dmitry Litinov, the uncle, and rat out his nephew to him, what do you think I'd get out of it? You think he's going to give us anything useful, anything helpful to unwrapping this? Of course not. They'd shut up Max and surround him with so many lawyers that we'd never hear another word."

"You could bring the kid in again," suggested the alderman, "threaten to tell his family what happened unless he talks."

"Sure, sure," said Frank, airily, "I could try that. But now that I've picked him up once, if I bring him in again it's a sure thing that the family will have their own lawyers on the scene, and Max isn't going to say a word if he thinks it'll get back to his uncle."

He leaned back in the booth, yawning slightly. "No, I just don't have the leverage on Max Litinov. In fact, the only person who does is Dmitry Litinov. And I *definitely* don't have that kind of leverage."

He paused.

"I mean, the only people who'd have that kind of leverage are business associates of Litinov, or people connected to his business associates, who could convince the Litinovs that we weren't interested in any of his larger business activities, just what the story is with this money to Bucholz, and that if we could get that story then our attention would naturally move on to other things. I mean, not everyone's attention… not some kind of get-out-of-jail-free thing, but at least an assurance that the Bucholz information wouldn't give us an edge in our other efforts to stop criminal wrongdoing, if you follow me.

"Of course," Frank threw up his hands, "I don't know any of those kinds of people, the kind of people who'd have some kind of leverage with Dmitry Litinov. Someone who could send him a message: that if Max makes a clean breast of all his dealings with

Bucholz, and convinces us he didn't have anything to do with the murders – which I'm actually prepared to believe, because I have another suspect in mind for that – that *if* those things happen, then I wouldn't feel compelled to devote resources I don't have to investigate a crime family that usually operates outside the city's jurisdiction."

"I can see what you mean," Stringfellow waved his hand to show Frank he could end his circumlocutions. "Let's say someone had a personal stake in Hayfield's shooting…"

"Let's just say," agreed Frank.

"And this person *also* had a way to get the attention of the Litinovs, to make them able to see the advantages of coming forward on this subject…"

"Bearing in mind that any persuasive methods used could not result in anyone getting hurt, no assaults or beatings or anything like that…"

"Certainly not," said Stringfellow, magnanimously.

"Then it might be possible for us to put the Hayfield case to bed and salvage the poor kid's reputation," concluded Frank.

The two men looked at one another. Almost imperceptibly, Alderman Robinson Stringfellow nodded his head. They didn't speak again. Stringfellow finished his drink quickly and walked out.

Frank unlocked his phone to find three text messages from his brother-in-law:

Why would anyone use the same gun to shoot three different people?, read the first.

Professionals would dump their guns and get new ones, the next one said, and Frank saw the third one provided the same answer he was thinking.

What if shooter didn't have a way to get a new gun? Like he was here from a foreign country?

Like a British Army officer.

Three hours later, while reading in bed, Frank heard on his police radio that someone had thrown a Molotov cocktail into a liquor store in the north suburbs, a store long suspected of being a central booking house for gambling operations. It was after hours and no one was hurt, but the fire damage was extensive. He pondered that for a moment, and decided he needed to take a shower. It almost worked.

Chapter 21

"I don't know," said Melody Kasson, two nights later, "but I think they could've done it."

Danny, Carol saw, was beaming with pride and bouncing up and down on his feet.

"There's this blogger, goes by the handle WarGod338, and he posted this about eleven years ago." Melody passed around printouts as the others munched on the popcorn that Carol had provided. "This guy posts a lot of stuff on Iraq, like he's sort of an informal clearinghouse for people who want to get some stories off their chest anonymously. A lot of them are pretty dark." She paused and swallowed. "I think this blogger really did serve in Iraq, and in the posts I've given you he's retelling a story that he heard from someone else." There were at least sixty pages. "Sorry, but I needed to include the comment threads, too. They have additional information."

"Why does this story stand out to you, Mel?" prompted Susana Melendez.

"'Cuz it mentions two duffel bags," said Greg Buhl, paging ahead. Then he realized who he'd spoken to and froze in silence.

"That," agreed Melody, "and, responding to comments, WarGod338 identifies his source as an 'MB' who lives in Chicago."

"Mark Bucholz," said Danny, in case that obvious connection had been missed by anyone in the room. It hadn't, and in either case they were all now reading too intently to listen to him.

Three large pallets stacked with huge amounts of cash for the American effort in Iraq, Carol read, were stored in a small warehouse filled with office supplies. There were three layers of guards, all from different units, and the guard duty was rotated at random. "MB" and his buddies took guard shifts from time to time, including duty inside the money room itself.

A log book recorded in triplicate any withdrawals from the stacks. Said withdrawals could only be done by an officer, in the company of another officer, and the guards were required to confirm the withdrawal order with a third officer from another unit before the money could be disbursed.

WarGod338 reported that MB found out the pallets of money were due to be moved by forklift to a new location, an armored bunker built for the purpose. It would be counted and the count matched against the log book before it was moved. MB traded shifts so that he and his friends worked inside the money room the last hours before the pallets were to be moved. Carol slowed down to read more carefully; this was almost crazy enough to work.

MB had duty first. He brought in five forged withdrawal forms, totaling millions of dollars in supposed disbursements (WarGod338 didn't have the exact number, apparently) and dated several weeks previously. He stuck them into the log amongst the genuine forms. His pal L (*Lars Gilbert,* she thought) went next, carrying in two standard army duffels. The inner-room guards were always thoroughly searched when they left. The guards searched L on his way out, and he was clean. They never noticed the duffel bags didn't come out with him.

G went next (*the late Glenn Beatty,* apparently) and he innocently stacked a couple of boxes on top of a shelf, cutting off one pallet from the view of the security camera.

The coincidence of letters struck Carol as another sign of the blog's authenticity. M and D – Marcus Kryevsky and Dwayne Tracy – were up next, and each filled one of the duffel bags with cash. They then locked and dragged the duffels to a dark corner of the warehouse, out of the way.

Andrew Ernst – called "A" by WarGod338 – was the last one in, and his job was to be on hand when the forklifts came to move the pallets. He helped count the money – which matched thanks to the forged forms - and also helped search the warehouse for anything suspicious. Every single one of more than a hundred boxes of copier paper were opened, but Ernst somehow kept them from looking at the two duffel bags in a corner. Duffels were so ubiquitous in the military that they might easily be overlooked.

And then the pallets were moved, and the warehouse became a normal warehouse again, with no security past a lock on the door. And two duffels filled with bricks of hundred-dollar bills, waiting for MB and his pals to saunter on in and waltz out with them.

Carol finished reading and looked at the others. Danny took the longest to finish, and he had a faraway look in his eyes as he did. Carol could tell he was imagining the scene, testing the story for weaknesses and flaws.

The others had found a few weaknesses of their own.

"Are we supposed to believe that their forged withdrawal forms passed muster?" asked Deniece. "And no one wonders why someone is carrying in duffel bags?"

"You block a security camera, and someone comes in to check it out, right?" added Greg, his curiosity completely overwhelming his shyness.

"I'd think someone would have noticed that they arranged to take the last shifts – didn't anyone think at the time that that was suspicious?" threw in Susana.

Danny started to answer, but was cut off by Melody Kasson, who stole his thunder. "The security camera probably wasn't monitored – just the recordings kept in case of future problems. And the military is used to people trading shifts; maybe they said there was a game on they wanted to watch, or a phone call they were waiting for from home."

"And the forged papers?" asked Carol.

"Who's to say they weren't eventually discovered?" asked Danny. "Maybe two months later, an auditor is going through everything and finds the forms. What does he do about it? He tells the higher-ups, and maybe they decide that they would rather keep things quiet than risk a scandal."

"Or," chimed in Melody, "the forms are still sitting on some desk, waiting to be processed. This is the US Army, after all."

Carol looked at the others. Susana (and therefore Greg) had skeptical expressions that probably matched her own, but she noticed Deniece Rogers nodding and typing on her laptop. "Deniece, what've you got?"

"Just… well, it's got a bit of a familiar ring, doesn't it? I mean, Bucholz really liked dramatic, elaborate things, didn't he? I've been researching him, and he's got a pattern. He bought his house for fifty thousand more than other houses in his neighborhood sold for at the same time. He plans and the spontaneously cancels a big overseas trip for him and his wife. He thinks big, to hell with the consequences."

Deniece concluded. "The guy who thought up a fifty-four million dollar robbery like this, he'd be just the sort of guy who would call a fake meeting and cancel it in order to free up a window for him to take a one-in-a-million shot at someone on the street below."

"Or approach his high school crush with a ten-thousand-dollar bracelet and imagine she would fall for him," added Danny, nodding in agreement.

"I agree he dreamt big," said Carol, pointedly. "I can recognize the type."

"But," Deniece went on, "that only shows how crazy unlikely this all is. I agree: this seems like the sort of plot that Bucholz might dream up. But it's a whole 'nother story to say he actually did it and got away with it. If it wasn't for the fact that Ernst, Tracy and Lars Gilbert all seemed to believe they had done it, I'd assume a caper like this would too easily fall apart in execution. I don't know... feels like we're missing something."

"Maybe there's someone else involved," said Greg Buhl. "I've been looking at the six of them, but who's to say there isn't a number seven someplace? Maybe an officer who helped cover up the forms and the security camera, something like that?"

Carol nodded and saw Danny do the same. "That sounds like a possibility. We'll bear that in mind." She stood up. "Anyone have anything else yet?" She looked around and got shakes of the head. "Melody, I want you to work with Deniece on this Major character – I think you have answered your piece of the puzzle. We'll meet back here in forty-eight hours."

Sitting in bed that evening, she happened to notice a news story about a parking lot full of luxury cars outside a Russian restaurant in Evanston, where someone had slashed every single tire and poured something acidic over the paint jobs on the fanciest SUVs. She paid it no mind.

Chapter 22

Frank Gaffney was on the phone with his sister for an hour the next morning, as she tried to wheedle something out of him in return for her scoop from the blogger. He stonewalled the best he could, resisting her threats to inform their aged parents that he was being "a big bully like he was as a kid," and ignoring her fraternal attempt at bribery when she mentioned that Danny was going to get a one of the newest flat screens and maybe he would want one, too. Eventually, once he heard the story that WarGod338 had to tell, he did reluctantly confirm that what Ernst, Gilbert, and Tracy had said more or less matched the blog post, and Carol hung up in triumph.

That meant Frank could go back to twiddling his thumbs, like he had for the past two days.

He'd had a long meeting with Lieutenant Halloran Tuesday afternoon, after he finished interrogating the three soldiers and typing up his report. She pointed out politely but with meaning that the murder of Glenn Beatty did not take place within Chicago city limits, that the murder of Kryevsky was in the hands of capable detectives in the western part of the city, and that the one murder that *had* been in Gaffney's jurisdiction, that of Willis Marden, was solved. She added that Reggie Hayfield's shooting was a tragedy, but he was healing nicely and there was no further evidence to pursue in the case.

She then noted, again with an overt firmness, that Harry Fiero – also arrested outside of CPD jurisdiction – had been formally charged and was being held pending bail, and that the Fireman was now keeping his trap shut on the advice of his attorneys, so there was very little to go on there.

And thus, it had been decreed. Mueller and Wright were handling their own cases. Patrol units were doing their normal beats. Even Frank's partner, Mike Levin, had been assigned an armed robbery case to work. Only Frank was left to work the Bucholz-Litinov-money angle. On the plus side, he'd finally gotten some time to work on his latest Thunderbird after hours. But in the office, he sat, biting the clicker on his pen, desperate for anything to break his way, or for his experiment in fraternizing with the enemy paid off.

To his great pleasure, it was the latter.

Responding to the phone call, he parked his car for the second time in the parking lot of Phil Swigert's law firm. Glancing around almost unconsciously for anyone looking to take a shot at him, he went in and was escorted to the same room where he'd beaten his head against the wall trying to get something out of Robinson Stringfellow. He admired the subtlety of the message.

Max Litinov didn't have Stringfellow's sanguinity. His suit was newly pressed, but his shirt had the kind of rumpling that comes from excessive perspiration, and his hair refused to obey commands and stuck out wildly all over his head. No, Max Litinov did not look the picture of health.

If Phil Swigert noticed any of that, he blithely ignored it as he politely brought coffee over for Detective Gaffney. He was still a jackass, Frank noted, just today he wasn't going to be a belligerent one.

"Mr. Litinov understands you want to question him about a supposed $450,000 he supposedly gave to a supposed friend. He also understands that, if he can show that it had nothing to do with the shooting of Willis Marden that your interest in the matter will dim." Frank nodded in agreement with the assessment.

"I have been instructed to relay the following to you," continued Swigert. Smart, thought Frank. Even if Litinov is going to spill the beans, he has a lawyer do it.

"My client was approached by Mark Bucholz close to five months ago. Mr. Bucholz indicated that he had left some personal valuables behind in Iraq, which he had entrusted to the care of a friend, a British Army officer whose name was never revealed to my client."

"Did Bucholz tell your client what the valuables were?"

"He did not."

"So," Frank said, turning to face Litinov, "you didn't know it was fifty-four million dollars?"

"Don't answer that," interjected Swigert, but Frank had seen the astonished expression on Litinov's face. Nope, Bucholz hadn't told him.

"My apologies for the interruption," said Frank with great civility, "please go on."

"My client was told by Mr. Bucholz that his friend in Iraq, the British Army officer, had contacted him again after a long absence. He was willing to help retrieve the artifacts in return for a payment of four hundred thousand dollars."

"Did he say how the officer was holding the items?"

"He gave my client reason to believe that they were somewhere on the grounds of the British Embassy, in a location to which the officer had access, but that certain… transactions would need to take place before the officer could retrieve the valuables."

Frank nodded. "Did Bucholz say how the four hundred thousand dollar figure was arrived at?"

"My client was told that Bucholz received an email from his friend, that is all."

"The idea was, Max here would give Mark the money, and then Mark would get it to the British officer, who would get the valuables to Mark, at which point Mark would sell the valuables and pay back Max?"

"Precisely. Mr. Litinov is a successful lawyer in his own right," Swigert couldn't quite conceal his sense of professional superiority, "and has substantial personal worth, so he was able to provide the money, which he asked an acquaintance of his, Mr. Fiero, to deliver."

"If the British guy needed four hundred, why was Bucholz given four-fifty?"

Swigert looked at his notes, purely for show. "Mr. Bucholz told my client that he expected he would have to travel to Turkey, Kuwait or someplace else in the region in order to receive his goods, and that there might be, well… *incidental* expenses along the way, with customs officials and the like."

"And you took Mark at his word?" Frank asked Litinov, again directly.

"My client has… had known Mr. Bucholz since they were five years old. He trusted him implicitly."

"What happened after you gave Mark the cash?"

Frank could tell that Phil Swigert was having the time of his life doing this. The lawyer paused to savor a fancy-looking coffee drink before continuing. He'd only offered Frank the regular stuff. "Mr. Bucholz provided my client with a mobile phone, and instructed him to communicate only via that device."

"Was anyone else involved in those phone calls? Anyone else have a phone?"

Swigert obviously didn't know the answer to that one, so he looked to Litinov, who spoke for the first time. "No, not that I know of."

"You're sure?"

Litinov resumed his muteness, only nodding.

"When was Bucholz supposed to get the goods?"

Frank could have sworn he saw the barest shimmer of discomfort travel through Phil Swigert's body. "Mr. Bucholz promised a return on my client's investment by the end of August. We presume that meant he would have obtained what he needed by then."

"Meaning he was late?"

"Yes. After the first week of August, Mr. Bucholz became extremely difficult to reach. It began to seem as though he was... avoiding my client."

Frank remembered what Danny had said after he met Janet Bucholz, and understood why Swigert's composure was slightly cracking. He was used to defending corrupt politicians and corner-cutting contractors, not violent gangsters.

"And is that why you threatened Janet Bucholz and broke her car windows?"

"My client admits to nothing of the kind," said Swigert, leaving the detective in no doubt that that was exactly what had happened. "He is close friends with the Bucholz family, and when Mark proved hard to reach it was only natural that he contacted Janet, to inquire after the well-being of his friend." Ah, there it was. For a couple of minutes Frank actually hadn't wanted to sock him on the jaw.

"When was the last time you spoke to Mark Bucholz?"

"He called Mr. Litinov about two weeks before he died. He came to see my client at his law office. He was in a highly agitated state."

"What did he say?"

"All he told my client was that he had made a terrible mistake and might not be able to pay him back. He told my client that he had been betrayed, but he declined to elaborate when pressed further. My client gathered the impression that Mr. Bucholz was trying to hide details from him."

"Did you threaten him, Max?" Frank asked.

Litinov may have been the scion of a crime syndicate, but he was still a human being. Frank saw him cringe at the memory even as Swigert smoothly responded:

"In no way did my client threaten Mr. Bucholz."

"Then why was he texting someone on the day of his death that his wife and child were in danger?" He looked the lawyer in the eyes. "Don't hold out on me here. I don't have the patience for it."

Swigert sighed melodramatically. "We are *not* holding out. My client did *not* threaten Mr. Bucholz. He merely stated to him an obvious fact, that my client's uncle – a man whose reputation precedes him - would not be happy to hear of this unfortunate turn of events, and that my client would not be in a position to dictate his family's actions."

Frank couldn't contain his outrage. "You told one of your oldest friends that your uncle was going to have him *killed,* and you don't think you threatened him?"

Litinov couldn't meet his gaze.

"And it wasn't even true, was it?" Frank saw Swigert grimace just slightly. "Your family had no idea that you'd pulled $450,000 out of the safe in your law office to give to your old friend from day camp, right? You told him your uncle was pissed, but your uncle didn't know anything about this."

The mood shifted, just for a moment, and Swigert and Frank were suddenly on the same side, arrayed against the younger sweaty man. "My client merely wanted to indicate the seriousness of the situation. It was, you may say, a bluff, intended to spur Mr. Bucholz to more zealous efforts to repay the loan."
"A bluff that led to Bucholz feeling so desperate that he resorted to murder," said Frank, nearly shouting. "A murder that drove

him in turn to commit suicide over the guilt. Has your client thought about that!?" He knew Litinov had. He could see it.

"My client had no way of foreseeing Mr. Bucholz's actions. Of course, he feels horrible about what happened, but he in no way accepts responsibility for a murder he didn't commit, didn't plan and didn't know about." Swigert was, irritatingly, finding a way to seize some moral high ground here. "All my client did was loan an old friend some money. A lot of money. He wanted to get paid back, as anyone would. It's not against the law to make a loan, even a large one, you know."

Frank didn't like letting it go, but knew he wasn't going to get anywhere trying to push it. Still… "Let me just reassure your client that *Mrs.* Bucholz isn't hiding any stacks of money from him. In fact, she is on the edge of bankruptcy. I trust, that as part of my… end of this deal, I suppose I can call it… that as part of this, your client will not feel it necessary to approach Mrs. Bucholz about any possible repayment?"

"You expect my client to simply write off $450,000?" Litinov squirmed in his seat. Yeah, they'd already discussed this prospect.

"A poorly-thought out investment, from which his only return is, hopefully, wisdom," said Frank, evenly.

Swigert bought time by jotting notes on his pad. Finally, he looked over at Litinov and raised his eyebrows.

"Fine. The debt is forgotten," mumbled Litinov. *Well, I didn't expect this to be fun, but sometimes life surprises you*, thought Frank. Frank decided he owed Robinson Stringfellow a beer.

*   *   *

Another weekend had come, freedom from classes, and Carol Alexander was in her element.

Your average person, she had always felt, was full of deep misconceptions about how research worked. We are taught about Archimedes' *"Eureka!"*. Newton being beaned by an apple. Ben Franklin and his kite. It's all about the Big Discovery. The Moment of Revelation.

It sometimes almost made Carol angry that people didn't understand how it really worked. There weren't a thousand pieces. There were a hundred thousand. Ninety-nine thousand were useless. The hard part was figuring out which was which. She thrived on this. Danny liked to try to help, but he was helpless at it. Very few people could sift, winnow, characterize, classify, synthesize and analyze data the way Carol could.

And no one, but no one, had as much fun doing it as her.

Melody, Deniece, and Susana had provided much of the raw material. TV broadcasts from 2007 available at a few clicks' distance. All the major British newspapers were online of course, but so were many of the provincial or city papers. The British military itself issued press releases and video in vast quantities. Then there was social media: Facebook and all its competitor cousins, blogs and chat rooms, and all the rest. Thank goodness Twitter was still new in 2007-08 – the volume of traffic would have been all but impossible to manage.

If there was a Major Nelson, a Major Murray, or Major Lewis who served in Iraq in 2007, he was somewhere in this mess of material. She had gotten the news from Frank that Cooper Stapley was having a hard time getting the British government to cooperate, as they considered the whole story too fantastical to be true. Carol didn't completely disagree with them, but she now had a burr in her saddle about this, and dove into the well of material with purpose.

From a story in the *Oxford Mail* she discovered a picture of officers returning from Iraq in early 2008. Three people in the picture had a major's insignia, but no names, and the date was unclear. The picture did, however, give the name of the military airfield where the troops had landed. That allowed her to find a regional BBC news report, reporting the arrival of soldiers to that airfield. There were no good shots of the soldiers, and no names, but from it she got the exact date of their return.

Half an hour later, she matched the date the BBC report was made with a military press release, announcing the rotation home of soldiers from a particular regiment to that same airfield. In just a few more hours she had identified thirty Facebook pages of soldiers from that regiment, and another seventy of close friends or family of those people. Soon she had close to three thousand pictures to sift through. Twenty minutes later she identified the name of one of the majors in that *Oxford Mail* photo.

By such means as these, as of Saturday afternoon Carol had list of nineteen British Army majors who served somewhere in Iraq in 2007 or 2008. For fourteen, she had photos as well.

At this point her husband's impatience gained a foothold. Carol wanted to keep searching, to bore down deeper into the data – add more majors to the list, find out which ones served in Baghdad, and more. Nonetheless, to his impassioned pleas she agreed to send what she had to her brother. Two phone calls to the feds later, Frank was comparing the names on the list with British military personnel who had arrived in the US in the past three months.

And there it was: Lt. Colonel (formerly Major) Charles Murray, who landed at Chicago's O'Hare airport at the end of July, en route to the Great Lakes Naval Air Station. And who was still in the country.

Chapter 23

And who Frank was not going to talk to, apparently.

He had shown the photo of Murray separately to Bucholz's surviving chums. All of them had immediately identified him as the major who helped them gain access to the vaults below the British Embassy. On the strength of that, he had convinced Lt. Halloran to appeal up the chain of command to let him and Mike take over the Kryevsky murder, which they could because it was within city limits. Frank relayed the news to FBI Agent Stapley, who reached out to the Pentagon to ask military police units at the naval base to detain Lt. Col. Murray and hold him for interrogation.

Which they had refused to do.

"This man is our prime suspect in two murders, and one shooting," pleaded Frank to the naval legal eagle assigned to give them the news. He could not have been a week over twenty-five years of age, and it galled Frank to have to beg a *kid*, but he had no choice.

"Just let us *talk* to him," added Mike Levin. The detectives had both had years of practice in the silent coercive power of the stare, and they were using everything they had ever learned as they sat in government-issue chairs facing him across a government-issue desk.

"Um… You see…" began the lawyer, stammering. "What y-y-you've got here isn't r-r-really, you know, evidence?" He found his mental footing for a moment. "You have three veterans who say they met him in Iraq, that's all."

"And who sent them emails for years, demanding cash payments in return for protecting their secret," added Gaffney, immediately regretting it.

"N-n-n-no, detective." A pause and a breath. "No. You have emails that these veterans *claim* are from him, but you have no evidence at all linking Lt. Colonel Murray to them. None." Little twerp sounded like he was pitying them.

"I could get that evidence," said Frank, warming, "if I could interrogate my suspect and search his computers and smart phones, if he has them." He regretted that right away, too.

The young lawyer, it seemed, was made of slightly tougher stuff than he had expected. "I'm sorry... um... detective, but all you asked for was for us to m-m-make Lt. Col. Murray available for questioning. You didn't say anything about a s-s-search warrant." Little bastard even managed to raise his eyebrows in a *touché* as he finished, but evidently knew better than to couple it with a smirk.

"No," said Frank, growing more agitated with every word. "We don't have a warrant. We didn't think we'd need one to get a little *fucking* cooperation from you, Lieutenant F..."

"What he means to say," said Mike, jumping in just in time, "is that we are eager, on our end, to do whatever is necessary to get a conversation with this man. Under any circumstances you would like, and at that time we would ask him to *voluntarily* allow us access to his electronic devices. That's what you meant to say, right Frank?"

Frank mumbled something that could have been agreement.

"Is there anything we can do to make that happen, Lieutenant?" Mike continued, sweetly.

The lawyer shook his head. "No, there isn't." He leaned in towards them, elbows on the desk, conspiratorially. Frank involuntarily looked around. They were alone.

Talking just to Mike, the lawyer went into an exaggerated stage whisper, which interestingly enough he could do with no speech problems at all. "You ought to know that my CO called the British Consul here in Chicago, and they blew their tops. They think your story about smuggled millions is laughable. The Brits made clear that they won't consent to any interview without serious additional evidence."

"Any chance they are willing to interview him for us?"

The lawyer shook his head.

"What's he doing in the country, at this base, anyway?" asked Mike.

Even more lean, and more stage whisper. "It's a ops planning team that is working out new tactical and strategic guidelines for land-sea cooperation against non-state insurgencies." He spoke it as though he had just shared nuclear launch codes.

"How about this, then?" Frank snapped, irritation still bubbling. "We're investigating three different crimes. For this fellow to have committed any of them, he would have to be off the base's premises. How about you check your logs and see if he was here when they happened."

"Well, the thing is... um... well... hmmmm." The young man gave it a thought. "I suppose we can probably do that. Give me the list and let me check."

"They're right, you know," said Mike to Frank, after the lawyer had left the room. "This story is too far-fetched to be believed. I'm not sure I can swallow it myself."

"I hear ya, I do," agreed Frank. "But if they're making it up, why did Mark Bucholz borrow $450,000 from his mob friend? Why did someone put a bullet in Reggie Hayfield and kill Kryevsky and Beatty? And, the big one, the question that started this all, why did Bucholz try to kill someone with a rifle from his office conference room, and who was that target, if it wasn't Willis Marden?"

"Has to have been Marden," countered Mike. "Why else would someone shoot Hayfield if City Guaranty and Trust wasn't somehow connected to this."

Frank grunted, unconvinced.

"Maybe the bank was going to launder this stolen money when it got back here," Mike said, then stopped himself, "which would have to mean they had money they were trying to launder. Damn. I don't like it."

"Tell me about it."

Their self-pitying reverie was interrupted when the lawyer came back in. His stammer came back with him.

"We-we-we checked th-th-the logs for th-the days you m-m-mentioned. Lt. Col. Murray has a lot of free time on, um, on this assignment. He was, was, he was off base for at least part of the day on each of the, uh, days in question."

"Gee," said Frank, sarcasm dripping. "Wonder what he was doing with his time."

*   *   *

He and Mike made it back to the station to find it abuzz with excitement. When they got to Lt. Halloran's office, they found out why.

"Stringfellow, Aldermen Fitpold and Spicuzza, fifteen city employees, three CEOs of construction firms and some of their minions, and former Congressman Cliff Lester. Racketeering, bribery, kickbacks, influence peddling, the works." She smiled. "Indictment was north of five hundred pages."

"City Guaranty and Trust?" asked Frank, hopefully.

"Not a word of it in the indictment." She tilted her head and shrugged her shoulders, sympathetically.

"Damn," said Frank, softly.

"How'd it go with the British guy?" asked the lieutenant.

"Struck out." He explained for a moment, watching his superior's face get redder and redder.

"Who the hell do these – why can't they just frickin' listen to us?" She threw her hands up in frustration.

"We hear ya," said Frank and Mike, simultaneously.

"I mean," she went on, "we all know that none of this make a ton of sense, but at the very least they should let us *talk* to Major Murray, just to see what he has to say." She rolled her eyes. "Sorry."

"What about detailing some uniforms to keep an eye on him when he leaves the base?" Frank suggested. "If they catch him doing something illegal then we can snatch him up, British Consul General or no British Consul General."

Halloran shook her head. "Too big a base – too many ways in and out. Plus, it's not within city limits. Plus," she added, "the photos we have of this guy are several years old. He looks nondescript enough as it is. Show this photo around the neighborhoods of the murders. Then you could go back to the case file and look at the whole thing again from the beginning. You've missed something, Detective.

"When God closes a door, he opens a window, Frank," said the lieutenant, gesturing the two detectives out of her office. "Find the window and crawl inside."

Chapter 24

"Here's what I'm still not getting," said Carol, as she closed the door on her Irregulars Monday evening. "I'm still not getting why Mark Bucholz decided to try to kill someone from the window of his law firm."

"You read the texts, hon. He was desperate with fear," replied Danny, as she moved a throw pillow to settle in next to him on the couch.

"Yeah, but that's the thing, isn't it? Sure, the Litinov money thing had him scared. Bucholz thought if he didn't pay them back, he or his family were going to get killed. I get that. But how do you go from being that scared to taking a shot at someone in particular, someone who hadn't threatened him? I mean, if he had tried to kill Max Litinov, to get him off his back, I could see that…"

"Right…" muttered Danny. Carol saw the wheels turning. "Hold on. You're onto something. Why *didn't* he try to kill Litinov?"

Carol nodded thoughtfully and took a sip of wine. "*Huh.* That *is* interesting. After all, if Litinov dies, it's possible he gets out from under the $450,000. And Litinov is in the mob – no one would look too hard at an honest taxpayer like Bucholz for the killing."

"So," continued Danny, "I think that tells us something about who Mark Bucholz was. Max Litinov was his friend from childhood. He couldn't bring himself to kill a friend. After all, Bucholz was no killer, right? What drove him to play sniper that morning? I think the answer is in that word in his last text message. *Traitor.* Somebody betrayed him, someone close to him."

Carol put her glass on the coffee table and picked up the thread. "Litinov threatened him, but Bucholz knew what he was doing when he borrowed almost half a million from the mob. He knew there was a risk. So, no, I agree," she said, with a hint of finality. "Bucholz didn't think Litinov was a traitor. He was trying to kill someone else."

The unspoken question hung in the air for a moment as each pondered.

She leaned up against her husband, and he brought his arm around her protectively. "Our prime suspect is Murray. He's the one mentioned in that text, after all."

"I don't disagree," said Danny, softly kissing his wife on the top of her head. "But how is it that he feels such a sense of betrayal from a guy he met once more than a decade ago in Iraq? Especially when killing the Major – Lieutenant Colonel – if that's what he was trying to do – cuts off any chance they have of getting the cash stash."

"Maybe they were closer than we thought. The other guys, Mark's buddies, did say they thought the Major was sending emails just to Mark sometimes."

Danny pondered for a moment. "That could be it. I don't know, though. Something's not clicking."

Carol turned her head to look up at him. She could see the wheels turning, but saw they didn't have traction yet. "I know what you want to do, sweetie."

He flashed an impish grin. "And what is that?"

"You want to go back and talk to Janet Bucholz again."

He laughed out loud, shaking the both of them as he did. "Can't keep any secrets from you anymore, can I?"

They sat in silence for a moment.

"I like that we're doing this together," he said after a while.

"Yeah. We make a good team, don't we?"

"We'd be nowhere if you hadn't made the Litinov connection, honey. And you found the Major. Pretty good work, if I say so myself."

"Yeah." She waited for him to say what he wanted, a process that took him a little time.

"I'd kind of… I don't know. I'd kind of like to do this more often."

"Alexander and Wife? Nick and Nora Alexander?" she teased.

"Why not?" he answered, with a grin. "Between the two of us we're a pretty polished package, aren't we?"

She sat up and turned to him. "Yes, we are." She leaned in and kissed him.

Their moment was disrupted by the *Dragnet* theme coming from Carol's phone. She had that set as the ringtone for texts from her brother. She clicked the phone open.

Major Murray dead. Tried to kill Ernst. Ernst shot but going to make it. Murray may have used THE gun.

Danny and Carol looked at each other, jaws open.

"Wow," they said together.

Chapter 25

This, thought Frank, *this* was a crime scene.

One room. Weapons on the floor. All relevant parties still on the scene. A single eyewitness whose story could not be gainsaid by the differing memories of others; not the ideal two witnesses, but close enough. It was so simple, Frank was already mentally typing up the reports in his head.

Which of course meant it wasn't Frank's case.

He was here through the courtesy of this suburban police department's single homicide detective, Jim Calderon, whose eyes widened as Frank and Mike Levin gave him the backstory, and who agreed to let them look at the scene and talk to the survivor.

Major Murray – Frank couldn't get used to the idea of calling him Lieutenant Colonel – was lying more or less on his back, near the sofa in Andrew Ernst's living room. Ernst had a "luxury" townhouse with an open floor plan, the living room and the kitchen taking up one large rectangular space, from the sectional sofa on one end to the kitchen island on the other.

"The kitchen island saved this guy's life," the Calderon was saying, pointing to the three bullet holes in it. "This fellow Murray must have aimed low."

"Common enough when someone's shooting in a hurry," agreed Frank.

Ernst, clearly, had not aimed low. Murray had two rounds dead center in his chest. Almost certainly died instantly. He fell where he stood, a .38 automatic still dangling off of one finger. It had a crude but effective-looking silencer on it. A .38 had killed Beatty and Kryevsky, and wounded Reggie Hayfield. Hello, friend.

Murray was dressed in civilian clothes, crisp and neat like soldiers wear things. He had a pencil-thin mustache that would have been slightly comical under other circumstances. He was definitely the guy in the picture Carol found.

Frank walked towards the kitchen as Mike continued discussing the case with Calderon. No blood splatter on the fifteen feet of carpet between Murray's body and the edge of the kitchen linoleum. Fair amount of blood in the kitchen, where the paramedics had worked on Andrew Ernst. A silverware drawer was overturned on the floor, blood on the handle. Ernst had pulled it out as he fell. In the middle of the bloody cutlery was a .45 automatic.

They had him up on the stretcher now, an IV dripping fluid and field dressings on two bullet wounds, one to the shoulder and one to his forearm.

"He winged me," croaked Ernst, a jagged smile on his face, eyes slightly unfocused by the morphine.

"How bad is it?" Frank asked the paramedic.

"If you're going to get shot..." she responded. "They basically grazed him, and it looks like the bullets went clean through." She gestured to the wall behind her. There were two more bullet holes in a cabinet door. "No major arteries hit. Frankly there's more blood than I'd have thought for these wounds, but the shock is mostly psychological. He's going to be in some pain for a while, and his arm will be in a sling, but other than that..."

"Can I talk to him for a minute?"

"The other detective has already worn him out pretty good…" she began.

"No, no… I'm all right," whispered Ernst. "I can do this." The paramedic gave him a disapproving look but shrugged her shoulders and nodded to Frank.

"How did Murray find out where you lived?"

"I called him." Frank began to interrupt but Ernst held up his other hand and stopped him. "I know. It was stupid. But fifty-four million is a lot of money."

"When we showed you his picture, we mentioned he was at the naval base," mused Frank.

"Right. I called over there and got through to him. I wanted to talk to him, see if there was a way to work out a deal for the money." He drew breath through clenched teeth.

"But he'd killed two of your friends."

"I know. My backup plan was to tie him up somehow after I found out what I needed about the money, make him fess up to the murders." He winced from the pain. "This was not what I had imagined."

"You should have known how dangerous it was, inviting him to your home."

Ernst shook his head. "Didn't. Bar down the street. The Red Lion. Public place. Thought I'd be safe."

"One of my guys already went down there. Confirms the story," added Detective Calderon from across the room.

"And then?"

"We met and talked. I told him we still wanted our bags. He didn't say much, but I knew he knew what was in them. I looked him over and thought he wasn't carrying a gun, so I invited him back here to talk in private." Ernst was at least a couple of inches over six feet and well-built. Murray, by the look of him, was shorter, thinner and older. Must have thought he could take him, Frank supposed, if it had come to it.

"But he did have one."

"I still don't know where he was carrying it. I walked to the kitchen to get us drinks, and all of a sudden it was in his hand." He paused, as a shudder of fear went through him. The paramedic put another blanket over him, vigilant about shock.

"Where did you get your gun?"

Ernst looked over to the kitchen island. "I bought one the other day, after Glenn and Marcus were killed. The store on 55th and Grand, forget the name. Took some target practice, too. He didn't want to kill me right away. I think he wanted to ask what we'd told you. Gave me time to back up behind the island. I got the gun out and we fired at the same time."

Calderon interjected. "Neighbor heard shots. She waited for a few minutes, not sure what to do, but then she heard someone calling out from here and called 911."

"That was me," Ernst said, unnecessarily. His face was getting paler and he was breathing harder. "I went down behind the island. I didn't know if Murray was wounded or dead, so I didn't want to get out from behind it to get the phone. So I started yelling."

He seized up for a moment, and the paramedic gestured Frank out of the way. "That's enough for now," she said, in a voice that brooked no argument.

Frank walked over to Mike Levin as Ernst was wheeled out. "Almost seems *too* simple, doesn't it?" Frank asked his partner.

"I know. Really wraps up a lot of loose ends, awfully neatly."

"I don't buy the whole story of why Ernst called Murray. Just seems too stupid."

"Maybe Ernst and Murray were in on this together," suggested Mike, not really sounding like he believed it himself, "had a falling out and started trading shots."

Frank thought about that for a moment. "I just can't see it. If they were in cahoots on the fifty-four million, they could have taken it and split the proceeds years ago. These guys only had access to the Major through emails from new email addresses. We saw them on Ernst's iPad and the others confirmed it. If the Major had decided to take the money, he could have just taken it and disappeared."

"Then tell me your theory," countered Levin.

"Ernst is the leader of this group of soldiers, right?"

Levin nodded agreement. "The ones who are alive, anyway, they look up to him. He's number one for sure."

"I think Ernst was acting like a leader. Wanted to avenge the deaths of his friends. I think he lured out Murray with the express intent of killing him."

Mike bit his lip. "Ernst invites Murray to a bar and talks to him until he thinks he's sure Murray doesn't have a gun, then leads him back here where he has a gun in his kitchen drawer."

"And then Murray spoils it by pulling his own gun."

Detective Calderon interjected, having overheard. "So, do I charge the guy? If it was his intent to kill Murray, should it matter that it didn't go according to plan?"

Frank put a hand out on the younger detective's shoulder. "You leave that to the state's attorney. I bet he'll say that no jury in the world would convict someone for defending himself in his own home, regardless of his motives."

"But then he's getting away with a cold-blooded revenge murder. He ought to be..."

Frank nodded. "But he won't." His phone rang. He looked at it and cursed.

Calderon looked at Levin. "His wife?"

Mike shook his head. "Worse."

"Is the Major really dead?" Danny Alexander's excited voice asked over the phone,

"You need to stop acting like this is some kind of game," admonished Frank. "One guy is dead and another nearly was."

282

"Sorry," said Danny, perhaps half meaning it. Then: "Talk me through the crime scene."

"I've got better things to…"

"C'mon, dude. You know this is my thing. Just walk me through the physical evidence. I might be able to catch something you haven't."

Frank grimaced, but he grunted anyway and proceeded to sum up what he had seen.

"This Major's a pretty bad shot."

"Most people are, Danny," answered Frank. "It's a lot harder than you think. Remember how he only hit Reggie Hayfield with one shot out of four."

"And there's no sign of blood spatter between Murray and Ernst?"

"First thing I looked for," confirmed Frank. "They weren't near each other when they were firing, and neither of them moved very much after getting shot."

"Right, right…" said Danny on the phone. "Or maybe not. GSR on Murray's hand?"

"Hey," Frank called out to the crime scene technician who was working around Murray. "Did you find gunshot residue on his hand?" He got a nod. "Yep, they did," said Frank into the phone.

"OK… ok…" Frank could hear his brother-in-law thinking on the phone. "OK… oh…. *Huh.* That totally could work."

"What could work?" he asked, impatiently.

"The bullets that went through Ernst's arm, they went into a cabinet?"

"Right."

"Are they still in there, maybe lodged into the back wall of the cabinet?"

Frank grabbed a latex glove and gently pulled open the door. "Good call. How'd you guess?"

Danny barreled on. "Is the sink wet?"

Frank looked over. "OK, tell me how you guessed…"

He didn't get to finish. "This is a luxury townhouse, right? Does Ernst have one of those big whirlpool-type tubs in his bathroom?"

"How the hell do I… fine, I'll go look." He walked down a hallway and found the master bedroom, then went through. "Yes, in fact, he does. Why on earth…"

"Is there any water in the tub, like it had been emptied recently?" asked Danny, almost exultantly.

"Water in the…?" He looked in. "Crap. Yes, there is a little water. OK, what have you got?"

"Come by the house tomorrow for dinner tomorrow. I'm making lasagna. I'll tell you all about it then, I promise. But do one thing for me. Ask if Ernst was wearing a jacket when he met the Major at the bar. And find the jacket."

"None of your shenanigans between now and then, Danny, all right?"

"I swear."

Frank didn't buy it. "Put my sister on the phone."

"Already listening in on the extension," Carol chimed in, startling him.

"Good. Then I need you to promise that you won't let Danny do anything stupid between now and dinner tomorrow."

"Oh, don't worry. We've talked. He's not going to do anything without my OK."

"Good." It wasn't until later that Frank realized Carol hadn't quite meant what he thought she had.

Chapter 26

Carol and "Chet" sat once again in Janet Bucholz's living room. The intervening days had been tough on her, Carol saw. Her eyes were hollow and red from too many tears and too few hours of sleep. Her body seemed to tremor slightly as she moved, as if an electric current was going through her. She had sounded almost robotic when Carol called to arrange this meeting, agreeing with a voice that suggested there was no real thought behind it at all.

"Janet, I'm so sorry for what has happened to you," Carol said, with real feeling. "I know it's only gotten worse for you."

"My lawyer says the police might still charge me with something, and that the family of the guy that Mark ki... the family of Will Marden might sue me? It's just too much sometimes." She smiled in a bright and cheery way that was obviously fake. Someone had raised Janet Bucholz to have manners.

"We don't want to make any more trouble for you, Janet, really," Carol sympathized, "but we're trying to learn a little more about how Mark had been behaving the last few months." She paused. Danny hadn't wanted to do the next thing, but they'd talked it over and she had prevailed. She'd try to get some answers out of Janet Bucholz, but she would do it honestly.

"You see, while I am a university librarian, we're actually her because we're helping the police." She saw Janet's eyes widen. "Please, please, we are not trying to get you into more trouble. We know you didn't do anything wrong."

"I need to call my lawyer?"

Carol acted like she didn't hear the question. "We also know that Mark wasn't trying to kill Willis Marden. He was trying to kill someone who put your life at risk."

"What?" Janet's face wrinkled in confusion. "You mean he was trying to kill... Max?"

"Max Litinov had broken your car windows, hadn't he?" Janet gave a small nod. "He also tried to scare you into thinking you would get hurt if Mark didn't pay him back some money he owed, right?" Another nod.

"Janet, we don't think it was Max who Mark was trying to kill. Max was bluffing. He lent the money without his family's knowledge, and he wouldn't have ever told his uncle about it. Without his uncle's muscle, Max Litinov isn't the kind of guy who would hurt you for real. He just tried to scare you. He isn't going to be trying that any more. You can forget about him." Janet didn't seem to quite believe it, but even so Carol saw her relax just a little.

"Why did Mark borrow that fifty thousand, anyway?" the widow asked.

"Actually, it was four hundred and fifty thousand dollars."

"What? But I only found..."

"I know. The rest of the money has been given to someone else. Mark thought he had a fortune coming his way, millions of dollars. He borrowed the money from Max to pay someone to get his fortune to him."

"Like one of those Nigerian email scams?"

"Something like that. The person who took the money, we think, is the person your husband was trying to kill."

"My husband's not a killer," she insisted, in a firm and question-mark-free tone. "I know they say they he fired the shots, but there must have been something else he was trying to do. Maybe scare somebody."

"Mark wasn't a killer, not at heart," jumped in Danny. They'd agreed he could ask questions this time so long as he stayed on script. "What he really was, was a dreamer, right, Janet? He liked to think big, didn't he?"

"Yeah," she said, looking up at the ceiling, reflective. "He was always talking about his big plans for us."

"And in the last few months of his life, he was more excited than ever about his plans, wasn't he?"

She nodded. "Yes. Something had changed, like he knew something he didn't before? He was so excited he couldn't even sleep sometimes. I asked him, and he just said that everything was coming up Milhouse." She paused. "He really liked *The Simpsons*," she added, mournfully.

"But at some point his excitement changed, didn't it?"

A nod *yes*. "First he started getting super nervous. He was just bouncing off the walls. Like a kid right before Christmas?"

"When did that change?" asked Carol.

"When we canceled the trip to Crete this summer."

"Oh, of course…" said Danny. "How did I miss that…?" Carol turned to look at him and saw a look of pure triumph on his face that immediately transformed into calculation.

He looked lost in revelatory thought for a moment. Wheels turning. Puzzle pieces assembling. Then he seemed to remember where he was and turned to the widow. "Janet, am I right that you actually got to the airport on your way to Crete when he turned you around and headed home?"

"Yes?"

"Were you by chance at the USO facility at O'Hare, waiting for your flight to be called?"

"How did you know that?"

"Mark knew the right people to let him in there, right, even though he wasn't active military anymore?" She nodded again. "Did Mark talk to anyone, anyone at all, for more than a few moments?"

She furrowed her brow. "Yes. I went to the bathroom and when I came out he was talking to a man in uniform? He broke off talking to him when I came out. That's when he told me we needed to turn around. I asked why, and he said something had come up at work and we needed to postpone the trip."

Janet, Carol noted, was remarkably uncurious. Apparently, she hardly bothered to ask why they were canceling an expensive vacation overseas. Or maybe it was the opposite; maybe Janet Bucholz had subconsciously known all along the trip wouldn't happen.

"Do you remember what the man he was talking to looked like?" asked Danny, hopefully.

Again the furrowing. "No, I'm sorry. I didn't really notice how he looked."

"What about his uniform? Do you remember that?"

"Mark always tried to explain uniforms to me, but I never paid enough attention."

"What about the color? No details, just the color of the uniform, or of the cap?"

"It was kind of a dark khaki, and the cap had a little peak on it, sort of?"

"British Army service dress, maybe," said Carol, who had spent many hours looking at uniforms over the last few days.

"The man he was talking to was British?" asked Janet.

"Maybe," she said, hastily.

"Like the British guy Andy Ernst got shot by? Is it the same guy?"

"It's something like that," Danny said, quickly, who to Carol's surprise was looking paler. His hand was shaking slightly. "One more question now about that trip. The fifty thousand dollars was found in a gym bag, Mark's gym bag, under your bed. Do you remember: did he bring the bag with him on the trip?"

"Why, yes, he did. I'd forgotten about it but I remember him putting it in the suitcase and thought it was a little weird? I didn't notice it later."

Carol expected Danny to explode with triumph, but instead her husband looked pained. She patted him on the arm and took over. "Janet, after the trip, what was his mood like?"

"He was real quiet for the first week or so, and then he was really angry for a couple of weeks – snapped everyone's head off. The last two weeks, he got quiet again, keeping to himself? Talking to himself a lot. That's what he always did when he was planning something big."

"Thank you, Janet, really." Carol reached out and took her hand. "I can't begin to imagine what you're going through. You've been a big help." She stood to go, and to her surprise Janet embraced her, squeezing tightly.

"Are you going to find out who's responsible for this?" she asked in a plaintive tone.

"We already have," said Danny. "Now we just need to prove it. And I think I know how to do that."

Danny and Carol exited Janet Bucholz's house a few minutes later. He was quiet as they drove. After well more than an hour, they pulled into the guest lot of a nondescript housing complex in the south suburbs. The police had gone, but there was still crime scene tape blocking off the front door to Andrew Ernst's townhouse.

"We can't go in," Carol reminded him as they got out of their car. Danny nodded affirmatively, eyes searching.

They walked up to Ernst's front door. Carol tried to peek in the window, but Danny stood off to the side, eyes unfocused, as the wheels turned. He shook it off, looked left and right. "Walk with me," he said, taking Carol's hand.

They strolled down the line of townhomes almost casually until they reached the end of the row. Danny turned the block and they peered around the corner at the detached single-car garages accompanying each townhouse. "Not exactly family-friendly parking," muttered Carol.

Danny muttered something unintelligible and suddenly his phone was in his hand. With his pitching hand his fingers were so agile he could type as well as most could with both hands, but they were shaking again and it took him a minute. He looked at the results and showed them to Carol.

"Of course!" she said, catching up. Then she caught up some more. She staggered slightly and felt faint. "Oh, Christ. When we went…"

Danny nodded, "We were seen, and they also saw…"

"And they needed a distraction and so they…" She sat down on the grass. Danny sat next to her. For a long moment they held hands but said nothing.

Carol wiped a tear from the corner of her eye. "We couldn't have known."

He nodded. "No. And we didn't do it, but I can't believe we were so dumb as to make this possible."

"Well," she said, with more determination than she felt, "let's make sure we finish it right." She looked down at the screen on Danny's phone and pointed. "This one first, I think?" They got back in their car.

When they pulled up Carol saw Danny's eyes flash. The mark of a true athlete, she'd heard him say many times, was the ability to recover.

"What is it?" she asked.

He pointed at the window of the little office where they'd just parked. A middle-aged man, hair thinning, was reading an actual paper magazine at his desk. "Can you tell what he's got?"

"No, not from here."

Danny grinned. "Becket Baseball Card Monthly." He reached into the back seat to grab a stray ball cap and opened the door. "This one's going to be easy."

It was.

Chapter 27

Lots to do:

Carol called Frank and had a long conversation. Frank called up Jim Calderon, the detective in charge of the investigation on Charles Murray's death, and made a few suggestions. They sounded just as stupid to Calderon as they did to Frank and he was almost too embarrassed to call the county crime lab about it, but in the end he did. Twenty-four hours later he had his results. Calderon didn't have to call the coroner about the other thing – it turned out the coroner had had the same idea and already checked it out.

Greg Buhl got the assignment of going to the county courthouse. Carol sent Susana Melendez to go with him, which so terrified Greg that he backed into a parked car on his way out of the lot. No one was hurt, if you don't count feelings.

Mike Levin drew the short straw, and sat down in a conference room with Danny Alexander and twenty six boxes of files in the Willis Marden shooting. Danny sorted through them to find the four large manila envelopes he was looking for, poured out their contents onto the table, and spent quite some time hunched over looking at them. At least, Mike reflected, Danny was using a magnifying glass, which was pretty old-school.

After he found what he was looking for, Danny went to a big box office supply store, and placed the biggest order that store had ever seen. It was a good thing Danny had the salary of a professional ballplayer, because he failed to read the fine print and only later discovered that the store did not accept returns.

Frank called Cooper Stapley, who flew in from DC, arriving – by Frank's estimate – some forty minutes after getting off the phone, in a suit whose pants had creases so sharp Frank reckoned they could chop wood.

Carol rented a truck, and over the course of a day she and the rest of the Irregulars moved the items from the office supply superstore to the space Danny had rented, where he drove them all nearly insane with his relentless micromanagement of the set dressing. Carol had to take him aside, after which he emerged red-faced and bought pizza for everyone.

Robinson Stringfellow sat in a jail cell playing solitaire. Phil Swigert had convinced him it looked more martyr-like to possible jurors to remain behind bars instead of posting the cash to make a million-dollar bail. He had his own cell, but he was bored to tears. The one bright spot was when the jailer opened the cell door and put a six-pack of cold beer on the floor. Non-alcoholic, and plastic bottles, but still.

Deniece Rogers and Melody Kasson had a ten-dollar bet over who could find the video on YouTube first. Deniece won.

Danny coached the Irregulars through the plan five times, which was four more times than any of them needed. He was so excited, though, they had a hard time saying no.

Frank made the calls to summon the audience. He had hoped they would refuse, but he was disappointed. Then he got to call Sam Richter, which he enjoyed much more.

*　　　*　　　*

"Thanks for coming, everyone," said Danny warmly as they all filed into the room. It was a large but ordinary storage unit at an ordinary storage place, the Suburban Storage Company, in the middle of a nondescript industrial park in the south suburbs. A large garage door opened to the outside, and the interior was unfinished and spare. A couple of space heaters were warding off the fall chill.

Carol was the only one who knew him well enough to pick up the traces of anxiety in Danny's voice as he greeted everyone. Then she noticed who was with Frank. She and Danny each grabbed an elbow and pulled Frank off to one side. "What is *she* doing here?" Carol asked.

He smiled widely. "Don't worry. Samantha agreed we're off the record. She just wanted to see the fun."

"You brought a *date*?" hissed Danny, incredulously.

Frank shook off their grips on his arms and straightened his tie with mock dignity. "Yes, yes I did. And you two can keep your mouths shut about it." He gave them a teenager's grin and walked back to Sam Richter.

Frank, Sam Richter, Mike Levin, Cooper Stapley, Dylan Connor, and Jim Calderon stood by the chairs provided for them, while Carol and the Irregulars positioned themselves nearest the little table with a coffee pot on it.

"Before we begin," said Danny, "come with me to the storage unit next door." He gestured behind him and they walked through. "I know it's not the same thing, but I think this room can serve as an approximation of the warehouse where the pallets of money were stored in Iraq back in 2007."

Everyone looked around. Six metal shelves stocked with boxes of copier paper were along one wall, with a video camera conspicuously mounted above. Along another wall were six more shelves with note pads, boxes of pens and pencils, folders, and binders, as well as a few dozen more boxes of copier paper. Three large unopened boxes, containing computers and monitors, were sitting on top of each other next to that. And so on.

In the center of the room, separated from everything else by at least three feet on each side, were two wooden pallets, with hundreds of reams of green copier paper in ordered stacks up to six feet high, with a handwritten sign reading, *"Pretend this is money,"* taped to one side. A three-ring binder filled with paper leaned up against one of the stacks.

Danny looked at his guests. Levin spoke first, "Close enough, I suppose, based on what we've been told." The others nodded. After a moment's pause Danny clapped his hands together and resumed his introduction, which Carol had seen him working on all morning.

"Thank you again for coming. You're here because you're working a case… well, really, a whole bunch of cases. The murder of Willis Marden. The death of Mark Bucholz. The shots fired outside Phil Swigert's law office. The shooting of Reggie Hayfield. The murders of Marcus Kryevsky and Glenn Beatty. The death of Lt. Colonel Charles Murray."

He opened his arms wide. "All of those cases, I believe, started here, back in Iraq a dozen years ago, with a crackerjack plan to steal millions in cash. Fifty-four millions, we are told."

"There's been one problem with that story, though," he continued. "A problem that has been bedeviling us all as we've been going through this case, and it's this: it sounds like something a twelve-year-old would dream up. The plan was so fantastic, so unlikely, so ballsy and dangerous, that it's more or less impossible to imagine it succeeding, or even being tried at all. And that's why I want to re-create the heist, step by step, to prove what really happened. The roles of the soldiers will be played by our in-house troupe." He swiveled grandly to one side and swept his arms in the direction of Carol and the others.

"This," he said, theatrically, "is our stage. But as an audience, we need to be in the next storage unit. Thankfully, this place had two open ones right next to each other. Will everyone please come with me?" He led them back outside to the first unit, furnished with assembled-from-a-box leather office chairs and a large TV screen, showing the feed from the camera next door. Bright orange extension cords rode along the ground between the two units.

There was a flutter of activity as people took chairs and arranged themselves. Carol was surprised at how docile everyone was being. Danny was doing a good job elevating the suspense.

"On the day they pulled off the heist, Mark Bucholz went in first, right?" he asked, getting a nod from Carol.

"Susana, will you do the honors?" Danny beckoned to Melendez, who reached into a bag and pulled out a file folder, which she handed to him. He opened it up to show three pieces of paper, each reading, "*Pretend this is a forged withdrawal form.*" He held up the sheets so that all could see, and then handed it all back to Susana. As she left, he explained, "Susana is going to do the first step, what Bucholz supposedly did that day. She is going to stick these forged forms in the log book that traveled with the money, so that a future count of the money would match the withdrawals even after fifty-four million dollars were taken."

On the screen, they watched her walk over to the binder and busy herself with the task. Danny clapped his hands together again to get their attention.

"While she works, let's jump ahead to the present. Mark Bucholz bought three disposable phones a few months back. One he gave to Max Litinov, and another he gave to a third person, unknown to us. It was to that third person that Mark addressed his last words, telling someone he called 'Major' that he had betrayed him, endangered his family, and deserved to die. Within a minute or two of sending that text, he fired his rifle from the conference room of his law firm, killing Willis Marden. What brought him to that point?"

"First though, I want you to note the invocation of the concept of betrayal. It's a big word, one that carried a lot of weight with Bucholz, one that he used to describe an encounter he'd had at O'Hare airport a few weeks prior, with a person who may have been in a British Army uniform." Everyone perked up at that as Danny explained what Janet Bucholz had told them.

"Mark liked the word betrayal, I suspect, because it had a dramatic flair, and Mark had a touch of theatricality in him. I know what that's like," he added, softly and a little wistfully. "It was his sense of the dramatic that led to this plan – the plan to steal millions from under the nose of the US military, without anyone being the wiser.

"What Mark had never quite learned was how to have the proper level of skepticism. This made him highly suggestible, a trait which led to his... tragic end."

Susana returned, nodded in Danny's direction, and sat down.

"Carol will now play the role of Lars Gilbert, who brought in two Army duffel bags, leaving them in a corner of the room out of sight of the security cameras." Danny walked to an open box on a table, from which he pulled two bags. "Would you be so kind darling?"

Carol took the bags from Danny, went out and was back in a moment.

"Next, it was Glenn Beatty, who moved some boxes of copier paper to cut off half the room from the camera." He nodded to Melody Kasson, who went out and was soon visible on the screen, sliding and piling a few boxes. In just a couple of minutes, half the other storage unit, and half the pretend money in the center of the room, was invisible.

"Marcus Kryevsky went next, and filled the first bag with money. Now, he did this out of sight, but for dramatic purposes I'll have Greg Buhl fill them up in view of the camera." He nodded towards the nervous young man, and in just a few moments, Greg was pulling reams of green paper off the pallet and loading them into a duffel bag.

"That's going to take a few minutes, so let's jump to the present again. Mark Bucholz was not a killer at heart. He didn't really have it in him. He only did what he did because he thought he had no choice – because in his desperation he became, if it's possible, even less grounded in reality than he had been before. When he failed and killed the wrong man, he was so distraught he drove to his old stomping grounds... and took his own life." He stopped for a moment to let that sink in.

"With Mark dead, only one person in the world knew that Bucholz had shot Willis Marden. This person knew it because Bucholz had been trying to kill them."

"Now this person... this person was in some ways the opposite of Bucholz. Extremely practical. Able to focus on the details. But, and this is important, not really suited for long-range planning. Didn't have the kind of vision Bucholz did, but great for on-the-spot tactical decisions. This person, too," Danny's expression darkened, "wasn't a killer, not to start with, but they knew how to be practical when they needed to, and so, they eventually turned into one."

"Once this person realized that Mark Bucholz had accidentally killed someone tied to the Stringfellow investigation they saw an opportunity. If the focus was on a possible Stringfellow connection their own role would remain hidden, as this person was not involved with Stringfellow at all. They saw on the news that the police were going to question Stringfellow. And this person took a gun, almost certainly loaded with blanks, and fired shots outside Phil Swigert's law office, with two detectives and a whole bushel basket full of journalists there to hear them." He looked at Mike Levin and his brother-in-law, who were considering the point with great interest.

"Now," Danny went on, "I made my mistake." He paused. "My first mistake, I should say. And my worst." His face reddened slightly and he took a deep breath before he went on. "I encouraged Frank to crash Bucholz's funeral. This other person was there, too, and they recognized Frank either from outside Swigert's office or from the TV coverage of Marden's shooting."

For just a moment, Carol saw Frank fidget nervously. Danny must have, too, because he stopped and held up his hands reassuringly. "Don't worry, Frank. I'm not about to go through this big setup as a way to accuse your girlfriend."

"She's not my girlfriend," Frank petulantly muttered, avoiding everyone's gaze as his face reddened.

Danny turned his attention to the whole group again. "No, the killer isn't here. I asked, but Frank wouldn't let me do that. But the killer did know we'd been at the funeral. Clearly, the police were figuring out too much, so this person needed to steer them back towards Stringfellow. They went to City Guaranty and Trust and waited outside to follow an employee home. They just picked someone at random, I think. It turned out to be Reggie Hayfield. For a day or two they tracked Reggie's movements, and then made their move, shooting Hayfield in an alley. Reggie told the police it was a man, but he wasn't really close enough to be sure." Carol saw several eyes perk up at that.

"I'm responsible for that," Danny said, a little more quietly.

"*We* are," said Carol, softly.

Danny smiled at her. "If we hadn't gone to the funeral, if we'd let things be, Reggie Hayfield never gets shot, and a lot of other bad things don't happen." He bit his lip. "I don't know if Beatty and Kryevsky should be on my conscience or not – I don't think so but I can't be sure – but Hayfield is."

No one seemed to know what to say, and things were quiet for a moment.

"Wounding Hayfield, not killing him, was the aim all along," added Danny, starting up again. "This person, like I said, wasn't yet a killer, but they were feeling increasingly cornered and desperate. They had been one step ahead of the others for so long, especially Mark, because Mark was adventurous and daring but not too bright. It was a strange feeling for this person, therefore, to recognize that connections were being made that they'd done their best to keep hidden."

"Now, wait," said Frank. "Ernst, Gilbert, Tracy, Beatty, Kryevsky were at the funeral. If they'd seen Major Murray, we'd have heard about it."

"Yep," was all Danny said. He turned and looked at the screen. Carol saw that Greg Buhl was closing the duffel bag, brimming over with reams of green paper. He then dragged it out of sight, and a moment later came in, breathing a little heavily.

"Folks, with your permission, in the interests of time, I'd like to ask that we agree to skip Dwayne Tracy's stuffing the second duffel bag, and just use the one for our purposes." He looked around as though expecting disagreement, but got none. "Deniece will then go in, playing Andrew Ernst's role. She will make sure the duffel is well-hidden, clear the blockage in front of the camera, and stand ready to mislead the soldiers who will soon be coming to move these pallets of money away."

They watched Deniece exit before Danny resumed. "So, who was this person? Who was willing to shoot an entirely innocent person to avoid a waft of suspicion carrying in their direction? After all, from the story so far, they were a *victim*. Bucholz had been trying to kill them, not the other way around. How could a desire for anonymity lead to gunplay?"

Danny looked around for a moment. "To answer that, let's go back to before Willis Marden's death, back to not long after these six soldiers pulled off the caper we're re-creating here. They took the duffel bags, and stored them in a secret vault under an outbuilding in the British Embassy in the Green Zone under the care of Major Murray. Everyone clear on this so far?" They all nodded.

"And it was just a few days later that they got an email, instructing them to deliver cash to the Embassy in the name of Major *Lewis*. They never saw Murray, then or after."

Carol could see wheels turning in brains, just a quarter step behind Danny, who hurried on, as if anxious to keep the spotlight.

"So," said Danny, "let me highlight what many of you are already thinking: we have no way of knowing who it was who sent that email demanding the money. It might have been Major Murray. It might have been another Major, named Lewis. Or it could have been anyone else who knew enough about what was going on. The person didn't even need to be there, if someone had passed them the information via email or something else."

"So, who was it?" demanded Frank, a little impatiently.

"I think it was the same person who shot Reggie Hayfield," replied Danny.

"Now mind you," he went on, "this is speculation. I think the person who sent that first email asking for money was doing it partially as a practical joke. A laugh. Nothing more. I think they thought the soldiers would refuse to pay, and was surprised when they did. And so, a year later, maybe because they were hard up for cash, maybe because they were just getting greedy, they sent the demand again. And again. And again. Five grand each for five years or so. Adds up, doesn't it?"

"And you're saying the person who did this *wasn't* Major Murray?" asked Calderon, clearly wondering how to square that idea with the corpse who had dropped in his jurisdiction. "Then why did he try to kill Ernst?" Stapley asked, confused.

"Well, now, he didn't try to kill Ernst," said Danny, condescendingly, "but we'll get back to that in a moment. Let me go on." He looked at Frank, who began to speak, then shrugged, let out an audible *ppppphhhttt* of an exhale, and waved for him to continue.

If any of them noticed that Deniece Rogers was taking a long time to get back from the other room, Carol saw, they weren't showing it.

"Now, again I'm guessing, but my bet is that this person was getting tired of the charade. Every year brought a renewed chance of discovery, after all, and, like I said, this person probably had started off doing it as a laugh. After five years, for reasons I admit I'm not clear on, they stopped making the demands for cash. If I had to guess, given what happened, I think Glenn Beatty or Marcus Kryevsky began to suspect something was amiss. This person stopped, having taken something close to a couple hundred thousand dollars from these veterans. They'd all come back from Iraq to a nice nest egg from their smuggling work with Litinov, and this person got a fair chunk of it."

"But a few more years passed," piped up Frank, nodding. "This person was burning through that money. It made them think about one more score."

Danny nodded. "Maybe. Bucholz was surely the logical target – he'd been the biggest dreamer of the bunch, the one most likely to cling to the fantasy that they could still get the fifty-four million. Even after they stopped sending money, he kept talking about it. And, of course, our killer knew Mark Bucholz had an in with the Litinovs. But it also might have been that this person simply wanted to stop Bucholz from thinking about the money. They hit upon what they thought was a perfect little plan.

"Mark Bucholz got word – I can only presume it was an email – or series of emails, maybe - to an account we don't know about – that the Major was prepared to let him have both duffel bags for a one-time, final payment of four hundred thousand dollars. This person knew how close Mark was to total insolvency, so they knew Mark would be looking for chances. Once he got this message, our mystery person thought, Mark would finally give up the dream, and this person could put the prank completely to bed, or Mark would somehow find the money. Bear in mind," said Danny, raising a finger, "at this point, the killer may actually have been trying, in a crazy way, to do the right thing. Maybe they hoped the large sum would scare Mark Bucholz off."

"Of course, no one in this story had Mark's extraordinary ability to dream big. Mark had a brainwave – a short term loan from his friend Max Litinov, who could be paid back as soon as they got the duffel bags back." Danny stood, and began pacing back and forth, speaking more rapidly as he told the tale.

"Mark also enlisted someone else to help him, someone to whom he gave the third disposable phone, and whom he entrusted to send the money to a person Mark assumed was Major Murray. And he prepared to carry out the plan that Major Murray had supposedly given to him: fly to Crete – a brilliant choice, just exotic enough to appeal to Mark's fancies, but not so dangerous as to scare him into asking the others to come with him - meet the Major with fifty thousand additional dollars for bribing the local customs officials, and take possession of the duffel bags."

"You can't carry that kind of cash on an international flight without all sorts of red tape," noted Stapley.

"My hope, Special Agent," said Danny, "is that you'll be able to check with Customs to see if Bucholz declared the money before he got on the plane. He also might have come up with a workaround. He was a smuggler, after all.

"That was supposed to be the end," said Danny, "and if not for one thing, the story *would* have ended there. Mark would have flown to Crete with Janet, with fifty thousand dollars in his gym bag, but the Major would never have shown up, and the emails were, I'm absolutely certain, going to stop. The duffel bags – to everyone's best understanding - were where they had been left, in the British Embassy, never to be retrieved. This person would have disappeared into thin air. No one would have been killed." Danny paused for a moment, reflecting. "In retrospect, I really wish the jerk had gotten away with it."

He stopped, as everyone took that in.

"But one thing went wrong. One little thing. A coincidence so crazy as to be the stuff of fantasy – except when we think about it, there were hundreds of ways this game could have unraveled over the years. Something like this wasn't a crazy coincidence, it was more or less inevitable. At O'Hare airport, on his way to Crete, in the USO lounge: Mark runs into Lt. Colonel Murray, on his way here for an extended assignment at Great Lakes Naval Air Station."

"Janet saw it, but I bet we can confirm it with TSA footage – every inch of an airport is under surveillance these days. It's Murray, I have no doubt, who Mark ran into. All it took was a minute or two of conversation for Mark to realize not only that Murray had no memory of Mark – they only met once in Iraq years ago after all - but also that Murray was not heading to Crete, not preparing to hand over duffel bags with cash, not the person to whom Mark and the rest had sent thousands of dollars over the years."

"Mark's life must have collapsed around his feet at that moment. He didn't have any money to pay back what he loaned Max Litinov. He had let down his friends. He had let down his family. Somehow, he had been betrayed. So, he wanted revenge."

"Mark Bucholz was not a smart man, but he was persistent, and after a few weeks of going back over things, doing some research, he had become convinced that he knew who was behind it. It was, in fact, the same person Mark had entrusted to help him. The person to whom he gave the third cell phone. Betrayal. And now Litinov was pushing for his money back, and the credit cards were maxing out, and Mark was getting desperate, and he went past his breaking point. He decided he had to kill this person. It may have been around this time, too, that Mark disclosed some amount of what he knew to Glenn Beatty and Marcus Kryevsky. I can't be sure there. Only the killer, if they choose to confess, can really fill you in on that part."

"The final text message, I think, was a final test of his theory, because he had to be sure he had the right person. On the corner where Willis Marden was shot, there is a coffee shop. Mark invited this person there to meet him, to chat. While this person was waiting in the coffee shop, Mark was setting up his rifle. Then he sent the text. If this person had been innocent, he would have replied, probably with some kind of "WTF?" text. Instead, this person proved their guilt. Once they got the text, they immediately got up to leave the coffee shop. To flee, for their lives. They walked outside, right into Mark's gunsights. Except Mark missed."

The audience was hanging on his every word, Carol saw, as Danny continued in a hushed voice. "That's why our suspect shot Hayfield. It was an attempt to move suspicion more firmly back to the Stringfellow investigation and local corruption. I admit, I was floundering for a while there. I *knew* that Bucholz hadn't been trying to kill Willis Marden, but I couldn't explain why he had been shooting in the first place."

He looked over, as did everyone else, to see Deniece Rogers coming back into the room. She looked at him and nodded.

"Excellent timing, Deniece, thanks," he said, sincerely. "So, let's go back to that motive, to Mark Bucholz's biggest, most fantastical idea. The next step, if I remember right, was for the money transfer to take place – a team of soldiers and officers moving the pallets of money from the warehouse to the new secure location. The first step would have been for the officer leading the transfer to review the log book and check it against the count. Detective Gaffney, could you fetch the log book from next door?"

Frank started to grumble, but his heart clearly wasn't in it. He got up, went in, and everyone else watched on the screen as he picked up the logbook and brought it out.

"Here we are," said Danny. "Now, we all saw Susana put the three forged forms – or at least our stand-ins for them – in this binder. Let's have a look." He held open the binder. The first page had *"Pretend this is a legitimate withdrawal form"* on it. "You see, there are lots of legitimate forms, too. The fakes would have been hidden amongst them. We know what they look like because we saw them before Ms. Melendez planted them."

"The inspectors would have looked at all the pages, to verify they were accurate." He handed the book to Mike Levin. "Will you do the honors, detective?"

Levin held the binder in his hands for a moment, as if trying to decide if this was absurd or exciting. Then he shrugged and opened it up. There were only a dozen sheets or so, and he paged through them quickly. He looked up. "All of them say the same thing as the first page."

"No, no," said Calderon, in confusion. "We saw her put the forged forms in there." He looked at Danny. "You switched the binders."

"Oh, no. No duplicate log books." He held up his hands and pulled up his sleeves, displaying his forearms. "Nothing hidden up here.

"So, the logbook has passed inspection and the big pallets of money have been moved. Now it's nighttime, and they all crept back to get the duffel bags out. Frank, Mike, will you recreate that? Bring that duffel bag, the one we saw Greg fill up with the green copier paper."

Everyone else waited in silence as they all waited. A moment later, huffing and puffing a little bit from the weight, they came back in, carrying a full and heavy duffel bag between them. They lugged it to the middle of the room, and set it down on the floor.

"And here we have it," said Danny. "A brilliant crime. After this, they made mistakes. They put their trust in the wrong place and left themselves open to blackmail. But the plan itself, Mark's plan, was brilliant in conception and, so it seems, flawless in execution. Take a moment to celebrate their brilliance by proxy. Open the bag and look at the green cash."

Frank reached down, unhooked a covering latch, pulled open the zipper, and stepped back as if he'd been zapped by an electric shock. The duffel bag was full of reams of copier paper. White copier paper.

Carol knew Danny had been waiting for the moment, and he must have been pleased by the collective gasp that filled the room.

"I admit it, I was wrong all along." Danny let that admission sink in for a moment.

"My other huge mistake. It took me so long to realize how stupid I was. I was *sure* they'd done it. They all seemed so convinced of it, and even though the plan was more than a little absurd, maybe it could have worked. But the skeptics were right. It was just one of Mark Bucholz's crazy schemes. Only one of those ever worked, because it was the only one that he could make happen through sheer self-confidence: he got the girl of his dreams." He caught Carol's glance and gave her a wink; she rolled her eyes.

He turned back to the cops at the table. "The scheme of Mark's was too complicated to work. And someone realized that right away. One of those soldiers knew that no fake withdrawal forms would ever pass muster, that the pallets of money were going to be counted and re-counted and the theft would have been discovered. The plan would only work if everyone else acted like complete idiots, and even though we are dealing with military intelligence, they couldn't count on it. And so, our suspect conceived of a second crime, the double steal – blackmail the other five soldiers for a crime that hadn't even happened.

"So Andrew Ernst," said Danny, briefly pausing to let the name sink in, "played along with everyone else, but when he was in the room, the last one of the group to be there, he emptied the money out of the duffel bags and replaced it with copier paper. He pulled the forged sheets out of the logbook. By the time the MPs arrived to count the pallets and search the room, everything was exactly as it was supposed to be."

"I'm all but certain Ernst was just pranking them. They were buddies. He was just having fun. He thought they would all balk at that first demand for a thousand dollars, and then he would show them all how he'd fooled them and get a laugh out of it. He underestimated the dollar signs in their eyes. They jumped at the demand for money, and gave it to Ernst to walk over to the Embassy, but it never made it."

"And so, every year, he did it again. All six of them got a windfall when they came back home, from the Litinovs, payment for the smuggling they actually did do. Ernst knew they'd have the cash to pony up five grand each. Eventually he got tired of playing the game, or worried someone was suspicious, and stopped. But Mark Bucholz, Mark the dreamer, just couldn't let it go, and so Ernst tried this last score, maybe to shut Mark up, maybe to grab one last bundle.

"Sometime after the funeral, Andrew realized that Kryevsky and Beatty knew something about it all, too, and now his prank had gotten too real to reveal. To protect himself from discovery, he had to kill his two friends. Of course," added Danny, with a touch of sadness, "it's also possible that Bucholz didn't say anything to those two at all, but that Ernst was just consumed with guilt and saw plots everywhere."

"Wait," said Stapley, holding up his hand. "They put the cash in envelopes and mailed it to far-off locations, usually London. Are you saying Ernst flew overseas every year to pick up the cash?"

From the corner of the room a timid voice piped up. "Ernst works for the Post Office," said Greg Buhl, glancing at Susana Melendez and turning seven shades of crimson.

Stapley looked at the other law enforcement professionals sitting with him. "Did any of us know that?" He got blank stares in return.

"Carol and her team did some pretty excellent work," said Danny, dramatically bowing in the direction of his wife. "Greg's workup of the soldiers was chock full of little details like that. You can guess, obviously, how Ernst handled this. He must have told his pals that he had a way to slip the envelopes with money past some kind of made-up postal security checkpoint."

"I've got a question of my own," said Samantha Richter. Everyone looked at her. "What? I can ask questions, too, right?" Frank caught his sister's eye and nodded towards Richter with a grin. Carol gave a conspiratorial nod in return.

Richter went on. "The soldiers *all* said they sat with this guy Murray and discussed a delivery of 'paper.' And he let them deposit their bags in the vault. Clearly, he thought they were smuggling something. Ernst didn't make all that up. What was it they were smuggling?"

"Just that. Paper," said Carol, coming over and pulling some files out of her shoulder bag. "Melody and Deniece have found dozens of references from blogs and social media posts about all sort of bureaucratic snafus in the Green Zone, among them a perennial shortage of office supplies where they were needed. The British had particular needs – their standard sheet is a different size than ours, but they needed American eight-and-a-half by eleven in Iraq. Two large Army duffels of copier paper could last a long time," she said, paging through the printouts in the files she held. "Our guess is that Andrew Ernst found Major Murray the first time while arranging to smuggle American copier paper to the British Embassy. He then had his idea for his prank, and brought his pals along to the follow-up he'd scheduled with Murray. They thought they were discussing a secret plot to steal millions. Murray thought they were discussing paper smuggling."

Melody and Deniece came over with a laptop, which they opened and placed on the card table. A video started, a grainy shot of a large room, amateurishly lit, with bunk beds occupying what looked like little vaults on either side of the room. "This is from a video tour of the British Embassy shot a little over three years ago," said Carol. "This is the vault room where the money was supposedly hidden. No hidden duffel bags. It's a dormitory now for embassy security staff. Whoever was getting the money from these soldiers wasn't using it to protect anything in this room."

Cooper Stapley looked impressed, and Carol could see that *that* impressed Frank.

Mike Levin went next. "Okay, so obviously there's no money hidden underneath the Embassy right now. And I agree that a prank by Ernst is more likely than these six grunts getting away with a fifty-four-million-dollar haul. But it's only speculation – a story just like the story the soldiers told us. Let's get back to the present and talk evidence. You obviously think that Ernst somehow rigged the shooting of Major Murray in his apartment, right? Let's get to that. What's the evidence?"

Danny nodded and looked at Detective Calderon. "Jim here was kind enough to help me with this. Frank called him up and asked him to look into a few things, and I called him myself to ask about a few more. It was really pretty ingenious." Danny could not keep a schoolboy's grin off his face. Carol couldn't help but feel proud.

"It was the silverware drawer that tipped me off," began Danny, almost professorially. He pulled a remote control from his pocket and clicked it at the screen. The video image from the next room was replaced by a crime scene photo from Ernst's home, showing the bloody cutlery. "Ernst said he reached for it as he fell and pulled the drawer out. But he was holding a gun, and had – in effectively the same instant – dropped Murray with two rounds in the chest. He had to be holding the gun with two hands, so it just didn't make sense to me that he'd have had a free hand to pull the drawer. Besides, pulling out a drawer so far and so strongly that it tips is harder than it seems. I just didn't buy it.

"He must have needed the silverware for another reason. There were sharp steak knives in the drawer. And, so, naturally, I thought of the bathtub."

Danny waited, and was rewarded when Dylan Connor took the bait. "Bathtub?"

"Ernst needed to fake a shooting, but he'd watched enough TV to know that that was hard to fake. If you want to fake a shooting, many folks think you just put the other guy's gun up to your arm and shoot yourself. Very bad idea. Blood spatter looks suspicious, and you could set yourself up for a flesh wound and end up bleeding out from a fragment or ricochet. Plus, once the sound of gunshots alerted the neighbors, you only had a couple of moments to clean everything up."

He put another picture up on the screen, the back of the cabinet in Ernst's kitchen. Two bullets were embedded in it. "But he had to have spent rounds to make this work, and he needed to have a wound that looked like a bullet wound. They found blood on both of these, as if they had gone through Ernst's body. He pricked a finger or something like that to get blood on them, gouged out the hole with a screwdriver, and stuck the rounds in as if they had gotten there the expected way. He used the screwdriver to make the bullet holes in the door of the cabinet, too."

"Nuh-uh," said Frank, skeptically. "A good crime scene investigator could tell the difference between a real bullet hole and a fake one."

"They did," said Jim Calderon, shamefacedly, "but only the second time they looked, after Danny asked me to have them go at it again. The first time they had no reason to think they weren't bullet holes, and they just didn't look that hard."

Danny clicked his remote to another picture, this time of the bathtub. It showed nothing past a perfectly normal bathtub. "He needed some spent rounds, so he did what anyone who watches TV does nowadays. He made a large gelatin block – you can find a dozen ways to do it on the internet – and put it in the bathtub and fired two rounds into it. Then he extracted the bullets and ran the hot water to dissolve the gelatin."

Danny turned to Calderon and gestured to the detective, who took over. "Ernst didn't think to clean the bathroom thoroughly, because he thought no one would look there. Or maybe he just didn't realize how far gunshot residue can travel, and didn't clean a wide enough area. We found plenty in the bathroom."

Danny pressed on, as chipper as ever. "Ernst got Murray into the house. I'm not surprised that Murray didn't recognize Mark Bucholz; they'd only met once and Mark had just been a guy sitting at a table. Ernst, though… Ernst was someone who'd smuggled office supplies to him, so the Major remembers him, and is more than happy to meet him for a drink. Once Murray was in the house, Ernst shot him dead with two in the chest with the gun he bought legally just the other day. He shot with the same accuracy he used when he deliberately wounded Hayfield and killed Kryevsky and Beatty."

"He walked over to where Murray was lying, leaving no blood spatter, because he didn't have any freshly-bleeding bullet wounds. Ernst put the thirty-eight – the one he used for the other shootings – into Murray's hand and fired three rounds with the silencer into the kitchen island, having left the magazine two light to even out to five. Little mistake there, by the way – a trained solider like Murray would have fired with two hands, but there was only gunshot residue on one."

The picture on the screen flashed back to the bloody cutlery. "Now Ernst went back to the kitchen and, with what I can only imagine was a lot of balls, punctured himself twice with a steak knife…"

"Nope," interjected Mike Levin. "Hold on. Bullet wounds and knife wounds look nothing alike. Even without any special training, Frank and Jim and I would have seen that at the crime scene right away."

"Yep, I agree," said Danny, amiably. "That's why I also had Detective Calderon here check out the garbage disposal in the sink."

He paused while everyone looked at Calderon. He shrugged. "Bloody bandages. Didn't all get eaten up by the disposal."

"*He* did *shoot himself,*" Gaffney suddenly said out loud.

Danny pointed at his brother-in-law. "He did, just not then and there. A day earlier, maybe, and in another location where he could bleed and it wouldn't matter. Took a chance on two light flesh wounds, then bound them up with field dressings, so that he wouldn't drip blood all over his home. Jim's people confirmed that Ernst wore a jacket to the bar to meet Murray; wanted to make sure he was hiding the bandages. Some blood inside the jacket, not a lot. Killed Murray, fired the shots into the island, then went over to the kitchen, removed his field dressings and tried to send them down the garbage disposal, then used a knife from the drawer to put holes in his shirt and to poke the wounds a bit so they started bleeding again.

"Anyone looking at the scene would see Ernst with two real bullet wounds, with the bullets already stuck in the cabinet. He had the height right and everything," Danny said with unfeigned admiration. "That was well-executed. The paramedic and the ER doctors may have thought the wounds were a little strange, but who on earth would re-open a bullet wound, right? The whole thing took less than three minutes, so that even if someone had called 911 right away he'd have been done before the first responders arrived. Most impressive. Really." Carol squirmed a little at how much Danny was complimenting a killer.

"I talked to the paramedic again yesterday," threw in Calderon. "She did think the wounds looked like they weren't exactly fresh, but she just never thought to say anything about it until I asked specifically."

"Compartmentalization," said Danny. "Division of labor. Everyone does what they're supposed to do, and that way they can do it faster. But if they don't all share what they know with each other, then things get missed. Ernst was in the Army, the poster child of the left hand not knowing what the right hand is doing. He counted on the paramedic not mentioning what it looked like to anyone else, especially since he was doing such an impressive job of looking freshly shot."

"All right, all right," said Frank, rising and walking over to his brother-in-law. He laid a hand on Danny's shoulder. "I believe you. Ernst faked the Murray shooting. You've got him on that. But that doesn't prove any of the rest of it's true. I'm not saying you're wrong, but even with all of your evidence any halfway decent lawyer could convince a jury to ignore the forensics and have reasonable doubt."

"Right," said Levin, walking over to the open duffel bag full of white copier paper. "You've got really good, concrete evidence about the shooting in Ernst's apartment, but all this," he pointed down at the open duffel, "is purely speculation. It's good speculation, I'll give you. But for us to move on it, we need something more."

Frank moved his hand off Danny's shoulder and patted him on the back. "We can take a run at Dwayne Tracy and Lars Gilbert, but if the story you tell is right, they won't be able to verify anything, except the part about Ernst handling the money deliveries through his job at the post office, and so far as they know he did that honestly."

Frank went back to the table, sat down and gave Samantha a smile. He shrugged his shoulders good-naturedly, and straightened his tie, radiating a tolerance Carol was sure he did not really feel.

"Um, Frank…?" said Danny, in the voice of a teacher trying to get the attention of a wayward sophomore. "Frank? Yes, over here, Frank. Who said we were done? You want proof? Let's try this on for size."

Carol came by Danny's side and handed him an envelope from out of her bag. "You forget that you let me look at some of the evidence the other day. I found something."

He opened the envelope and pulled out some photographs. "Your team collected hundreds of pictures taken by bystanders of the Willis Marden crime scene. Printed them out, even, for you Luddites in Homicide. The guy who was walking right behind him when it happened took these three, and I blew them up a bit."

He held them up. A crowd of people, one of them without doubt Andrew Ernst, staring slack-jawed at the lifeless body.

"I know you went through these with a fine-toothed comb, Frank, but when you were looking at these Ernst wasn't a person of interest, so you never noticed him, right?" Frank nodded, clearly lost in thought. "It's hard to see, but in one of these pictures Ernst is clearly holding a flip phone. A cheap flip phone, a burner. It's the phone on which Ernst had just received a text message, a message which made him get up and leave the coffee shop where he was waiting to meet Mark Bucholz. Made him get up and leave and almost walk into a bullet that went into Willis Marden instead." He stood over the photos on the table in silent triumph, his wife beside him, as the others looked carefully at them. There was a moment where no one moved, then Frank reached for his jacket pocket, trying to get his phone from his just-too-snug suit.

"Hold off one minute before you call the lieutenant, Frank," said Carol, rolling her eyes in the direction of her husband. "She'll be here in a minute, anyway." She playfully poked Danny in the arm. "Go on, tell 'em."

"You see," said Danny, almost to himself, "something still didn't fit. It was the story of when Detective Mueller went to pick up Ernst. Just didn't make sense, the way it played out. Ernst gets out the window of his condo or townhouse or whatever and gets at least a two, three-minute start on the police. More even, because we looked, and the back of that apartment complex is connected up to different roads than the front. For the detectives to get around and get after him cost maybe another minute or two. And yet... and yet, within 10 minutes, the cops chasing Ernst are *ahead* of him, and Detective Mueller had to turn around and come towards him from the front to box him in."

Danny spun his finger next to his head. "It sounded crazy. Even a complete idiot knows to get as far away as possible as fast as possible. Even on residential streets you can go at least four or five miles in ten minutes, and the search radius for law enforcement would have quickly become too large to handle. A three- or four-minute lead is usually all you need.

"But why was Andrew running at all? After those first ten minutes, he was ready to be picked up – the first car that flipped on its rollers got him to pull over quietly. So why was he so panicked to get out that window when the police arrived?"

Danny again paused, but this time either no one was willing to take the bait, or no one knew what to say. His eyes darted around, looking, for just a moment, and then he shrugged his shoulders. "He had something he wanted to get rid of, is what I thought."

He paused again, clearly waiting for someone to respond.

"He really likes to ham it up, huh?" said Samantha Richter in a loud whisper to Frank.

Danny smirked at his brother-in-law and continued. "It struck us all as odd that the same gun was used in the Hayfield, Beatty and Kryevsky crimes. My first thought was that this meant the person who had the weapon couldn't legally buy a gun here – like a foreigner, like Major Murray. But then it occurred to me that the universe was bigger than that. It included anyone who, for any reason, didn't want to buy a new gun. Buy a gun, there's a record, something that can be traced back to you."

"Now, lots of people can get guns without going through the proper channels. That's why I knew Litinov didn't do the shootings. But for ordinary citizens, people who aren't criminals, it's not that easy to find out how to buy an illegal gun. You could end up drawing a lot of attention to yourself, or worse, getting hurt, and still have no idea who to talk to in order to get one. Ernst *is* a criminal, but not the kind with connections. He used the same gun because he couldn't get another. It takes a fair amount of work to get hold of a reliable gun illegally."

Danny playfully, smiling in response to the blank stares he was still getting. "Ernst ran out the window because he needed to hide that gun. He'd kept it on him, foolishly, because he thought it would be days before anyone made the connection between the two murders. He wasn't prepared for one student's devotion to his studies" - he flashed half a grin at Greg Buhl, who turned eleven shades of purple – "to figure out the link between Kryevsky and Beatty so quickly."

"He ran. And hid the gun. And then he made it look like he had been fleeing the police, and got caught in no time. After he had hidden the gun."

Danny paused once more to savor the moment, and Carol audibly groaned.

"And this is why we're meeting here, in this boring little storage unit in the middle of nowhere."
"Just half a mile from Ernst's home," Jim Calderon said, catching on. "Right off the road that Ernst would have taken when he drove off that day."

"Gold star, sir," said Danny. "Armed with nothing more than my considerable charm, I got lists of clients from the owner of this establishment, who it turns out is quite the baseball fan." Danny unfolded a list from his pocket. "'*Ernie Andrews*' is a pretty lame pseudonym to have used on the lease," he chuckled, "but there's a security camera and they store the footage for thirty days." Carol pulled out a flash drive and plugged it into the laptop. Danny continued. "I was even on the owner's fantasy team for a little while this year before he traded me for a southpaw. He was happy to let me look at the footage. This is from the night Ernst was picked up. You can see him drive in, and leave three minutes later. More than enough for a warrant, I'd think, right?"

He looked at Frank, who couldn't quite conceal his rueful smile. "And Lieutenant Halloran?" he asked.

"Will be here in just a few minutes, I hope, with that warrant."

*   *   *

A half hour later, a convoy of vehicles drove past open chain-link gates into the lot of the Suburban Storage Company. It had been agreed that Danny, Carol and the team could watch, provided they stayed at a safe distance so that no one could charge them with tainting the search. Samantha Richter wasn't with them; Lt. Halloran and the State's Attorney had drawn the line at journalists. Danny's suggestion to call Andrew Ernst and invite him to look on was not taken with the seriousness with which he had meant it.

An officer cut the lock on the storage unit, and Frank rolled up the garage door and peered inside. Danny and Carol stood on their toes, trying to get a better look as a crew of officers and forensic experts went in.

They waited for more than an hour like that, holding hands in silence. Greg Buhl, Melody Kasson and Deniece Rogers stood in a circle, spinning each other stories about what might be found. Susana Melendez was on the phone with her mother, listening to another interminable story about some apparently dreadful behavior by her Aunt Rosa.

Eventually Frank Gaffney and Mike Levin emerged from the storage locker carrying a large cardboard box. They beckoned the civilians over as they set the box on the trunk of a squad car.

Frank began removing the bagged contents, one at a time. "Three boxes of .38 ammunition, the exact same brand and type used in the shootings of Hayfield, Kryevsky, Beatty, and at Ernst's home."

He pulled out the next. "A spare clip for a .38 automatic that fits the weapon recovered in Murray's hand in Ernst's condo. Also, a fair amount of blood and a couple of bullets wedged into some thick boards."

"This was a fun bonus," said Mike Levin, pulling out the next evidence bag. "A set of license plates. These plates were reported stolen ten days ago from the parking lot of a mall not five miles from here. The first three letters of these plates were reported on a green four-door sedan – like Andrew Ernst drives – that was seen near Marcus Kryevsky's home on the day he was shot."

"Why on earth didn't he ditch those?" mused Carol out loud.

"Cocky bastard," replied Frank. "He never thought anyone would find this place. He paid for it in cash under an assumed name, and there was no address or phone number on file, either. He had a combination lock, so there was no telltale key anywhere. We could have gone through his life with a fine-toothed comb and

324

never had a clue this existed." He looked up at Danny. "Good find, man. Really." Danny blushed.

"Now," said Frank, "the *piece de resistance*." Frank did his own dramatic pause, which he bungled by almost knocking the box off the trunk of the car, before reaching in an pulling out two more bags.

"In my left hand is a burner phone, with a familiar text message still on it. In my right hand is ten thousand dollars, part of a stash of nearly four hundred thousand in a large box with Mark Bucholz's fingerprints on it."

Danny, Carol and the Irregulars burst spontaneously into applause as Mike Levin called on the radio for the officers watching Ernst in his home to go ahead and arrest him.

*   *   *

It was a more muted celebration than they'd expected. First, of course, everyone was tired. Frank and his partner Mike had spent the rest of the afternoon filling out endless reams of paperwork, and were far from done. Melody, Deniece and Greg had dashed home to catch up on the schoolwork they had been neglecting for too many days. Carol had a stack of papers to grade in the hours before the party began.

More important, though, was that the thrill of the chase was wearing off, and the sadness of it all had begun to sink in a little bit. Carol saw it most with Danny. On the drive home after the search, he'd been high as a kite, bubbling over with energy. But as the evening wore on, he grew more pensive, more somber.

Carol was already feeling it, because the next day she had promised to drive over to Janet Bucholz's house and talk it all over with her. She'd had a word with her brother about it, and Frank thought there was a small but real chance that Janet would get the fifty thousand back, given that it had been part of a more-or-less legal loan, and that Bucholz hadn't sought the loan in connection with any actual crime. She hoped it would help. Poor girl wasn't the sharpest knife in the drawer, but she didn't deserve this. Of course, neither did Willis Marden, and his family might get all of the money in a civil suit.

And so the party broke up within two hours as, one after another, people begged off to head to sleep, back to work, or for some quiet reflection on their own. Cooper Stapley left first, to catch the redeye back to DC. When he got up off the Alexander's couch, though, his suit jacket was rumpled just a little, and Carol thought that gave Frank some solace. Frank spent almost a half hour on the phone with Samantha Richter, who was burning the midnight oil writing up her sensational scoop, leaving out Danny Alexander's name, as she'd promised. Her editors had been happy to cooperate on being selective with some of the details in return for so much other inside information.

Susana Melendez left next, and was overheard whispering with Deniece and Melody about the date she was headed to. Four quickly-consumed vodka tonics later, a Lyft came to take Greg Buhl back to his apartment.

Melody Kasson spent most of the evening drilling Danny with questions, probing every aspect of the case. That produced an exceedingly rare moment of embarrassment from Danny, who realized that his grand dramatic summation had left out the discovery in the county records office that Mark Bucholz was Andrew Ernst's executor and prime beneficiary of his will. If he'd been his executioner as well, he may have had a chance to pay back Max Litinov. Having satisfied her urge to show up Danny, Melody left, dragging Deniece with her.

Mike Levin had barely seen his kids in days, and he was next to go, hoping to put them to bed before another late night at the office.

That left Carol with her husband and her brother, who both sat quietly, lost in their own thoughts.

She looked at them, one to the other. Her brother had had to swallow a lot of pride to let Danny and her help on this case. Already, she knew, Mueller and Wright were off someplace trying to take the lion's share of the credit, and Frank would probably let them rather than argue it out. He never walked as tall as he used to anymore. Too many hard cases, too many long nights. Carol was glad she had made the time the day before to accidentally run into Sam Richter at the newspaper office and ply her with stories about what a great older brother she had.

Frank could use a little of what she had with Danny. Even after all of this, she was still a little mad at him, but she was proud of what they had done together. He was proud, too, she knew, and the energy he'd drawn from this had sustained him through a tough couple of weeks. They hadn't even watched a baseball game since they went to Mark Bucholz's funeral. Now, with this behind him, he could focus on getting back into shape and making it to spring training someplace next year.

He wasn't going to stop with this, she knew. He'd never dominate a pitcher's mound like he did ten years ago. He needed something else to give him that rush, to get his juices flowing. This was just what he wanted, and, maybe, just what he needed.

And when the sadness and horror of it all caught up to him in the middle of the night, as she knew it would, and he thrashed about and groaned in his sleep, she would be there to hold him. And then he'd do the same for her. And that was enough.

THE END

Made in the USA
Las Vegas, NV
05 February 2022